How to Build a Boyfriend from Scratch

Sarah Archer's writing has been produced for Comedy Central and published in numerous literary magazines. She has worked in literary management and film and television development on projects including *House*, *Concussion*, *Roots*, and *Girls Trip*. *How to Build a Boyfriend from Scratch* is her debut novel.

How to Build a Boyfriend from Scratch

. . . . . .

SARAH ARCHER

HarperCollins*Publishers*

HarperCollins*Publishers*
1 London Bridge Street
London SE1 9GF

www.harpercollins.co.uk
1

First published in the USA as 'The Plus One' by G.P. Putnam's Sons,
a division of Penguin Random House LLC, New York 2019

This edition published by HarperCollins*Publishers* 2020

A catalogue record for this book
is available from the British Library

ISBN:
PB: 978-0-00-833515-1

Printed and bound in Great Britain by
CPI Group (UK) Ltd, Croydon CR0 4YY

MIX
Paper from
responsible sources
FSC™ C007454

This book is produced from independently certified FSC™ paper
to ensure responsible forest management.

For more information visit: www.harpercollins.co.uk/green

To Gunnar, who is perfectly human

How to Build a Boyfriend from Scratch

one

. . . . . .

Of the three people standing onstage, only two of them were people. But that was totally normal to Kelly—one of the *people* people. Along with Priya, her best friend and fellow robotics engineer (the other *person* person), she looked out over the audience filling the brightly lit demonstration room: a field trip of fifty or so kids, squirming and grouchy under the cloud of that early January gloom. The children were freshly reinstitutionalized after two halcyon weeks of holiday break, the feral spirit of pajama days and pumpkin pie breakfasts still smoldering in their eyes. And now it was up to Kelly to win their wandering attention.

"I'd like you to meet Zed," she began tentatively, gesturing to the robot standing beside her. He was one of the first projects she had worked on five years ago when she landed her coveted job at Automated Human Industries, AHI, *the* boutique cutting-edge robotics company. Zed made a modest impression at first glance, his body a four-foot-tall construction of steel ligaments and exposed wires, his face a flat panel. "I know he looks pretty basic," she continued, trying and failing to eclipse the gleeful Pillsbury Doughboy noises issuing from four girls in the back as they took turns poking each other's stomachs. Kelly was not the most confident performer. This was a young woman who, when playing a tree in her third-grade play, had gotten stage fright—despite not having any lines—and dramatically fled the theater. Which had not been easy, seeing as her legs had been bound together in a trunk.

But now her voice grew as she got excited, talking about her work. "But at the point of his creation, Zed had a greater scope of motion capabilities than anything else on the market. He was our first build with our patented predictive stereo vision—"

A tinny ring from the front row announced that a sandy-haired boy had just won a game on his contraband phone—and threw Kelly off her flow. Robbie, one of her coworkers here at AHI, bustled over and extended a hand. "Phone," he commanded. The boy dutifully dropped his thousand-dollar smartphone into a red plastic bucket of other thousand-dollar smartphones, glass hitting metal with a thump. Robbie had jumped at the chance to play phone wrangler today, ensuring that—even though none of the company's newest technology was on display—no junior spies filmed the program for their parents, two thirds of whom probably worked at competing tech companies here in Silicon Valley. He clutched the bucket with a sort of protective satisfaction and retreated to his position on the sidelines, from which he watched the rows of children like a prison guard. Sometimes Kelly couldn't believe that she had dated him.

She refocused. She was determined to get through to these

students. Or at least to half of them. Maybe one? Just a small one? But so many were talking to each other that they could barely hear her. The whole detailed presentation she had perfected and re-hearsed was falling apart in practice. "So we started with some-thing called stochastic mapping, which is, um—" She faltered. Her eyes darted irresistibly toward the exit. She felt another "fleeing tree" moment coming on.

"It's kind of easier if you see it first," Priya gently interrupted. "Who wants to see this guy in action?"

"Yeah!" a couple of the kids responded, sitting up. Kelly relaxed as she looked across at her friend, grateful for the intervention. Priya was better at this type of thing anyway. She could get a smile out of a statue.

"Shall you do the honors, madam?" she asked now.

"I shall, mademoiselle." Kelly clicked the remote in her hand and Zed beeped into life, his blue eyes blinking on. More of the children looked up, their attention caught. "So he can walk, of course." She pushed the mini joystick on the remote forward and Zed took a few steps, his movements more fluid than his rough form seemed to indicate.

"But big deal, right?" Priya asked the crowd. "You guys have been walking for years." Some of the kids giggled.

"But he can also walk *sideways*, which is pretty cool." Kelly tog-gled to the right on the remote, sending Zed into a side-to-side grapevine movement. "And if you add in the arms—"

Priya pressed a sequence of buttons on her own remote and the robot added a rhythmic arm movement to his routine. "Zed's got some major moves." The kids in the audience started clapping.

"Observe." Kelly swept the joystick around, and Zed whirled in a perfect, whip-fast pirouette, stopping on a dime. The sandy-haired boy let out an involuntary "Whoa!"

"Way better than my moves, I have to admit," Kelly said.

As the crowd laughed and cheered, Kelly sneaked a grin at Priya. They had officially won these kids over with the sweet smell of science. They were superheroes. Now she spoke confidently as she started to explain her process. This was her favorite part: the magic of engineering, the ability to imagine an impossible-to-solve problem, then slowly break it down, unpiecing it until it became possible.

"So how do you teach a robot to walk?" she asked the crowd. They were silent now, utterly rapt. "Imagine you were trying to give someone else the ability to walk for the first time. What would you need to give him?"

"Feet!" one child cried.

"Good, that's the first thing." She was actually starting to enjoy this. "What would those feet need to be able to do?"

But the buzz of another phone, conspicuous in the quiet, cut her off. Her eyes shot instinctively to Robbie, waiting for him to nab the culprit. But Robbie's glare was fixed squarely on her. "I'm so sorry," she muttered, fumbling her own phone out of her pocket and striking the Ignore button. She could almost physically feel everyone watching.

It had been her mom calling, but she could have guessed that even without looking at the screen. It was *always* her mom calling. She cleared her throat and tried to resume the presentation, but she had lost her train of thought. "So . . . the feet. The feet would need to be able to balance flat on the ground, right? What else?"

She felt a smaller rumble in her pocket as a voicemail registered, where it would sit alongside the five or six other voicemails from her mother that could be found on Kelly's phone at all times. She could already hear what this one would say: "Are you coming to family dinner this weekend?" (Yes, Kelly came to every family dinner, every two weeks like clockwork.) And "Are you bringing a date?" (No, it's a family dinner, that would be weird.) Of course, Kelly was rarely dating anyone anyway. But that wasn't the point.

Diane's energetic voice filled Kelly's mind so loudly that she failed to hear the kids shouting answers at her in the audience. "Sorry, what? One at a time," she said. Just moments ago she had been doing so well. She had asked her mom time and time again to not call while she was at work, but Diane just never seemed to think that Kelly's work was too important to interrupt. "How about balance?" she tried again. "Wait, I just said that. Um—"

Priya gave her a sympathetic glance before stepping forward again. "What did you just say? You, the boy in the awesome Spider-Man shirt? That the feet have to talk to the brain? That's right. You have to figure out how those feet are going to know what to do."

This time Kelly stepped back, allowing Priya to take over for her. She had lost the nerve to try again.

The drive from AHI to her parents' house that Sunday wasn't far. But passing from the sweeping, glass-bound corporate giants of North San Jose to the leafy suburban streets of Willow Glen always gave her the feeling of entering another world. Maybe she became more of the girl she was growing up there, less of the woman she was now.

The Suttle house was a neat ranch-style home that looked as modestly middle class as ever despite the million-dollar price tag the tech boom had hung on it. The sage-green painted exterior was nice enough, framed by solid bushes and a white bench tucked beneath a shady oak tree, but it gave way to an interior that had, in the decades-long war of attrition that was her parents' marriage, become almost entirely her mother's territory. Pillows with an indefensible number of tassels, framed flower prints jockeying for wall space, a menagerie of china and glass figurines—Diane had difficulty saying no to anything beautiful, or at least cute, or at least, well, whatever was appealing about the life-sized sculpture of a cat that glowered at them from the mantel. Family portraits from years gone by had the five Suttles smiling down, pressed and perfect, from every room. But the actual family tableaus formed in these rooms were never so idyllic. Kelly took a heavy breath as she entered the house. Something about the numerous clashing pots of potpourri, the unidentifiable cooking smells, the thick fug of repressed childhood emotions, made the air more difficult to breathe here. Kelly loved her family. But sometimes she thought it would be easier to love them if she didn't have a career that kept her so close.

As she emerged into the kitchen, she looked to see what her mother was cooking, but her spirits fell when she saw her ladling an ominous, gelatinous something onto plates. The older she got, the more Diane embraced a sort of culinary Russian roulette, throwing ingredients together with abandon, and the results were as likely to be toxic as inspired. Kelly could already tell that tonight would be a miss. Meanwhile, Diane talked in a stream to Clara, Kelly's twenty-five-year-old sister. Clara had a Disney princess thing going on: she wasn't a supermodel, but with wide, round eyes and a sunny smile, she was the sort of pretty that made babies smile at her automatically in checkout lines and customers at the vintage boutique where she worked want to give her the sale. Her strawberry-blond head bobbed, listening raptly, while she pushed some parbaked rolls into the oven. Beside her, her fiancé Jonathan, an overgrown but good-natured jock getting soft in the middle since college, dutifully pretended to be doing something with the butter to look busy.

Across the kitchen, Kelly's older brother, Gary, was half visible under his young daughters, who were summiting him like mountain goats. Kelly knew that there were three of them—triplets, in fact—but sometimes suspected he had picked up an extra one somewhere, like a leaf stuck to his hair. They made way too much sound for three humans and with the way they ran around, really, who could tell how many there were, or what was happening at all? It was like that game where you try to guess which cup the penny is under. The only possible solution is that there's a secret fourth cup. They were just reaching the age when they were developing truly distinct personalities, and Kelly was half thrilled at watching their minds blossom, half terrified at the notion that all three girls could now run and turn doorknobs.

"I talked to the florist about the camellias," Diane was saying as she fluttered around the kitchen, her sleeve of bracelets clinking, her dark hair motionless in its eternally perfect coif. Clara's wedding, which was eight weeks away, was the topic du jour—it was the topic du *every* jour, taking the place of the gossipy stories that Diane usually recounted from Blush, the bridal shop she ran. "It's vital that she understand. Gary, can you grab me the salad tongs?" Diane didn't seem to notice that Gary currently had a shoe in one hand, an upside-down toddler in the other, and an Anna from *Frozen* doll in his mouth. Kelly dove into the room and scooped up the toddler while Gary seamlessly plucked the tongs from their container.

"Ah, Kelly, you're here, finally. Hand me the lettuce spinner?"

Kelly struggled to perch her niece on her hip while extricating the lettuce spinner from a top shelf.

"So if we go with peach, that would mean—"

"White for the ribbons," Diane finished Clara's sentence. "And then—"

"Those other sashes for the bridesmaids, exactly," said Clara.

"The ones you showed me a while ago?" Kelly asked.

"Which were those again?" Clara said, busily setting the butter on the table while Kelly offered the lettuce spinner rather aimlessly, trying to catch her mom's attention. Diane seemed to have forgotten that she wanted it in the first place.

"Um, I don't know, they were in a catalogue?"

"They're all in catalogues, Kelly," Diane asserted. "Don't worry about it, we'll tell you what to wear on the day." Kelly set the lettuce spinner on the counter and pulled her niece closer to her instead, making her laugh with a funny face. She sensed that her energies were better expended there.

"Oh, hi, Dad," she said, just noticing her father. His stillness in the whirl of motion around him had camouflaged him into the room.

"Hi, Kel," he responded, not looking up from his white paper. Carl was always reading or scratching at something for his job as a civil engineer with the local water utility, but he never discussed his work with the family. For someone who worked so closely with technology, he spent an awful lot of time doing things the analogue way, and Kelly suspected this was because of Diane's strict "no devices at dinnertime" policy. If he was working on a notepad, Kelly's mom interpreted it as legitimate and let it slide.

Kelly's father was one of those fifty-five-year-old men with a beard and glasses who looked like he was born a fifty-five-year-old man with a beard and glasses. Trying to imagine him as a young boy, a twenty-year-old, even, was ludicrous. His crescent of close-cut, early whitened hair never seemed to grow, get cut, or fall out. His favorite armchair was so molded to the angles of his body that he didn't sit in it so much as wear it. And in the same way, he wore his marriage to Kelly's mom. When they met, he was studying bio-chemistry, she theater. They were married before they graduated. A boiling, opposites-attract passion carried them through the first few years. By the time it cooled, Gary was there, and so was a mort-gage, and a long future that seemed pretty much planned out. Di-ane's silliness and flair for the dramatic didn't age well, and Carl's analytical intelligence became boring. They were married now more out of habit than love, though he never appeared to notice such things.

Diane thought often of such things, but was so willfully roman-tic that she saw only a long and happy marriage, a model for all the young brides-to-be at her shop. So she chattered on blissfully obliv-ious to her husband's disregard, which was probably the secret to their "success." She focused on the perfect image of her marriage in their family portraits and Carl focused on his work, neither looking at the flesh-and-blood spouse in front of their eyes.

Growing up in such a household, Kelly, an innately rational little girl, had had no choice but to review the evidence of her parents' marriage and conclude that fairy tales were a load of fluff and bunk. With such a mismatched model of love, relationships had always seemed to her at best illogical, at worst a source of pain. And so she poured herself into her Legos, which turned into computers, which turned into intricate robotics systems. Machines made far more sense than people.

While the family ate dinner, or worked the chicken around on their plates to make it look eaten, the topic of conversation was, of course, still Clara's wedding. Several important facts were established. Gary's wife, Gina, an ER nurse with an insane schedule who couldn't be here because she was working, because she was always working, hadn't gotten a dress yet so, yes, Gary had picked out something for her that was color-scheme appropriate. Yes, Jonathan had passed Diane's hair advice (instructions) on to his groomsmen, and it was duly received. And yes, Carl would take a dancing lesson for the father-daughter dance. This was news to Carl.

"A dancing lesson? It's a wedding, not a cabaret."

"Carl, this is your only daughter's wedding—"

Kelly looked around the table to see if anyone else noticed. They didn't.

"And you're going to learn to dance," Diane said in her I-mean-business voice. Carl's face stiffened, even his glasses stiffened, but Clara cut in with a gentler tone, her eyes glimmering with sincerity.

"It's just one lesson, Dad, and it'll make things so much easier. This way you won't get up there at the wedding and feel like you don't know what to do. You'll have learned everything beforehand; you won't even have to think about it."

"Oh, fine, that's all right then," Carl grumbled. Kelly gulped on her chicken. How did Clara do that? How did she always say the right thing?

But she was quickly distracted by the inevitable question. "So, Kelly," her mom asked brightly, "have you met anyone recently?"

"Well, a boatswain from the Philippines just asked me to connect on LinkedIn, so . . ."

"You know what I mean, a man!"

"No, Mom, since you asked me last week, I have not found a husband."

"No need to be snippy. I just want what's best for you. After all, you are already twenty-nine; I would think you would gladly take my help in the situation. And luckily for you, I met someone!"

"Congratulations, dear. Will I be invited to the wedding?" Carl asked, not looking up from his salad.

"I mean for Kelly, obviously."

"Mom, I don't—"

"Oh, is this the one you were telling me about?" Clara interrupted Kelly excitedly. "I think you'll actually like him, Kel."

"Please don't—" But Kelly failed again.

"Give it a try. Worst that happens is this stranger murders you on the first date, and then at least you're not dying alone," Gary said, slicing food for two of the girls across his own untouched plate. His expression was so straight that few people but Kelly would have been able to tell he was joking. And even she wasn't convinced.

"I really don't want—"

But now Diane cut across Kelly. "Will everyone please just let me finish?" Oh, how rude of me, Kelly thought. "His name is Martin and he's Donna's sister's neighbor's son. He's a realtor and a tennis player and just adorable and best of all, he's the same height as Gary, so everything will be symmetrical in the pictures!"

"What pictures?" Gary asked.

"At the wedding, obviously."

Kelly couldn't let this go on. "Mom, I don't care how good this guy looks next to Gary, I'm not marrying him."

"Not your wedding, silly. Though who knows! I mean for Clara's wedding. Oh, and I almost forgot. He has a cocker spaniel." Diane sat back, satisfied. The man had a cocker spaniel.

"It's perfect, right, Kel?" Clara beamed.

"Wait, so you guys just went and found a plus one for me?"

"I know how you dread these things," Diane said. "Now you don't even have to worry about it."

"What makes you think I don't already have one?"

"Well, you don't—do you?"

Kelly spluttered. "That's not the point! I don't want to go to my sister's wedding with some tennis-playing jerkoff I don't even know."

"But you will know him. I set up dinner for the two of you. You've got almost two months to get to know each other."

Kelly looked to her father. "Dad, you'll pose next to me in the pictures, right, so everything looks good? I don't need a plus one?"

"I would, but I probably wouldn't live up to your mother's standards. She's never called me adorable."

"Gary? Is anyone going to stand up for me or is my whole family happy to just pimp me out to a strange man off the streets?"

"Honestly, I'd be thrilled to have another guy at the family table," Gary admitted. "My doctor said if I don't start exposing myself to people other than Gina and the girls, I will lactate."

"Kelly, this is ridiculous. You have to bring someone," Diane insisted.

"Why? Who cares?"

"Who cares?" Diane set down her fork. Kelly sensed that she had asked the wrong question. "A wedding is a house of cards, Kelly. If you mess up my seating arrangements, all hell will break loose. And all of my friends, my family, my industry colleagues will be there. The eyes of the Bay Area are on me. I am a bridal professional and this is my daughter's wedding! This is my Triple Crown!"

"Wait, so are you the horse in this scenario?" Kelly couldn't resist asking.

"I think she's the jockey." Gary caught her eye before looking away, masking a grin.

"Please, just give him a chance, Kel," Clara said. "It's one dinner. I think you'll have more fun at the wedding if you have someone to talk to, and I won't have to worry about whether you're having a good time. Please? For me?"

Kelly sighed. Clara's sweet tone was much harder to say no to than her mother's quasi-mania. She had a feeling she was about to meet a cocker spaniel.

two

· · · · · ·

Kelly wondered, as she prepared for her blind date the following Saturday, why other girls seemed to love the getting-ready process. In movies this was always a snappy montage that involved trying on various colorful outfits and throwing them off over your head like a jovial idiot who doesn't understand how hangers work. Instead, there she was, in her drab apartment, staring sadly into her closet. It was like Eeyore shopping for a *quinceañera* dress.

Well, drab may be a little harsh—Kelly had a perfectly nice (for Silicon Valley rental prices) one-bedroom with square, modern lines, granite countertops mottled with black and sienna brown, and broad windows offering views of the small, flat park across the street, where dogs ran through the cropped grass and kids played soccer. Her IKEA décor was neutral and tasteful, if rather plain. She tended to choose items in neat, geometric shapes, pieces that had no possibility of clashing with each other or cutting the space in the room into any of those awkward, too-small-to-have-a-function wedges of unfillable air. It was easiest to go basic, she figured— safest. Pick out something inoffensive and you didn't have to devote any time and energy to thinking about it, or worrying what other people would think. There was no way you would look back at that rectangular beige couch and think you'd made a horrendous mistake. She couldn't imagine a world where home décor served any higher purpose than to do no harm.

The same philosophy extended to the wardrobe she was now peering into as if she expected it to offer her some magical, glamorous outfit she had never actually bought. She might as well have been looking for the portal to Narnia. Kelly owned very little in the way of going-out clothes or even casual clothes, because she did very little going out or casual-ing. Most of her items were work oriented: blouses in cream or taupe, skirts and trousers with simple lines. In actuality, her office was rather forgiving of the "artist/ techie/genius with beard lice" types who worked in the Engineering department, many of whom dressed like college students who had rolled out of bed just in time for class. But Kelly wasn't the type to indulge in such informality.

She swung out one of her three dresses and looked it over. A high neck, but at least it was sleeveless. Nothing says date night like a pair of arms. It was a basic, lightly fitted shape in a sturdy material of forest green. She worried that the green might be too matchy-matchy with her eyes. Then she worried that another color might not match enough. Before sliding it on, she snapped herself into a too-small, one-piece bathing suit she had brilliantly repurposed as a form of budget shapewear, repeating "It looks good, it looks good" in her head like a mantra while it rearranged her internal organs.

Kelly met her own eyes in the mirror as she blow-dried her light hair. Her routine here was more about correcting her features than playing them up. She twirled a round brush through her hair as she blew it out to eliminate its natural waves and create a simple, straight shape. She smoothed foundation over her freckles to cover them up. Her face and nose were a little longer than she would have liked, but she had learned through precise application how to rectify them with contouring. She actually liked her green eyes; just a little mascara and oyster-colored shadow was all that was needed there. She left her lips bare—this was a first date, after all, and the last thing Kelly wanted was to go overboard.

She stepped back and surveyed herself in the bathroom mirror, trying to imagine what she would think if she were meeting herself for the first time, pondering the question that has troubled mankind since the ancients: Hot or Not? Would she want to date herself? Not that she wanted to date Martin. But that didn't mean that she didn't want *him* to want to date *her*.

That would sure show her mom, and Clara. They had assumed she couldn't get a wedding plus one on her own. As much as Kelly loathed to even formulate the thought, preferring to stow it safely in the back of her mental closet, with the dust and the fifth-grade gymnastics costumes, she knew that she was a failure in her mother's eyes—and Kelly was not someone who accepted failure. She breathed out a contented little sigh just imagining her family's shocked faces if Martin came back for a second date—if he *actually* liked her.

Kelly had always relied on data, and the models of her parents' marriage and her own disappointing relationship history gave her little logical basis for predicting the arrival of true love in her own life at any point in the future. Her two previous boyfriends had been guys who looked great on paper, but made her even less happy than she had been alone. Still, a little illogical hope kept flickering, telling her that love might still be out there after all. Her stomach clenched in a way that was only partially the fault of the bathing suit.

She swiped on a little lipstick, just in case.

Martin knew the waiter at the restaurant, a French and Vietnamese place in Alum Rock with glowing saffron-colored walls, and Kelly naturally took this to be a bad sign. She harbored an instinctive suspicion of these people who seemed to know everyone. With a pang, she visualized the modest Friend count on her Facebook page—that couldn't have made a good impression when Martin had likely online-stalked her prior to meeting.

Martin wasn't bad looking: sandy hair, features a little blunt and Germanic but good-natured, and wide shoulders. He looked like someone who got outside often, but always for recreation, not for a living.

He started the conversation by asking about Kelly's work. "So I heard that you do some kind of Hall of Presidents thing for work? Isn't that that show at Disney with all the animatronic presidents? That seriously creeped me out as a kid. But I mean, totally cool if that's what you do."

"No, it's not really anything like that," Kelly said with a small laugh. Already she felt embarrassed. Diane told everyone that her daughter basically worked at the Hall of Presidents.

Martin went on. "Oh, cool. Yeah, I'm a realtor, I do residential spaces in East San Jose. I kind of fell into it through family, but I feel lucky because I actually love it. I love working with people."

"Mm-hmm." Kelly smiled while taking a sip of water, hoping that her face didn't betray that she could relate to that comment about as much as if he had told her he liked taking long walks on the planet Xanadu.

In the ensuing silence, Martin glanced around, then, spotting their waiter, Tony, quickly stopped him. "Could I get another Amstel when you have a second? Thanks, man."

Kelly thought back anxiously to how quickly she had responded when Tony took their food orders earlier. Of course she had Googled the restaurant menu beforehand and figured out what she could order so there would be no surprises. Prawn noodles? Too messy. Papaya salad? Too fussy. Ahi tuna? Just right. Though the beef shank did sound good. But it might be an uncomfortable bedfellow with the bathing suit. Naturally, it was exactly what Martin had ordered.

She glanced up to see him looking around the restaurant with a polite aimlessness, drumming quietly on the lip of the table with his fingers, broad and flat like tongue depressors. And she pulled out of her own anxieties enough to realize that she clearly was not being a very good date. If she wanted to achieve her ambitions for a successful night, it was time to ratchet up her conversational acumen. Besides, a twinge of guilt lit within her. Martin really was trying.

"I'm not sure how closely you follow all the news out of Silicon Valley," she said, leaning forward, "but there's this amazing new development called 'visual foresight' we've been working with. We can program robots to teach themselves how to predict the outcome of different behavioral sequences. They're basically learning to see the future."

19

"Awesome," Martin replied, with an easy smile. "That is definitely cooler than the Hall of Presidents."

"I like to think so. That's what I love about this field—you take anything you can imagine, and you can find a way to make it a reality." She smiled back at him, lighting up. She was crushing this first date thing after all.

"So robots can predict the future. It's like *Minority Report*. I love that movie."

"Well, not exactly. The machines use dynamic neural advection, calculating what will happen in the next frame of a video. The really exciting part is that they're teaching themselves, learning autonomously."

"So wait, maybe it's more like *Rain Man*. Like, if you took a robot to Vegas, could it predict what the dealer's going to do? Are you taking orders yet?" He laughed.

Kelly stopped, her hopes sinking. She could think of literally zero good responses to this. He was staring at her, waiting for her to continue the conversation, to say something, anything—

"I have to go to the bathroom," she blurted, standing abruptly and knocking the table so that the ice in their glasses rattled. She recognized too late that the worst response of all had been to imply that she had to drop a super emergent deuce.

"Oh, sure," Martin said politely. He stood and moved to her side of the table to help pull out her chair. As he did so, he extended a hand around her lower back, as if to usher her out—and that hand went straight to her butt. He didn't squeeze it, didn't precisely cup it, but he definitively, 100 percent touched it. Kelly's eyes flew to his face, which was entirely nonreactive. She couldn't tell if he even recognized what was happening. A swift analysis determined that either he was copping a feel before dinner had been served, or that her butt didn't feel anything like a butt, and both prospects were so worrying that she was clueless as to how to react.

"Um, thank you," she mumbled, and slipped butt-first from his grasp. But somehow when she started walking, instead of going toward the restroom in the back, she started toward the door. Some primal fight-or-flight instinct was taking over, and evidently Kelly's ancestresses had been the ones who bowed meekly before the mastodon and bid it a pleasant day. She was fleeing.

Clearly, she reasoned with accelerating speed, the whole evening was down the toilet anyway (nearly literally). If she turned around and headed back to the table now, Martin would be obligated to ask why she had thought the restroom was somehow invisibly concealed by the front door, like some sort of Platform 9¾ situation. She would be obligated to provide an explanation, which would mean she would be obligated to come up with an explanation, which would mean she would need to think a heck of a lot faster than she was thinking right now. Then the rest of the evening would pass in tense small talk about wine and weather while Martin was obviously fixating on her mysterious lap around the restaurant, and she was obviously fixating on whether or not her mom had paid Martin to give her some human contact, the lack of which in her "already twenty-nine-year-old" daughter's life Diane was always lamenting, and really, did Kelly want to subject herself and Martin to that? Of course she didn't. Besides, if she left now, Martin's pal Tony certainly wouldn't charge him for her tuna, and he wouldn't stay for dessert or order another drink without a date, ergo, Kelly was granting him a significant savings by walking away from the night now. Maybe fifty dollars? If he invested that right, it could be five thousand dollars by the time he reached retirement. Clearly, Kelly was taking the only logical course. This was a successful and reasonable termination of the night.

As she pushed open the door, its chime jingling, she looked back just enough to glimpse Tony and Martin gathered by the table, both gaping at her in bewilderment.

Kelly clattered down the sidewalk as fast as she could in her sensible heels, cursing the frigid winter air and the fact that the only parking spot had been on the other end of the strip mall. The faster she moved, the sooner she could get to her car and vent her emotions by blasting NPR. She needed to drown out her thoughts: Thoughts about the million and one more graceful ways in which she could have handled that situation. About how she couldn't find a plus one on her own and couldn't even hold on to the one that was handed to her. About how dating, the soul-sapping square dance of trying to find the right guy, sucked. About the fact that she really did still want to find the right guy, in spite of all the bruises that come with cracking your heart from its exoskeleton. About the growing suspicion that she couldn't find the right guy because she wasn't the right person.

As she finally reached her black Accord, her still-empty stomach creaked in protest.

As soon as Kelly got home, she stepped out of her dress and unpeeled her swimsuit. It was like skinning a grape. She felt better. Until her phone buzzed. She knew even before fishing it from her purse what the screen would say, and sure enough, it was her mom. Of course Diane would be waiting anxiously for a report of the night's events, probably envisioning a fairy-tale evening that had ended with Kelly stretching onto her tiptoes for a magical kiss, kicking back one foot like the heroine in a rom-com. Instead, here Kelly stood in her half-lit apartment with a very confused date somewhere alone in another part of the city and a Target Juniors bathing suit around her feet. She couldn't talk to her mother. Not now.

She walked into the kitchen, pulling up Priya's contact on her phone instead. Priya she could talk to. Priya she *needed* to talk to.

Priya shared Kelly's intellectual curiosity and analytical mind, but not her *over*-analytical mind. She was relentlessly open, sometimes to the point of TMI, but her endless ability to laugh at herself and others had often sapped the power from Kelly's neuroses. It was lucky, really, that they were forced to work together for long hours back when they had been paired on the Zed project as AHI's newest hires. Otherwise Kelly would probably never have attempted to get to know Priya, or been able to let Priya get to know her. But something about finally getting a robot to execute a perfect spin in place, at three a.m., after imbibing enough Red Bulls to make your toes twitch, really cements a friendship. Now, tinkering beside Priya in the lab was one of Kelly's favorite parts of her job.

Kelly told Priya her tale of woe while she fixed herself a favorite late-night meal: Campbell's tomato soup with popcorn, and soon Priya's laughter was coming so loudly through the phone it nearly drowned out the popping from the microwave.

"You just walked out of the restaurant? You literally did that?" Priya gasped.

"I mean, it wasn't that bad, really. Not as bad as it sounds," Kelly protested grumpily.

"After you told him you needed to poo?"

"Well, I didn't tell him—"

"I love you. This is amazing. This is the greatest moment of my life."

Kelly finally had to laugh. She felt a little better. "But what am I going to do? You know my mom; I can't just go to the wedding alone, like a normal person."

"Uh, normal people don't go to weddings alone, but whatever. Just find a date."

"Oh, sure, why didn't I think of that? I'll just go out and find a date."

"It honestly doesn't have to be that hard, Kel. I promise."

Maybe for Priya. Priya had a mixed history with men, but getting a date was never the hard part. Men found her attractive: her features were unremarkable, but with her good teeth, abundant dark hair, and long legs, she gave a general impression of youth and prettiness. More than that, she was fearless with guys. She never hesitated to ask them out, and it was rare that they didn't say yes. She loved meeting new people and would give almost anyone a chance.

But once the date began, things tended to go downhill. The same openness and lack of guile that drew men to her like magnets tended to repel them with the same force. She would reveal off-putting truths about herself on a first date. She was ruthlessly honest about her initial impressions of men's naked bodies. But as often as Priya failed to get the third or fourth date, she forged ahead. She would laugh it off to Kelly, asking breezily why she should get hung up over one guy, anyway, when there were so many others out there to sample? Kelly noticed that she never seemed to learn anything from her failures, but then again, who was Kelly to give dating advice?

"Getting a date *is* that hard," Kelly persisted. "Otherwise I would have done it already."

"Uh, hello, have you heard of Tinder? We literally have an Amazon for lonely penises."

"I don't want a lonely penis," Kelly said.

"For this, you do. Just sign up for a dating website. You'll find someone in no time. We live in Man Jose. The odds are good."

"But the goods are odd," Kelly mourned. "Maybe there's just not anyone out there for me. Maybe I'll be a cat lady, except instead of cats, it'll be those robotic comfort seals from Japan." She ate a spoonful of soup. "Actually, that sounds kind of nice."

"No excuses. There is someone out there for literally *everyone*. Just keep an open mind. Or . . ." Kelly dipped a piece of popcorn while Priya paused dramatically. "Come out with me! I'll help you find a man. I'll get you a whole freaking Boy Scout troop. But, you know, of grown-ups. There's this awesome new bar in Menlo Park—"

"I don't do bars."

"Come on! The night is still young! Get your heinie over here and I won't let anyone touch it unless you sign a consent form first."

"It's just not my scene, Priya, you know that. Besides, I'm tired. I'm actually falling into bed right now." Kelly popped another piece of popcorn in her mouth. She could almost feel Priya squinting on the other end to make out the noise.

"You're not in bed. You're eating popcorn and tomato soup, aren't you?"

"Good night, Priya."

"Imagine how much better that soup would taste if your robust young lover were spooning it between your eager lips."

"Good *night*." Kelly tried not to snort with laughter into her soup as she hung up.

The next day, Kelly was actually glad to be spending her Sunday morning at Gary's small, stucco house in Santa Clara, babysitting her nieces. She needed a task that kept her mind from drifting to other things. Not that she didn't have fun spending time with her nieces, but she got it when her brother called these few hours spent running to Costco and to the dermatologist to get his plantar wart frozen off his "me time." Playing Baby Einstein games with the girls while their father was on hand to swoop in at the first signal of a potty training disaster was a whole different experience than being alone with them for four hours, the only thing standing between them and the kitchen knives. Now Gary was due home any minute and Kelly was exhausted.

"So what piece looks like it could fit with this piece?" she asked Bertie, the oldest by a few minutes, holding up a gray plastic wheel from the top-of-the-line Lego set she had splurged on as her Christmas gift. Bertie rummaged through the pieces spread on the floor and came up with a gray spoke. "Yes!" Kelly beamed, helping her lock the two together. "And what fits with this one?" She offered a red block. Bertie carefully scrutinized the piece, then responded by taking it and placing it calmly in her own mouth.

"No!" Kelly wrested the piece back just as she saw the quickest of the girls hurtling into the next room, naked from the waist down. "Emma? Where are you going?"

She gave chase and emerged into the entryway to see Gary coming through the front door. A Costco box in one arm, he easily scooped Emma up in the other, just in time to keep her from making her grand escape into the street. "Hi, Emma. Nice fashion statement," he said.

"I swear she was *just* clothed," Kelly panted.

"Where are Bertie and Hazel?"

"In the living room. Or at least they were twenty seconds ago, so by now they might be on Jupiter. Do you have any more boxes in the car?"

She accepted the keys Gary tossed at her with some relief as he walked calmly into the living room, bouncing Emma gently on his arm.

As Kelly and Gary put the groceries away, the girls happily comparing the animal crackers from the boxes they had pulled from the Costco boxes with glee, she regaled him with the story of last night's date with Martin. It was a little easier to laugh at after a decent night's sleep.

"Mom's going to kill me," she sighed, rearranging the produce in the fridge to fit a bulging bag of grapes.

"Eh, just maim, probably," Gary replied.

"If I show up at that wedding without a date, she'll lose her mind. She'll sell me to some other family on the black market."

"Not sure there are too many couples out there looking to buy twenty-nine-year-old children, but it could happen."

"Don't you have any single guy friends you could set me up with?" Kelly pleaded, turning to look at her brother.

"Single guy friends? Kelly, my entire life is spent between preschool, Mommy and Me, and these four walls." He gestured around the house. "I murmur Nickelodeon theme songs in my sleep. I know the origin story of flipping Caillou. What about any of that makes

27

you think I have single guy friends?" He put a bag of oats in a cabinet then turned back around. "Although there is this one guy," he said slowly.

"Who? As long as he's free on March seventh, I'll take him."

"No," Gary shook his head, thinking. "It wouldn't work."

"Why not? Is he married? Is he a felon? We don't need to let that come between us."

"He's too similar to your exes. Robbie and—what was that guy's name from college? The one who didn't want you to meet his parents until after you'd gotten your teeth whitened?"

"Nick. So? It sounds like your friend's my type," Kelly responded.

"That's the problem. Your type isn't working."

It was true that Kelly's relationship history read like a warning label for women everywhere. Both Robbie and Nick, the college class president with the gargantuan list of extracurriculars, had looked good to Kelly on paper, but made her feel bad about herself in real life. Spotted in between were a few short-lived flings, if "flings" can describe a series of dignified lunch appointments with coders who ended each date with a hug as tentative as if she were an electric fence.

"You ended up miserable both times," Gary went on. "I want you to have something better, not the same thing all over again. It's not a good match." He broke down the boxes and stacked them by the recycling bin. "Thanks for helping out today. I'm a new man without that wart."

"Yeah, sure," Kelly said, with the slightly deflated feeling that she was being dismissed.

On the ride home, she couldn't help but wonder if she had just sealed her own doom again. She was sure that Gary was genuine about wanting the best for her, but she questioned too if hearing about her behavior on the date with Martin made him reluctant to burden any of his friends with her company. She already knew she was a mess. But was she that much of a mess that her own brother couldn't recommend her? As she pulled into the parking garage beneath her building and shut off the engine, she wondered grimly if Caillou was single.

three

· · · · · ·

Back at work that week, Kelly sat in a room that was open, square, and full of lights: fluorescent ceiling beams, glowing computer monitors, and a bank of control panels with switches, knobs, and blinking indicators. Beside her was Dr. Masden, a psychologist whose black eyes angled up in a very attractive way that she would have seen if she weren't nervously avoiding those eyes. Opposite them, an oversize monitor displayed a digital waist-up image of a being named Confibot. The image looked essentially like a man, sporting short, combed blond hair and a small-check plaid shirt. But where a human face should have been was a set of dotted lines over a blank white space: two oblong rounds for eyes, a triangle for a nose, a straight line where a mouth would go, really just the suggestion of features.

"We need to pin down his range of facial options before we can settle on a final set of features," Kelly was saying to the psychologist.

"Then we can start building him. So, say, what face should he make when he greets a user who's just woken up?"

"A pleasant smile, I would think," Dr. Masden answered.

"Well, yeah, but I need you to tell me exactly. Like, here." Kelly scooted closer to the doctor's computer monitor on the control panel, blowing up the diagram of Confibot's head in front of him so that it was minutely imaged under a set of gridlines. "Show me specifically how his mouth should be positioned."

"There's no one way it *should* be positioned, Kelly. Human behaviors aren't that precise."

Kelly shook her head, clicking into a folder on her own computer to display tile after tile of saved files compiled from her own research and the focus groups and surveys that AHI's marketing team had done. "This is my research so far on microexpressions alone. Human behaviors are *totally* precise." She knew that her own instinct to apply a mathematical, logical viewpoint to everything in life was one of the things that made her so good at this job. It was essential to the physical building of a robot, to giving it hard skills, like teaching Zed how to walk, and it was why she had always chosen to stay more in the mechanical and electrical engineering lane at work, focusing on building the "body" of the robot, so to speak. Confibot was the first project she had led—the first time she was also in charge of the "brain." Her concrete, analytical way of thinking had always worked before. Just because she was grappling with something far more conceptual didn't mean she was about to change her methods now.

Confibot was also the highest-stakes project in her career thus far. Anita Riveras, AHI's CEO, had tasked each of the engineers in her Consumer Products division with inventing a caregiver or assistant robot—one of the market's hottest niches. In three months, their inventions would all be pitted against each other for investor funding. Kelly had decided to create the most believably humanoid robot of the bunch, capable of the most nuanced social interactions, based on the astounding body of research she had uncovered about the health and lifestyle benefits of companionship. If she could get Confibot just right, she knew she stood a real chance at winning this.

"There are very specific, scientific ways that people react to different gestures, expressions, tones of voice," Kelly continued now.

"Well, how would you respond?" the doctor asked. "Think about what you would want in a robot who's taking care of you and living with you. You shouldn't discount your own instincts here."

"Instincts may be your business," she insisted. "Data is mine. The science has to be there to back up every choice I make."

"Then I'm providing you my insights as data. I'm a trained psychologist," Dr. Masden pressed. "I'm here to give professional guidance."

"But that's not good enough! I mean, not that your insights aren't good," she said quickly, turning to the doctor, hating the way she could feel her cheeks instinctively flush as she did. Frankly, the fact that AHI had brought in the hottest psychologist in Santa Clara County to assist her on the project was just rude. She had enough on her plate between working on Confibot and worrying about having to admit to her mom how the date with Martin had gone. Not to mention now needing to find another date on her own. For Kelly, social interactions with any element of uncertainty were a source of stress more than excitement. She was a woman who wondered what she had done wrong when the cashier didn't wish her a good day.

She needed to get started on building Confibot's physical model, but first she had to get past this task of designing his face and voice and mannerisms so she would know what to build. She needed to focus on facts, not Dr. Masden's "insights."

"The way that Confibot interacts with users has to be perfect," she asserted. "There are already other caregiver and companion robots out there on the market. If we're not the best, we might as well not be out there at all! And the only way Confibot's going to be the best is if he's the most realistically human."

"Kelly, to replicate a human, you have to understand humans."

"I do! Why do you think I took six semesters of biology in college? I understand how the human body works, how animal bodies work. I know how to translate those structures into mechanical form."

"I'm not talking about the body." The psychologist looked away for a second, pursing his lips as if searching for his next words. "Designing a personality is a nebulous thing, Kelly. You're never going to get anywhere if you're so tied down to the data. I'm only trying to say that you might want to approach this in a different way." He put a palliating hand on Kelly's arm. Instinctively, she jerked away and crossed her arms. Dr. Masden looked taken aback as he abruptly withdrew his hand. It seemed he hadn't even realized he had put it there in the first place. "Sorry, I—"

"I won't be approaching it that way!" Kelly declared. As soon as she heard how weird that sounded, she tried to laugh, but the sound came out as more of a tubercular bleat. Dr. Masden's eyes were increasingly confused and also very deep and black and olive-shaped—

"I'm sorry if I made you uncomfortable just now, I wasn't even thinking. I never want our work environment to be less than professional," he said.

Kelly stiffly crossed her legs below her crossed arms, walling herself behind a defensive pretzel of limbs. Great, she thought, let's do the one thing that will make the situation more awkward and talk about it. It would be so much simpler if everyone could just do what she did and suppress their emotions, stuffing them in the back of the closet, right next to the childhood traumas and the performing-in-your-third-grade-play-naked-and-then-all-your-teeth-fall-out dreams.

"I'm not comfortable. I mean uncomfortable."

"It's just that you seemed a little uncomfortable when I put my hand on your arm, just now," he continued. "I didn't mean anything by it, I just express myself physically. I'm a very expressive person, but I realize it's unfair to make assumptions about your communication style since we've only been working on this simulation together for a week."

"Well, I've been working on it for months before you got here!" Kelly exclaimed. The anxieties simmering in her had been lit to a boil. She felt the tug of that same old instinct to flee the scene, yet this was her project—she couldn't. She was trapped. But maybe it was time she blew up the room instead of trying to tunnel out. After all, she reminded herself, she'd been quite content back when she began developing the Confibot simulation all on her own. Then this guy had to come and get his big—not big, average, definitely average—hands all over her. That is, all over the project. Insinuating that she didn't understand people. So much of why she had gone into engineering in the first place was because it didn't ask her to try to make sense of people, who, let's face it, were often nonsensical anyway. This was her safe space, and he had breached it. But it didn't matter; she didn't need him. Sure, he was responsible for providing all the psychological bases for the interactions they were architecting, but that was soft science. Kelly, red cheeks and all, stared the doctor down.

Dr. Masden scraped back in his own chair. "I wasn't aware that you felt that way."

"I guess you weren't paying attention," she replied.

But now Dr. Masden didn't look confused. He looked insulted. "I'm a psychologist. Not to flatter myself, but I pay pretty close attention to people's behavior."

"Then stop! You're here to help develop the simulation, not analyze me. Which you're doing a pretty poor job of anyway."

"You think so? All right, then, here you go. Normally I charge hundreds an hour for this, but you're about to get it for free." Kelly tried to hold her crimson face high as the doctor leveled his searching gaze on her.

"You're a control freak."

"Is that the clinical term?"

Ignoring her, he plowed forward. "You're smart and you're good at this job and you know it. But part of why you're good at it is because you're a perfectionist. Any unknown variables that are introduced might mess up your perfect little world. And another human being is an unknown and unknowable variable, and in this case I'm the lucky one crossing your path. For the first couple days I thought you were just a little shy, but now I can see that you're constantly on edge, with antisocial tendencies bordering on aggression. Any suggestion of friendliness is enough to upset you. Who knows what kind of crazy, frightening, fun, sad, unpredictable things could happen if you made a friend, or more than a friend, so why not just cut it off before it even starts? Better to have people think you want nothing to do with them and leave you alone than for them to find out everything that's wrong with you. I wondered initially why you cared so much about developing a companion robot. It's pretty obvious now that you're so interested because you're afraid that you yourself are going to end up alone, and guess what? If you don't change, you will."

Wow. Kelly had thought he was just going to call her uptight. Her entire being froze. She pondered how long she could go without making a response. If she just stayed still long enough, eventually she would be left alone. Eventually an asteroid would collide with the Earth and render her whole predicament irrelevant.

"I'm sorry. That was way out of line."

Kelly's eyes focused to realize Dr. Masden was looking at her, his own face now flushed. She was embarrassed, she was frustrated, she was flustered, and all she wanted was to get the doctor out of the room so this moment could end. Strike first, regret later. It was the safest tactic she knew.

"When you spend all day picking apart other people's flaws instead of acknowledging your own, I guess it comes naturally."

The doctor shook his head and pushed himself up from the chair.

"Good luck, Kelly." And with a slam of the control room's back door, he was gone, leaving her, once again, alone.

Kelly swiveled back to the control panel, unconsciously kneading her hands. There came the regret. What would happen to the Confibot project? Would the company find a replacement psychologist? Would they pull the simulation entirely? Did everyone think of her the way Dr. Masden did? Were they right?

Kelly had always known she was an introvert. She was awkward, sure, and not a brilliant presenter or performer, but essentially a functioning person. But maybe she had it all wrong. Maybe Martin had been relieved rather than bewildered when she made her untimely exit. *Antisocial tendencies bordering on aggression . . . everything that's wrong with you . . .* The bulbs on the control panel misted into a glittery haze, like Christmas lights seen through an icy window, as Kelly's eyes filled.

She squeezed back the tears, embarrassed, reminding herself that she didn't have time to loaf around the office, blubbering like a too-short kid at a roller coaster entrance. After all, without a partner, she had more work to do than ever. The soft science stuff didn't seem quite so minor as she pondered tackling it without a professional guide. She adjusted her chair and got back to work.

Kelly had never made a trip to the principal's office, but she imagined now that this was what it must feel like. The airy prism in which she waited for her boss, however, was considerably more chic than a public school office. Sculptures of fluid silver filaments were scattered with effortless grace among awards, books, and photos on the white oak shelves, and a broad desk, arched like a ship's bow, speared into a sweeping view of the palm-tree-lined avenues of San Jose. Through the frosted glass of the door, Kelly could read in reverse the letters "Anita Riveras, CEO."

As Kelly studied Anita's carefully curated photographs, she smoothed her already smooth blouse self-consciously. Even in miniature, Anita's presence was formidable. The angles of her cheekbones, her sleek black bobbed hair, even her offered handshake all somehow aligned into a careful geometric construction. Kelly wondered what she would look like with a bob, if people would take her more seriously if she had Anita's expensive yet effortless-looking hair. She tried looping up the edges just to see.

The door swung open decisively and she dropped her hair, simultaneously catching her foot as she stood up too fast. She had a tendency to hurtle through life like she was running a one-woman three-legged race. But Anita swept to her high-backed chair like she didn't see.

"Have a seat, Kelly."

She fixed Kelly with a clear gaze. There was nothing visibly judgmental about it, but Kelly felt judged. Anita could do that. She let the silence hang for a moment. Her chair was a curve of pristine white leather. The weightless ease with which she sat in a chair with no arms was conspicuous, as if she had bought that chair just to show off her mastery of the art of sitting.

"I'm sorry about what happened," Kelly blurted out.

"What did happen, Kelly?"

"I just . . . it was a personal issue between myself and the doctor. It had nothing to do with the project."

"But it does. Because you needed him to complete the project, and he's no longer here."

Kelly's throat felt parched. "Are you—do you mean that I can't complete the project?"

"It's your project, Kelly. You tell me. Can you?"

There was a right answer to this. Kelly's confidence rose. "Yes, I can. Please let me, you know how much Confibot means to me."

"You say it means a lot to you, but from your performance, I have yet to see why. Convince me."

"There's so much we can do with it." Kelly's words came faster

39

now as they pivoted to her work, flowing with liveliness and ease. Talking about Confibot brought out her fervor for science, awakening the little girl who used to take apart Gary's Speak & Spell and rebuild it again and again until she knew exactly how it worked. "If we can create a fully convincing android, with which people can interact as if it were a human, we can take robotic caretaking to a whole new level. Users can develop meaningful relationships with their Confibots, making them true robotic confidants. If you look at the research about the effects of companionship and mental stimulation on health outcomes, the physical and lifestyle devastation of loneliness is astonishing, I mean, it can increase your risk of everything from dementia to heart disease to arthritis to—"

"Old people are a gold mine," Anita mused, her eyes trained far out the window.

"I—I'm sorry?"

Anita sat up smoothly in her chair, focusing on Kelly. "The Baby Boomers are on the brink. When they crash, I plan to be ready to reap the dividends." Not exactly how Kelly liked to think of her own work, but she bit her tongue. "Confibot's commercial potential is massive, we both know that." Anita waved a hand tipped with bone-painted nails. "The success of your project hinges on your ability to complete an android that can pass for human, and you're the closest of our engineers to achieving that. And with that technology, we can go anywhere."

"I am? I mean, I *am*. Thank you. It's been thrilling to see how close Confibot is coming to real humanity, and I—"

"According to current projections, you're the closest," Anita corrected. "But other companies, even some of your own coworkers, have been logging astonishing progress as well." Sitting back again, Anita looked pleasant, unhurried, yet still radiating a cool intensity.

Meanwhile, Kelly was sweating like a lumberjack. "Right, so . . . I'll get back to it, then?"

"You are directly competing with these coworkers for investor funding," Anita went on, as if Kelly hadn't spoken. "And if you win the competition, you will be directly competing with the creators of every other robotic caregiver and assistant device in the world. The company that comes to market first gets to charge a premium. Anyone who lags behind has to cut prices to compete. So if you cannot make AHI the first to market, I will find another engineer who can." She scrutinized Kelly with eyes that were impossible to read. "Confibot is the first project that you've spearheaded," she noted. "Your first opportunity to bring one of your own ideas to life. As such, it requires high-level project management skills on which you have not yet been tested. You're building more than a physical robot here. You are designing a whole person. And if you fail to make this work, you will not be afforded such a high-level opportunity again." Kelly tried to gulp, but her throat was so raw, so dry, that it stopped halfway. "Robotics engineering is a human discipline, Kelly. It's collaborative, it's interpersonal. If you fail to think on this level, you will fail as an engineer."

Every time Anita said the word "fail," the blood in Kelly's ears pulsed painfully hot. Her boss was calling her interpersonal skills a failure. Dr. Masden had called her pathologically antisocial. What was she doing wrong? Was she that incompetent at things that appeared so basic for everyone else? Was she writing her own doom in her career, her relationships? Would she push everyone away forever?

"I'm taking a sizable risk on you, Kelly," Anita was saying as Kelly forced herself back to the surface.

"And I'm grateful for it. I won't let you down."

"No." Anita looked at Kelly with a placid smile. "You won't."

Kelly held herself together long enough to make it out the door. As soon as she was down the hall, she allowed her knees to turn to jelly, pressing her back against the cool wall, lifting her face to the fluorescent-lit ceiling. She didn't know what she was doing wrong, but it was clear that there was something. When she came to a dead end in her work—a limb moving at an unnatural angle, a memory fault—she would force herself to back out of the situation and look at it from a bird's-eye view, searching for a new way in, trying something different. And here, she had to do the same thing.

When she walked back into the lab several minutes later, Priya was already there. She rose from her chair. "Finally, let's get lunch. I was about to eat my intern. Also I have to show you these sick pictures my friend posted from this new club called Sadie Hawkins. I'd totally take you there if you weren't still being No-Club Nancy." Priya began fishing out her phone, but Kelly interrupted her.

"I'll go."

"What?"

Kelly looked at Priya with resolve. Here was something different she could try. It wouldn't solve her problems with Confibot, but taking any action would make her feel better about herself right now.

"Let's do it," she said firmly. "This weekend, I'm ready to try out the clubs."

four

· · · · · ·

Kelly's second thoughts about this scheme hit her immediately. Priya buzzed for the rest of the week, ready to plan them the perfect night out, whipping out her phone at random moments to show Kelly the latest bar that they just had to try, or a Pinterest mood board of hairstyles that she knew Kelly could definitely rock. Priya went out with friends virtually every weekend, it seemed, but Kelly was her going-out white whale, and her electric anticipation of this weekend was at a high. Meanwhile, every time she brought up their plans, Kelly was vividly reminded of the last time they had gone out together, more than a year ago: she had ended up with her shoes in her purse, her drink in her lap, and her dignity somewhere in the next town. She may have tried to gaze flirtily at a man across the bar while drinking seductively from her cocktail and ended up sticking her straw up her nose instead. She chose not to remember.

Yet here she was Friday night, at Priya's high-rise apartment in North San Jose, sitting squashed between pink, orange, and gold pillows on the bed while Priya battled wills with her eyeliner. "Are you sure you won't let me do your makeup?" Priya asked.

"I already did it," Kelly said, watching Priya attempt a winged eye with her liquid liner. Every time she fixed one eye, she had to add more to the other to even it out, and the effect was increasingly alarming. Kelly had already worked her way out of Priya's offer to dress her by reminding her of what she did to her own clothing last time. She would be more comfortable in her own jeans and shirt. It was just a simple black top, but it had gold buttons on it, which she had convinced herself would demonstrate to the world that she was a free-wheeling partier.

"*Finally* you're coming out again. We are going to scorch this club tonight," Priya asserted, pausing to assess her handiwork. "We are going to slay on the dance floor. *Flay* on the dance floor. Flog it to a pulp."

"Nasty." Kelly wrinkled her nose.

"Come on, it'll be fun," Priya urged. Kelly wasn't sure that her definition of fun looked like Priya's, but with "antisocial tendencies bordering on aggression" ringing in her ears, she knew that she needed to give it a try. Part of why she so seldom agreed to go out with Priya was because a night out with Priya was a *night*. As much as Kelly adored her friend, she was convinced that she was harmlessly certifiable. Her historic hijinks ranged from commandeering the PA system at the grocery store to announce that the vegetables had gained sentience and were on the attack to giving the department store Santa Claus a lap dance and nearly a heart attack in the bargain. But as long as Kelly could stay out of the spotlight herself, she enjoyed Priya doing her thing. Maybe having a best friend who was "the crazy one" allowed Kelly to be anything but.

Priya did manage to get Kelly to borrow some of her shoes—a pair of nude heels with gold studs all over them. Kelly had to admit, they looked pretty good as long as she was standing in front of the bedroom mirror, holding on to a chair back for dear life. Logically she knew that the way to walk in them was just to transfer her body's weight onto the front halves of her feet. But her body didn't seem to grasp the concept.

While Kelly pondered physics, Priya scrutinized her own butt in the full-length mirror with a painter's meticulous eye. "I'm going to give you a very precious gift," she announced.

"A Tesla?" Kelly asked.

"Better. My three rules for dating in Silicon Valley."

"I'm the one who grew up here," Kelly reminded her. "I should be teaching you about Silicon Valley."

"Uh, no, the fact that I grew up in New York is what makes me an expert. I've been outside the bubble. I have perspective. You could have a guy come up to you and act like a total tech bro and not even know it because the air around you is so dense with tech bros."

"Okay, so what are the rules?"

"Numero uno: Don't go out with anyone who works in robotics. He'll hack your phone while you sleep, looking for company secrets."

"How do you know that?"

"Just guessing," Priya said innocently as she stuffed things into her purse: her phone, lipstick, keys. She threw in a tin of mints, took it back out and tasted one, grimaced, then tossed the tin back in anyway. "Two: If a guy tries to pick you up by telling you that he's employee number whatever at a certain company, run. That's a 'douche crossing ahead' sign if I ever saw one." She slung her purse onto her shoulder and paused. "Unless he's, like, number four and it's Facebook. Then you go for it. Get that coin, queen."

The girls headed for the door. "And number three?" Kelly asked.

"Everyone in Silicon Valley works way too hard during the day. So if you're going to go out at night?" Priya gave her a sly smile. "Have some fucking fun."

They could hear the muted hubbub from inside the bar all the way up the bustling Menlo Park sidewalk as they approached. Inside, Kelly regarded the trendy exposed ductwork and glowing blue lights with a wary eye. Priya dove into a group of guys like a puppy into a snowbank, but Kelly inched her way more slowly into the dauntingly fashionable crowd. She settled at the bar first and tried not to stare at the bartender's hairstyle as he mixed her drink. His head was completely shaved except for a long tuft at the top, gathered into an aggressively perky ponytail. Maybe she was supposed to stare at it?

"All of our ice is made using water unlocked from the melting polar ice caps," he informed her, sliding her a glass. "It's the purest water on Earth. Twenty-three dollars." Kelly dragged out some cash.

Just once she would love to be at a fancy bar or restaurant and have an unfamiliar cocktail delivered to her table, like in the movies. No, make that a fancy dessert with some sort of froufrou chocolate thingamabob on top. "Oh, I didn't order that," she would say.

"I know, mademoiselle," her waiter with the pencil-thin mustache would reply as he gestured across the restaurant. "That gentleman did."

And she would look across and see, smiling mysteriously at her, the most dapper, debonair, dashing—

46

"Is this seat taken?"

Kelly turned to see the most dapper, debonair, dashing man she had ever seen.

Well, not quite *the most* dashing man, but this guy was certainly cute, with hazel eyes and rounded lips. Kelly stuttered.

"No, I'm alone," she said. Probably unnecessarily.

Hazel Eyes laughed, slinging himself onto the stool. "Well, that's lucky for me." She blushed vibrantly enough to be visible even through the neon-suffused gloom of the bar's atmosphere. He nodded at her drink. "Did you get the line about the ice caps water too?"

"I did."

"To global warming. It may kill us all, but at least it tastes good." He raised his glass and clinked it against hers with a mischievous grin. Kelly restrained herself from swiveling to look behind her and make sure he was really smiling at her. Was it possible that all she had to do was show up at a bar and within minutes, she'd found a man who was cute, charming, and interested?

"I'm Kelly." As soon as she offered her hand, she regretted it, recognizing that it was cold and clammy from her drink. But he shook it without hesitation.

"Reece," he said.

Kelly nervously switched her crossed legs and, in the process, kicked Reece in the shin. "Sorry!" she blurted.

"No worries—wow, killer shoes. Mind if I take a look?"

"Um . . ."

He bent and lifted her foot, nearly placing it in his own lap, examining her high heel with a practiced eye. "I *love* women's shoes." Kelly felt her bubble burst. Of course. The good-looking guy who was actually expressing interest in her had a foot fetish. She had a sudden vision of Reece sitting next to her at the family table at Clara's wedding, calmly conversing with her mother while holding her foot in his lap and stroking it.

She pulled her foot back, and Reece looked up, surprised. "Sorry, I didn't mean—" But he cut himself off as another cute guy, this one with shoulder-length black hair, approached, smiling. Kelly found herself momentarily distracted. Priya was actually right. This wasn't so hard. She straightened, smiling back at him.

But then Reece stood up and turned to Black Hair and gave him a long, deep kiss. Very long. Very deep.

He turned back to her, smiling every bit as broadly as he should after a kiss like that. "This is my boyfriend, Marco. Marco, you have got to check out Kelly's shoes."

Kelly stood from her stool, setting her feet, or rather, her shoes, which were apparently her chief attraction—and they weren't even her shoes—firmly on the polished concrete floor.

"I've got to go," she said abruptly.

"Okay—oh, wait, did you think—oh, no, honey, I'm sorry." Reece laughed.

"You shouldn't give people mixed signals," Kelly responded hotly, before she could stop herself.

"It's just small talk," Reece insisted, but Kelly was already pushing her way into the crowd, away from the bar, slipping on her heels as she went. "Try putting your weight onto the fronts of your feet!" he called after her.

Kelly managed to locate Priya and extricate her from within the recesses of a dense knot of men. "There you are!" Priya said. "Did you meet any cute boys?"

"Yeah, but they got to each other first. Can we go yet?"

"Have you found a date yet?"

"Can't you just find one for me?"

"Can't you stop being a pussy?"

"Priya."

"Kelly."

"I really just want to go home."

The serious look that Kelly was giving Priya must have translated through the gloom because Priya took her by both hands. "We're not going home. You need a date, and I want to see you have some fun for once! You work so hard, you deserve that! Live your life!"

"Okay, okay," Kelly acquiesced.

"Look, this is a tough crowd. And they all take themselves way too seriously anyway. The last guy I met just went on and on about how he only uses free-trade mustache pomade."

"Don't you know any other bars? Like, preferably somewhere where there's absolutely no pressure to be cool?"

Priya's eyes lit up. "Girl. I've got this."

One Uber ride later, they arrived in a visibly grimier part of town outside a club named, with an impressive show of shamelessness, Bodies. Kelly gestured to the sign, where the "i" flickered repeatedly. "This *bodes* poorly," she said.

Priya gave her side-eye.

The interior was eerily similar to how Kelly imagined it would be to shrink down, Magic School Bus–style, and travel to the inside of one of her own organs. The atmosphere was dark, humid, and hormonal.

As difficult as it was to hear over the bass-charged soundtrack, Kelly and Priya found themselves approached by guys almost as soon as they wedged themselves next to the bar. But no guy who talked to them got further than three sentences before making some dubious claim about the down payment he had just placed on a condo in Los Altos Hills, or his app's stratospheric IPO. They were the sort of statements that were off-putting enough in broad daylight, but were made even worse when shouted incongruously over lyrics that were mostly thinly disguised metaphors for fellatio. Everything in Kelly was telling her to flee again, to throw in the towel—after taking a thorough shower—but she truly wanted to make this work. All she needed was someone she could see enough times over the next month and a half for it to not be bizarre to invite him to her sister's wedding. Was that really so hard?

Priya turned her back to the bar and rested her elbows on it, gazing out over the heaving dance floor. Finally she pointed to a guy with spiky black hair. "Him," she declared. "Go get him."

Kelly crinkled her nose. "Why him?"

"Because I want his friend," Priya said, eyeing the guy next to him. Kelly shook her head, smiling.

"How am I supposed to ask this guy for a date when we can't even talk?" Kelly yelled. The music would only be louder on the dance floor, the belly of the beast.

Priya spotted the platform where a rainbow-haired DJ was hunched over a laptop, zoned out and nodding. "Chillax, I'll take care of that. All you have to do is get yo' man."

While holding a real conversation was impossible, it seemed that approaching within five feet of another person and making eye contact was all that was required of a courting ritual at Bodies. Kelly pursed her lips, furtively eyeing the movements of everyone dancing around her, assessing how to imitate them—her past few attempts at dancing had left her with as much faith in her own skills as in the structural integrity of a sandcastle. Fortunately, the courting ritual had been half the battle, as dancing at Bodies also seemed to consist mostly of proximity. But her partner came closer and closer, gyrating, running his hands repeatedly around her hips and over her jeans. Kelly gulped, but told herself to just go with it. Dancing was actually less awkward than any of her conversations had been. She smiled at the guy and he smiled back. Maybe she should give him a chance. It was time she moved in and completed her task.

"I'm Kelly, what's your name?" she asked Spiky Hair. She couldn't call him that forever.

"Totally," he nodded.

"I'm Kelly," she shouted.

He leaned in close to her neck, his nose on her collarbone. Kelly flinched instinctively, but then tentatively leaned her own nose toward him, attempting to mimic the bizarre dance move. But then he sniffed deeply and shook his head. "You smell fine to me," he yelled. This was not working.

Suddenly the bass halted mid-pound. As a slower, less ear-rattling selection began, Kelly glanced at the DJ's stand to see Priya there, giving Kelly a thumbs-up. Kelly smiled as Priya swayed, getting into the jam, a throwback Mariah Carey tune. Now this Kelly might be able to work with.

She turned back to her guy. "I'm Kelly," she tried again.

This time he got it. "Stan." He nodded, pointing at himself. Kelly cleared her throat.

"Do you—" But just when Kelly was about to make her proposition, a new voice entered the fray, battling Mariah's and losing very,

very badly. Priya had apparently gotten too deeply into the jam. Having somehow procured a mic, she was singing along, loudly, joyfully oblivious to the melody.

"This isn't a karaoke bar!" some guy shouted at her.

"It is tonight!" she cried, soliciting a smattering of laughs and cheers. "Come on!" A few people started singing along halfheartedly.

The time was now. If they didn't get out of here soon, Priya's "singing" was liable to get her arrested for a noise violation.

"Do you want to hang out sometime?" Kelly tried again. Just as she got the words out, Priya unleashed a howl so resounding, so soulful, so reckless in its treatment of pitch, that Kelly worried every glass and eardrum in the place might break. Kelly turned to look at her friend, who had one arm raised in the air in triumph, swaying to the music.

She turned back to Stan only to find there was no Stan. She wheeled around and worked her way through the pulsing couples around her, wondering if they had just gotten separated, but he was nowhere to be found. A hot wave of embarrassment flooded her. As soon as she had finally gotten up the courage to ask a guy out, he had vanished.

Another man, this one wearing a vest with nothing under it, slinked up to her. "Girl, are you from Mars?" he asked, "Because—" He stopped and just stared at her, sipping his drink, apparently trying to remember the rest of the line. He found himself a spot and sat on the floor of the club to think it over.

"Please go home," Kelly instructed him wearily. It must have taken some pretty potent substances to give him worse conversational skills than her. Looking around, she realized that half the club was now singing along with Priya, cheering her on. Kelly gave a moment of silent admiration to her friend. Priya had truly pulled a Priya.

As she wailed the last note, Kelly pulled her off the platform to the mingled cheers and boos of the crowd.

"Why aren't you dancing with someone?" Priya shouted.

"Because I'm unattractive and have no social skills," Kelly said.

"What?"

Kelly just shook her head, not wanting to repeat herself. "Spiky Hair vanished."

"I'm going to get a drink, you want one?" Priya shout-asked.

Kelly shook her head no, but Priya held on to her. "Can you spot me some cash?" she asked. "I'll pay you back at work."

Kelly reached into her jeans pocket, where she had slipped some cash at home, not wanting to carry a purse all night. But the pocket was empty. Frantically, she checked all her pockets, turning them inside out—nothing.

"What's wrong?" Priya asked.

"Is it normal for a guy you dance with to keep feeling you up around the hips?" Kelly said.

"It is when you've got an ass like that!" Priya swatted her playfully.

But Kelly sighed. "I think that jerk pickpocketed me when we were dancing."

"What? No way. Where is he?"

Priya shouldered her way through the masses, trying to spot the culprit, the fire of justice in her eyes, but Kelly stopped her. "Can we please just go?" She wasn't sure which was worse, being ghosted because a guy didn't want to go out with you or because he had just robbed you blind.

Kelly wrestled with herself as she sat in front of her laptop that night, unable to fall asleep. Logically, she knew that online dating had long been destigmatized. Everyone did it. Normal people. Non-murderer people. She knew two separate couples who had gotten married after meeting online. But something about it still felt to her like giving up. Like admitting that even though she lived in the man-mine that was Silicon Valley, the traditional means by which humans had found mates for millennia had failed her. Or, more accurately, she had failed them.

Then again, she knew it was unwise to make assumptions about something without verifying the reality of those assumptions. Suspicion was the enemy of knowledge. Could she justify ruling out online dating without testing her hypotheses against it?

After all, she reasoned, signing up didn't mean she actually had to go on dates. She could make a profile just to see what was out there, from the safety of her home sweet browser. She never had to actually even talk to anybody, come to think of it. And most of them probably wouldn't trace her IP address and come to her house to hack her apart with an axe, right? What the heck, she thought. She was feeling reckless.

Kelly found a site that offered a free trial membership and had the least painfully posed stock people on its homepage. The first thing the profile asked for was a picture. She took a selfie, then uploaded it before she could scrutinize it and think better of it.

The first few questions were pretty simple—basic physical attributes, religious and political affiliations, education and career highlights. Then it asked what she did for fun. Into Kelly's mind immediately flashed an image of herself at home in a Slanket, eating a cake she'd made for one person in a mug in the microwave, watching one of the terrible, wonderful movies Mary-Kate and Ashley Olsen made before they became eccentric old ladies of the Upper East Side. Even Kelly sensed that this was probably not the impression she wanted to give a man. She wracked her brain for anything that normal people might do for fun. Biking. Bicycling? She put down biking.

And now a new image flashed into Kelly's mind: a new version of her. This New Kelly was biking down an idyllic sun-washed street, the folds of a colorful dress swashing over her knees, her naturally wavy hair lifting in the wind and looking, for once, impeccable. She was pedaling expertly and easily. And she was smiling. Beside her on his own bicycle was a man. Kelly couldn't get a clear visual of his face, but she knew that he was smiling too. They pedaled along in perfect synchronicity, passing simultaneously under the same shadows and the same golden patches of sun.

Real Kelly found herself smiling too. While she had no actual desire to take up biking, she had to admit that it would be nice to have someone to pedal with. What if this was it? What if tonight was the night she found not just a wedding date, but something much more?

Her heart was beating entirely too fast as she navigated to the next section. Then the site started asking questions that she found increasingly unreasonable. She scanned the list: *Where do you see yourself in ten years?* Clinging to a raft, stranded in the glacier melt that used to be San Jose. *What do you want out of a relationship?* To prove to my mom that I'm not single. And sure, it would be kind of nice to be curling up in bed with someone right now instead of sitting here alone, answering these questions. *What makes you happy?* Uh . . . does the fun night in the Slanket count?

Kelly paused. She was not accustomed to failing a test, but she knew that she didn't have the right answers for any of these questions. Say the perfect man really was waiting for her on the other side of this questionnaire. What did she expect to happen? That he would fall for her immediately and they'd bicycle away into the sunset? Kelly's heart began to thump more slowly, more painfully, as she realized that more likely, she would send him pedaling as fast as possible in the opposite direction—like Dr. Masden, like Martin, like everyone else. Best-case scenario, it would happen immediately. Worst case, it would happen after she'd fallen for him just enough to really, really not want for that to happen.

It was time to enter her qualifications for a man. Kelly rationalized that it was necessary to be specific. A whole host of unpleasant potential eventualities lurked on the other side of this page: awkward mismatches, wasted time and energy, heartbreak. The only way to reduce the odds of these potentialities was to provide the most robust possible data for the website's algorithm. The site suggested writing something simple and friendly like "Looking for a guy who works hard, plays hard, and loves to laugh. Must love dogs!" Kelly almost laughed aloud. That could describe literally anyone.

Height: 5'10"–5'11". Athletic build. Symmetrical smile. Master's degree in a scientific field. Ambitious professionally but laid-back personally. Sense of humor. Love of animals. Love of movies. Love of Twinkies. Close to his family emotionally, but not physically. She didn't need another mother breathing down her neck. Good at board games, but not better than her. Likes mountain vacations. Likes Harry Potter. Likes the Talking Heads. Knows how to cook but can afford to eat out. Prefers hand-drawn animation to CG. Wears V-necks. Wears boxer briefs. Doesn't wear yellow. Drinks martinis and knows how to make them. Has been to at least three different countries. Has been to at least ten different states. Cares about his friends but not more than about her. Doesn't eat prunes. Has a good heart.

Something manic had taken over Kelly. Maybe it was the alcohol, or maybe it was a subconscious knowledge that the more difficult she made it to find someone, the less likely it was that she'd have to face whatever might come next. Because *anything* could come next.

She finally finished her list, clicked Submit, and waited while the site spun its wheel.

five

. . . . . .

While Kelly waited for her results, she realized that she didn't
even know how this was supposed to work. Would the dating site find her perfect match immediately? She had a fleeting image of a guy materializing at her door. She tried to calm herself: she would probably never go on a date with a stranger from the internet anyway. She probably wouldn't have the guts to even contact him. But there went her heart again.

"No match found," the site said in unnecessarily large letters. "Try deselecting some of the attributes you've chosen in your ideal partner."

There it was in crystal-clear pixels: written proof that her perfect person did not exist. No woman could be expected to find this mythical man if even a computer couldn't. Kelly sighed, a sound edged with both disappointment and relief. Here was another flood to douse her flicker of illogical hope that love might be out there for her. Even if the site had presented her ideal partner, would she be the ideal partner for him? If she'd never seen a true model of love, it stood to reason that she would never be able to replicate it herself. It was easiest to just close out of the site and forget the whole thing. Yet up rose the tiny flame again, still flickering. She still wanted love, maybe even needed it on some encoded biological level. *The physical and lifestyle devastation of loneliness is astonishing* . . . She grimaced as her own words to Anita came back to her. Even Dr. Masden had said that her research was relevant to her own life.

So cocooned was she in her own thoughts that when her phone rang in the silent apartment, she jumped a full inch off her chair. Kelly squeezed her eyes shut and inhaled. Since her date with Martin, her phone held seven unanswered calls, ten texts, and four e-mails from her mom. If she didn't satisfy Diane's curiosity soon, either her mother or her phone might combust.

"Kelly, why do you have a phone if you're not going to answer it?" her mom asked as soon as she picked up. "Why aren't you answering my calls?"

"I just haven't had a chance, I've been busy with work."

"You're always busy with work. One day you'll be at the office and wake up with ovaries the size of currants and realize you're dying alone."

"That's not how ovaries work, Mom."

"I didn't call you at this hour for a physics lesson."

Kelly cupped her forehead in her hand. "You want to know what happened with Martin? It didn't work out."

"What did you do?" Diane asked.

Kelly bristled. "Why do you assume I did something? He was the one who got too personal."

"It was a date, not a bank transaction!"

"It was a *first* date, and he crossed a line." Kelly hesitated. "It was embarrassing, okay? It was bad enough the first time without having to talk about it again."

Diane's tone softened. "Kelly, Kelly, Kelly. All right, you don't have to tell me the details."

"Thank you. Now I'm kind of trying to get to bed."

But Diane wasn't finished. "But what will I do with you, dear? You're already twenty-nine. You can't go on like this forever."

"I think you mean *only* twenty-nine."

But Diane was on a roll. "By your age, I was married with two kids, and a third on the way! Gary was married at twenty-seven. Your sister will be married in less than two months, and she's only twenty-five. I'm getting worried for you. Who will take care of you when you're old and alone?"

"Socialized medicine or the apocalypse, whichever gets there first. I can take care of myself, Mom. For someone who talks about me being twenty-nine like I'm some Bronze Age corpse fished out of a bog, you don't seem to realize that I'm an adult."

"All right, then, who are you bringing to the wedding?"

"I don't know! The Jolly Fucking Green Giant!" Kelly threw her left hand up in exasperation.

"Kelly Suttle. Do you think this is all a joke?"

"I think it's a party, not a Navy SEAL operation, and you're taking it way too seriously."

"Oh, so it's just a party. The biggest day of your sister's life and my life's work is just a party."

"I didn't mean—"

"When I started in the wedding industry here, this was just

another middle-class town," Diane forged on. "Now it's one of the most expensive zip codes in the country. Everyone expects the moon! Last week a bride demanded that I find her a dress that changed color according to her mood. I'm not Merlin. These people think that I'm a Google and they can just enter their dreams into me and I'll spit back whatever they want—"

"I met someone," Kelly blurted out.

"You met someone?" Diane was utterly confused. "Do you mean on LinkedIn again?"

"No, a guy. I went out tonight with Priya and met this guy and we really hit it off." Kelly winced, biting her lip. Palliating her mother might buy her some time. Or she might have just royally screwed herself.

"You met someone!" Diane's tone was suddenly full of sunshine. "Who? What's he like? What's his name?"

"His name is—" Kelly drew a panicked blank. She looked wildly around the room. A spotlighted billboard caught her eye through the window—*eSan, for all your hardware cleaning needs.*

"Esan. I mean, Ethan. His name is Ethan."

"Ethan, Ethan. I like it, it's a good name. What does he do? Where does he—"

"I really have to go, Mom, it's been a long night."

When Kelly got off the phone, she threw her head down tiredly on her desk. If only it were so easy to create a boyfriend out of thin air.

Kelly didn't sleep long that night, but she slept hard. Her lower back aching from the heels, she tossed fitfully between dreams of Anita hovering over her shoulder while she tried and failed repeatedly to build a tower of blocks, and a laughing Mariah Carey advancing menacingly toward her, brandishing a shoe like Priya's, but with the gold studs grown to lethal, torturous spikes.

Then Mariah morphed, transforming into a handsome young man. He held Kelly's hand, leading her through what at first looked like a nightclub, but turned out to be a high school gym, lit with swirling colored lights for prom. They drifted through slow-dancing couples, pausing to watch Clara and Jonathan get crowned prom queen and king by none other than Diane. The triad smiled approvingly at Kelly and her date in the audience.

The handsome man turned Kelly away from the stage. "Dance with me," he said.

"I don't know how," she protested. Then he removed a giant key from the small of his back, like a wind-up toy, and handed it to her.

"You have the key," he said.

Kelly woke up with a hangover, a backache, and a plan.

I t was Saturday, so Kelly knew she would be fairly undisturbed at work. But to be safe, once she had taken the elevator up to AHI's floor in the corporate tower, she did a quick walk around—empty. She was on track. She breezed down the hall to the lab, clutching a red and white bag from the hurried purchase she had made at Target on her way in.

In spite of her hurry, Kelly took a second to appreciate the lab after she firmly locked its door. She loved this space, but she couldn't always get it to herself. Now, empty, silent except for the low thrumming of machinery, it had the cavernous atmosphere of a cathedral. It was a sort of space-age Geppetto's workshop: brushed steel cabinets and counters, banks of computers, and 3-D printers mixed with limbs, eyes, torsos, hair, all in various states of half-formed humanity. Scattered around the workstations were a hoop with six casters attached to it; a flexible polymer band, sinewy with wires; a periscope-type contraption with an infrared sensor on it—skeletal fragments of the other engineers' works in progress. At the back of the room, a few completed prototypes of earlier android models stood sentry, each progressively more believable than the last: a smooth white robot humanoid only in posture, a boxy male with clawlike metal hands, a young blond woman with waxy-looking "skin." The scene might have been creepy to some, but to Kelly, it was home.

She had been making a mental inventory all morning—she knew the stock by heart, having had a hand in the creation of much of it herself—and knew there were enough completed spare parts to service her need. They would require some alterations to make a harmonious whole and, of course, the actual combining of the parts would take some doing. But Kelly had been putting in extra hours already, working out the kinks in anticipation of making her physical model of Confibot. And unlike Confibot, this model wouldn't require exquisite precision of response. It didn't have to align with a specific vision of user compatibility. It could just be what she wanted it to be, meaning it would be much more straightforward to assemble. For once, she could just follow her gut.

As Kelly raced around assembling parts, she realized she didn't know what to make him look like. She rolled a tray of glass eyeballs from its shelf, assessing them: a hundred varieties of iris color, pupil size, corneal tint, veining. It would be safest to go ordinary. Draw as little attention as possible. But her hand hesitated over the center of the tray with the midrange colors, as if reluctant to actually pick one up. *Live your life*—the words Priya was always telling her echoed in her head. The usual rules were clearly already out the window here. The adrenaline was pumping. With swift decision, Kelly's hand moved to the outskirts of the tray, toward the set of eyes her own had gravitated to first: a crystalline, almost lavender, shade of blue.

Well, then, why not go all the way out? As Kelly modeled her ideas on the computer-aided design software, then made them reality with the help of a 3-D printer and a shopping trip through the lab's existing parts, she decided to let her heart, or something south of her heart, be her design guide. Ordinary be damned. She draped coffee-brown hair in waves over his tanned forehead, carefully working around the minuscule, fragmented solar panels integrated into his scalp as a power source. She made his hands long and clean, chiseled at the wrist. She sculpted the heck out of his butt. It felt a little creepy. But it felt a little good.

Luckily, the normal biweekly family dinner had been pushed since Diane was traveling to a trade show. Kelly had the weekend to herself, and she stayed in the lab the entire time, catnapping in her chair, leaving only for bathroom breaks and vending machine trips where she picked up bags of Fritos and cans of whatever had the most caffeine in it while furtively hiding her face from the security cameras. At one point she heard the window washing crew making their rounds. Later, an employee stopped by an office down the hall, presumably to pick something up, giving her a shock of adrenaline so strong it left her weak. As an employee, she had every reason to be here—but still. What would happen if anyone discovered what she was doing? There was no way her hard-nosed boss would allow her to enter the hallowed doors of AHI ever again if she knew that

Kelly had taken thousands of dollars' worth of company equipment to build herself a boyfriend. News would spread rapidly within the robotics industry—it was exactly the sort of kooky schadenfreude fodder that tech bros would crow over on Reddit, and for the rest of her life, any time a potential employer or date Googled her, this story would be the first result.

Priya would be sympathetic, but she would still think that Kelly had lost it when she heard of her plan. They would never work together again and, probably, they would drift apart. And Kelly would basically be handing her family, who already thought she was so inept that she could never find a plus one on her own, a certificate—signed, framed, and embossed in gold—confirming that exact fact. More than ever, she would be the odd one out, the slightly dotty, slightly desperate girl. As Kelly thought about it, she stopped working, her hands clenching over her screwdriver. She stood to lose *everything*.

But then she looked at the work in front of her and almost jumped. She had been so focused on racing through the details that she hadn't stopped to look at the big picture. And while the picture was still being painted, it was already incredible. This was far and away the most complete, the most convincing, the most beautiful android she had ever made. Even with his torso still an uncovered collection of plates and wires, he looked . . . *human*. She knew that this was possible, of course; it was exactly what she had been aiming for in all her months of preparatory work on Confibot. But to see it actually happening was thrilling. In fact, she realized, this might be the very thing to help her with Confibot. What better way to perfect her creation before the presentation than to have another model prebuilt to observe? The research gains she stood to acquire more than outweighed the extra time she would need to put in to rebuild the Confibot parts she had scavenged this weekend for Ethan.

Still, Kelly needed something more concrete to control the risk. She needed a deadline. She grabbed her phone and tapped open her calendar. In bold, red letters, she set an appointment for March eighth titled "You Know What." She would take Ethan apart the morning after Clara's wedding. Having a plan, structuring some order into the chaos, allowed her to breathe a bit more freely. She just had to keep Ethan's origins a secret for six weeks, then she would return all of the parts to the lab. No harm, no foul. She wouldn't lose anything, and she stood to gain so much. She steadied herself and dove back in.

Eventually she turned off the 3-D printer, connected up the last wires, and dressed her robot. He even made the cheap slacks and button-down she had picked up at Target look tony rather than plain. But the thing of beauty was still just a thing. The shapely jaw was slack, the bright eyes dull. It was time to Frankenstein him.

Kelly knew the software was all essentially in place, most of it designed by herself. But it was still in the testing stage and hadn't been fully run yet. Her focus had been on conducting the social research necessary to determine how an android should interact with users, not yet on programming in those interactions and traits. She would have to make some tweaks and improvise as she went, but even then, it might not work. She feared she could very well end up with a Swahili-speaking pedophile with Tourette's.

Kelly ran some simulations on one of the lab's computers, making minor changes, gaining a cautious confidence as she went. It wasn't until it was time to make her programming selections that she realized that she had the opportunity to create her ideal man.

She had already made him physically perfect, so why not do the same cognitively? But defining perfection in terms of mind, of heart, of personality was a much trickier proposition.

Then inspiration struck, and she almost laughed aloud—of course, she had already designed her ideal mate. She accessed her list of requirements from the dating site and went to work, elaborating and fleshing out the profile as she programmed. A man should know how to tie a tie, change a tire, and train a dog. He needed to speak English, of course, and let's throw in Italian, and Mandarin is important . . . oh, what the heck. She didn't have all day. She gave him access to all of Google. She knew she was taking a risk in making this man so extraordinary, but she didn't have time to cherry-pick, and frankly, she didn't want to. The more Kelly programmed, the less she was making *a* man, a breathing biped who could stand next to her in photos, and the more she was making *her* man.

She imported the rudimentary responses to social cues she had been developing, but worried there were holes there . . . she'd been responding to social cues for twenty-nine years and still hadn't figured it out. She brushed the thought aside: this would have to do. She'd rely on his machine-learning capabilities to fill in the gaps as they went.

The essential thing was to ensure he was entirely under her control. Give herself the ability to reprogram him, to turn him off and on, to mitigate as much as possible the crazy factor of what she was doing. She ensured that she could access his system from her own laptop so that she could make changes as necessary at home. And as an analogue backup, she fitted a panel in his lower back with a set of switches—fundamentals, like on, off, and sleep mode—just in case. With everything that could go wrong with this plan, it was reassuring to feel that physical manifestation of control under her fingers.

And finally, it was done. Or rather, he. Tingling, exhilarated, Kelly flipped the On switch. And stirring into life in front of her was the most amazing man she'd ever seen. He looked around the room a little, gaining his surroundings, but when his eyes found Kelly, they stopped. He smiled. "Hi, Kelly," he said.

six

. . . . . .

On Monday morning, Kelly had difficulty getting out of bed when her alarm jackhammered its way into her consciousness. She had fallen asleep so deeply when she finally arrived home just a few hours earlier, that her brain was stubbornly refusing to follow her body into Awake People Land. She sat up, yawning, propping her arms over her bent knees. Through the fog, the memory of an odd dream resurfaced . . . she had a watery image of herself guiding a stranger into her car in the parking garage at work . . . leading him into her living room, pulling up his shirt, and pressing a button on his back. Coffee. She was going to need a soup-bowl-size cup of coffee.

When she trudged into the living room, she started. There, sitting on the couch, was the man. Definitely not a dream. Though he was dreamy, even in his vacant-eyed, lifeless state. Kelly felt a flutter of excitement. She had just built the most advanced creation of her career. It was time to see how he worked. Suddenly she didn't need the coffee anymore. She located the button on his back and powered him on.

A thousand imperceptible motions started at once, but the effect was that he suddenly looked stunningly, palpably alive. Ethan turned and beamed at her. "Good morning, Kelly," he said.

"Um, hi," she replied.

With the morning light wafting through the window, picking up the glint of Ethan's white teeth, the jewel-like facets of his irises, the copper notes mingled in the waves of his perfectly groomed hair, Kelly became very aware that she was standing there in the same rumpled clothes she'd had on since Saturday morning, with no makeup on and her hair probably doing a fair imitation of a tangled set of earbuds. But she shook herself straighter, reminding herself how illogical it was to be self-conscious. In the "Are intelligent robots beings with rights?" debate, Anita's stance was a staunch no. They were machines meant to turn a profit, and she was adamant that her engineers think the same way. Kelly had been taught early not to anthropomorphize her creations. You could never maintain the rigor and objectivity of science if you developed an attachment to your work. But while that mind-set was Kelly's accustomed pattern in the lab, here at home, stripped of the clinical accoutrements of steel and soldering irons, she was finding it took a conscious effort to maintain the same kind of distance. Especially when this creation was already so anthropomorphic.

She strode past Ethan into the kitchen and pulled down the makings of her favorite guilty pleasure breakfast: a box of Cheez-Its and a jar of Nutella. She dunked with vigor. Working herself blind all weekend had really worked up an appetite. "Come here," she called to Ethan, and he dutifully approached the kitchen. "Want one?"

He accepted the Nutella-topped Cheez-It as if it were the greatest gift anyone had ever given him. Which, technically, it was. "Thank you, Kelly. This is so generous of you."

"It's a Cheez-It, not the Hope diamond," Kelly responded. She watched with some anxiety as he chewed and swallowed, but he simply smiled back at her. She gave herself a little internal high five. This was the first time she had built a comprehensive food and drink consumption pathway, including programming Ethan to dispose of his own masticated food waste in the bathroom, and so far, everything was looking peachy. She crunched a Cheez-It with glee. "There's nothing on this Earth I love more than Cheez-Its and Nutella," she mused.

Kelly had an extra bounce in her step as she got ready for work, singing that annoyingly catchy new Taylor Swift song in the shower, flipping her hair back like a mermaid when she was done blow-drying it. When she walked back into the bedroom, she jumped again. There Ethan was, sitting at her computer, his face aglow with a sort of bright-eyed shyness. He leaped from the chair. "I hope you don't mind me using your computer, Kelly," he said. "I wanted to give you a little something."

Peering at the monitor, Kelly saw that he had found his way to her design program. And on the screen was a bouquet of digital flowers, exquisitely drawn in a rainbow of pixels, yellow gladiolus flaring above a shimmer of violets, the colors more real than life. The image rotated slowly, showing fifty or more unique flowers bundled into the arrangement.

"Why did you do this?" Kelly asked, utterly baffled. She hadn't commanded him to give her flowers, hadn't programmed in anything of the sort. Immediately she was intrigued to understand this unforeseen behavior of her creation.

"I know that they're not as nice as real ones," Ethan responded anxiously. "But since I have no means to buy anything, I determined a drawing to be my best alternative—"

"But why flowers? Why give me anything at all?"

"To make you happy, of course. Do you not like them?"

Kelly stared at the bright image sweeping softly around the screen. She realized that she'd never been given flowers. "I do," she said after a moment. "Thank you."

She finished dressing and moved out to the living room, Ethan following behind. Her mind swirled with questions and ideas. Already her robot was surprising her with the unanticipated independence and creativity of his actions. Though she wasn't quite sure what she had anticipated. She was eager to learn more, but she would have to switch him off so he didn't do anything else surprising while she was at work.

As she stepped into her ballet flats and looped her bag over her shoulder at the door, she looked at Ethan. His face was luminous with all the excitement of his first day on Earth. And the feeling was catching.

Kelly hung her bag back on its hook. "Come on," she said. "I'm calling in sick."

She had known that, sooner or later, she would have to take Ethan out in public. Though the thought of walking out into the world with him made her stomach churn with anxiety, she decided to bite the bullet. She had to assess how other people reacted to him before she could risk him meeting her family. Besides, she'd already played hooky for the first time in her life.

Half an hour later, Kelly and Ethan stepped through the wide automatic doors of Safeway. She had figured that the grocery store would be a relatively safe place for her companion's debut—quotidian, judgment-free (this wasn't Whole Foods, after all), full of people, but unlikely to contain anyone Kelly knew. Still, she swiveled her eyes so rapidly between Ethan and the other customers near the entrance that she nearly swung them loose. She clocked the potential threats like an undercover operative: nine o'clock, a woman in a brown trench coat testing the softness of a baguette. At two o'clock, a young mother gently wheeling her toddler back and forth in the cart while she waited at the deli counter. An older gentleman in a tweed cap tentatively selecting his jar of chilled pickles, dead ahead.

But as she wrested loose a cart and edged into the minefield, her heart rate began to relax. She and Ethan were just . . . two more customers. Nobody looked at them strangely. Nobody looked at them at all. And suddenly, Kelly felt a warm surge of pride. She had never seen a humanoid robot as realistic as Ethan, but the fact that he was here now, out among the unsuspecting public, and nobody knew a thing, confirmed that her work was that good. She was exhilarated.

An involuntary smile slipped onto her face, and when she looked from the other customers across to Ethan, she noticed that he was smiling too. Gaping may have been more accurate. He gazed at the plethora of items in the store. "Where does one even start?"

"Come on." She pivoted him by the elbow. "I'll show you."

Kelly had always hated grocery shopping. She wasn't much of a cook—she found the whole process unnecessarily messy, unpredictable, and time-consuming—yet she refused to relinquish control over her own selections by taking advantage of one of the grocery delivery services proliferating in the Valley. Now with Ethan at her side, she saw the commonplace store with new eyes. He knew what all the products were, of course, but marveled at the very quantity and selection of them. He asked her questions that she didn't know how to answer, but wished she did, like "Why are there seven varieties of Diet Coke?" and questions about herself she'd never considered, like "How do you decide which flavor of Jones Soda to purchase?" They fell into a natural routine, Ethan pushing the cart and Kelly pulling from the shelves, checking off items on the list on her phone. His smarts came in handy in the produce aisle. When Kelly went to pick a watermelon based on color, he picked the candidates up instead, deftly judging their weight and knocking for a hollow sound before placing the winner in the cart. "This one," he said with confidence. He knew that the best avocadoes were from New Zealand and that red grapes, at this time of year, should come from Chile. He instantly calculated the best deals per unit. She started to feel like she was part of a team. The mundane aisles took on a novelty for Kelly; the colors were dialed up, the fluorescent lighting cheerier.

As they rounded the aisle into condiments, Kelly noticed a middle-aged woman glance at Ethan for one second too long. Her pulse thrummed—this was it. The woman was full-on staring at Ethan. Just as Kelly was reaching for his arm, moving to steer him away before the woman could question them, or catch them, or whatever she was about to do, the woman caught Kelly's eye, smiled, and offered a small wink before turning back to the vinegars. Kelly looked at Ethan and realized he did stand out here, but not because he looked like a robot. Against the everyday setting of the grocery store, his planed cheekbones and strong jaw were cast into even sharper focus. He was gorgeous, a twenty-first-century Paul Newman. As she pushed on down the aisle, side by side with Ethan, she held her head a little higher.

Normally Kelly beelined for the self-checkout. Her past interactions with store employees involved, at best, neutral silence, at worst, the sorts of embarrassing mishaps that led her to now read too much into every nuance of the interaction, trying to avoid saying the wrong thing and coming off as cold in the end. But now, feeling cocooned within her bubble of two, she went along with it as Ethan steered the cart to the nearest cashier, even smiling at the man. "How are you?" she asked as she and Ethan stacked products on the belt.

"Pretty good." He held up her box of Velveeta. "This stuff is my guilty pleasure."

"It's my cardinal sin," she admitted. She gestured to the rubber divider for the belt. "I've always wondered, what happens if two people forget to put the divider between their groceries? Do they just have to go home and make a life together?"

"Yep. Grocery store law."

Kelly laughed with him. The whole thing was so easy. For once, as she left the store, she realized she hadn't even bothered to track whether or not the cashier wished her a good day.

At home, Ethan pitched in to put the groceries away, helping out in particular with the elusive top shelves. Kelly had resigned herself to an acceptance that the packages stuck at the back of those cabinets would never again see the light of day until the San Andreas

Fault shook them down. But here was Ethan, organizing them with aplomb.

Kelly settled at her desk in the bedroom to get some work done, drafting a parts request for the lab supply manager, scanning the latest issue of *Cybernetics and Systems* on her tablet. But as the day went on, her mind wouldn't stay put. Flush with the coup of a successful grocery store trip, she itched to take Ethan out again. If his company had done so much to improve a boring errand, what would a night on the town with him be like?

Besides, there were too many distractions for her to focus here anyway. Priya kept texting to ask if Kelly was *totally sure* that she didn't need her to come over and bring chicken soup or a medical evaluation helicopter or anything. The sick day had raised some alarm bells—normally Kelly was the sort to work through her own funeral. And her mom had been trying doggedly to reach her since Saturday to continue the conversation about this Ethan person. Kelly gave up on working. She glanced into the living room—there he sat on the couch, politely awaiting her next instruction. First she needed to sit down with him and figure out who this Ethan person was.

You could tell that the shops and restaurants on Santana Row were expensive even if you never breached their doors. The minimalist compositions behind the plate glass of the store windows, the doormen with wired earpieces and folded hands, the gusts of sandalwood air exhaled from the open doorways—even the spotless street exuded a feeling of "invitation only." Most of the district held little appeal for Kelly, who would rather blow a paycheck on a high-speed charging dock than a belt. But in the few times she ventured out there, one spot had always caught her eye: La Vigna. More accurately, it had caught her nose. The smells of garlic, wine, and rosemary perfumed the Italian restaurant's entire block. She had wanted to try the place for years, but would never have dared to venture past its tall, sculpted oak doors alone. But now, walking through those doors at Ethan's side, she thought she might actually fit in. She had changed into her trusty green date-night dress, and it somehow felt more festive tonight than it had when she went out with Martin.

The stiff-faced waiter came for their drinks order just as Kelly was trying surreptitiously to adjust her bra under her dress. She swiftly dropped her hands, hoping he hadn't noticed, and picked up the wine list. She went by price, choosing something that wasn't the cheapest but wasn't the most expensive, since none of the names meant anything to her anyway. "We'll have a bottle of the—" And it was not until she reached the end of the sentence that she realized she had no clue how to pronounce the name, which had an indecent number of consonants. "The Mmblggrwgitz," she tried quietly, as if lowering her voice would hide the fact that she didn't know how to pronounce the word, yet somehow still get the correct name across.

"Pardon?"

Kelly cleared her throat. "The house red," she said. Maybe this whole evening was a bad idea, she considered. Of course she didn't fit in at a place like this. Then she looked across the table at Ethan, who offered her an easy smile. Each time she saw him, she had to blink, taken aback. He was just so good-looking, he almost didn't look real. Of course, he wasn't real, she corrected herself.

Dinner was as flavorful as the fragrances had advertised, and

Kelly and Ethan sampled each other's wine-glazed roast and leek risotto with enthusiasm. She was discovering yet another benefit of being paired off: you get to try twice as many dishes. Ethan's conversation was so easy that she forgot that it could have been hard. His speech was eloquent, if stiff, and while he brought no real personal experience to any topic, he was so voracious for details of Kelly's experiences, so genuinely absorbed in her words, that it was easy for her to chatter throughout the night.

"One of my coworkers in the Commercial Products division is working on this really cool new aquatic robot. It moves with a sort of undulating fin system that allows it to go really fast."

"A corollary would be the cuttlefish," Ethan responded.

"Exactly!"

"Perhaps an analogous system could have potential for subterranean exploration. Think of the musculature of the earthworm."

"You're right." Kelly paused with her fork halfway to her mouth, considering. "I never thought of that. I should suggest that to him." Normally Priya was the only one she could have these types of conversations with. She thought back to her attempt to discuss robotics with Martin, which had gone over with all the success of a paper umbrella. In contrast, Ethan's literacy and intelligence were astonishing. He could understand any topic she brought up. In fact, he could teach her a thing or two—or twenty.

"I can suggest a selection of literature on the topic that you might find elucidating," he went on.

Now Kelly frowned. Ethan's intelligence was almost too much. His voice itself was great, but his speech patterns and vocabulary were too formal. He understood colloquial phrases only in an academic way. Before she could ever introduce him to her family, she had to get this right. She had to make him sound like a twenty-first-century American.

"I think we need to dumb you down," she declared.

Ethan was confused. "What do you mean?"

"You're getting it already!" she joked. He didn't respond. "Never mind, just—you have the whole internet in your brain, right? Read through it. I want you to look at websites that Americans use every day—Reddit, Twitter, CNN, whatever—and just try to imitate what you see there. Common expressions, slang."

"I should talk like people on the internet?" Ethan repeated dubiously.

"Yes," she said firmly, taking a decisive bite of risotto.

"*Buona sera!*" A robust voice jolted them from their conversation. A short man with full gray hair and a laughing red face barreled toward them. In each hand he held a shot glass full of a velvety substance, which he placed before Kelly and Ethan. "Chestnut velouté. An amuse bouche for *la bella coppia*, courtesy of the house."

"Thank you," Kelly and Ethan said in unison.

"And what are we celebrating tonight?"

"Oh, nothing, just—dinner," Kelly responded.

"Dinner is not nothing! Dinner is something to celebrate! You are young, the night is young, the moon is full." Kelly was fairly positive she had seen a crescent moon on the way in, but even she wanted to allow herself to be lifted on the gust of the ebullient romance of this man. "You need anything, you ask for Paolo." He gave a short bow, hand over his middle. "This is my house. I am the house!" Paolo turned away, laughing.

Kelly turned to Ethan. "I wonder what '*la bella coppia*' means."

"The beautiful couple," he translated instantly. Kelly had never seen herself as beautiful, and when she had been in a relationship with Robbie—and with Nick from college—she had never quite felt a snug fit with the word "couple." But now she smiled.

The prim waiter glided their way, refilling their water glasses with decorum. "And how are you finding everything?" he asked.

"You'll never guess what happens next," Ethan answered.

"Pardon?" the waiter said again. They seemed to be testing his limits of the word tonight.

"You have to see Victoria's Secret model Alessandra Ambrosio's Malibu nip-slip to believe it."

Kelly dropped her fork to her plate with a clatter. The few surrounding customers who hadn't looked over at Ethan's declaration were looking now. She coughed, trying to choke down her food before speaking. "Everything's great," she said. She looked at Ethan—did he have a glitch?

"Would you care to review the wine list again?" the waiter asked.

"Seventeen struggles all curly-haired girls know. Me AF," Ethan answered.

"No wine, we're fine!" Kelly cried. A few diners around them snickered. The waiter's eye began to twitch alarmingly.

"These Asian babes are sick of being alone," Ethan continued, entirely straight-faced.

Dear heaven. He was talking like people on the internet.

"We don't need anything, thank you," Kelly gasped, not meeting the waiter's twitching eye. "We're fine." He left her with an expression that clearly indicated that he didn't believe they were.

Ethan called after him as he walked away, "Is this the most satisfying pimple popping video yet?"

"Ethan, stop!" Kelly said.

"What?" he asked. "Or no: 'What happened when I spent the night in a haunted hotel. Not clickbait. Parentheses, emotional.'"

"Stop doing that! I didn't mean for you to literally talk like people on the internet. I just wanted you to sound normal."

"As in colloquial? Casual?"

"Yes," Kelly responded, her chin tucked nearly to her chest, her fingers clutching her temples, too embarrassed to look up.

"Oh. Sure. I can do that." Ethan picked up his fork and began digging in again. It wasn't until a moment later that he stopped, noticing that Kelly wasn't eating. "Is something the matter?"

"Um, yeah. You just humiliated me," she said.

"I did?" Ethan's voice was horrified. "I'm so sorry! What did I do to embarrass you?"

"Talking like that! The whole restaurant is laughing at me!"

Ethan looked around at the other diners. In fact, they had all gone back to their own meals, the incident already forgotten. "I'm sorry, I must not understand. I don't see anyone who's laughing at you."

Kelly's eyes ventured upward. Ethan was right. "Well, not *now*," she muttered. She guessed it would be safe to return to her dinner.

When the waiter returned for their dessert order, Kelly was deliberating between panna cotta and cornmeal cake when Ethan set his menu down with a firm gesture. "I'm sorry, but none of these will do," he said. "What Kelly likes best is Cheez-Its and Nutella."

"Pardon?" the waiter repeated, wearily this time, as if resigned to whatever gauche lunacy they were about to throw at him.

"Ethan, I don't—" Kelly started, feeling her face start to flame again. As if she hadn't had enough embarrassment tonight, now Ethan was revealing her bizarre tastes to the waiter. And now Paolo appeared, overhearing.

"Is there a problem, my *bella coppia*?" he asked with concern.

"Is there?" Ethan asked, looking at Kelly with even greater concern.

It was true, she had already been through embarrassment tonight. But what did it really matter? As she glanced around the restaurant again, she saw only people who were living their own lives, not judging how she led hers. And damn it, Cheez-Its and Nutella did sound really good.

"Do you by any chance have Cheez-Its and Nutella?" she asked.

Twenty minutes later, out came Paolo, guns-a-blazing, nearly literally. The candles on the plate in front of him simultaneously lit the artful Cheez-It house with Nutella mortar on the plate and his beaming face above. "Never say that Paolo's chefs are not resourceful!" he crowed. *"Cheeez-Iiiiits!"* he sang theatrically as he set the plate down and left with a bow. Okay, that was a little embarrassing, but Kelly still found herself having fun.

The candles made each silver facet of the cutlery handles on the table glitter and dance. Kelly blew out the flames, then handed a cracker to Ethan before plucking one off for herself. "Here," she said. "Good, right?"

Ethan nodded emphatically. "It is without a doubt the best thing I've ever eaten."

Kelly laughed.

seven

. . . . . .

Within a week or so, Kelly began to worry less about whether someone would recognize that Ethan was a robot, or look askance at him in any way.

At home, they were building a routine together, with shared take-out dinners and TV time before bed. (Ethan "slept" on the couch in a low-power sleep mode, a state that allowed him to breathe and stir.) Every morning, he designed her a new digital bouquet while she got ready for work, each one a unique combination of colors and exquisitely rendered textures, sometimes incorporating surprising materials like seashells or Romanesco cauliflower, even branching out and using flowers that were entirely his invention, lavish tendrils of blue or prismatic constructions that were mathematical, yet delicate. Each evening, he bounded to the door when she came in, ready to hold her hand while she slipped out of her shoes.

For someone so naturally self-conscious, there was a delicious freedom in having a robotic boyfriend. It was impossible for him to judge her. He had no exes, no other women to compare her to. She had literally programmed him to be loyal to her. When she walked around the apartment in her mismatched underwear, or in one of her favorite at-home comfort uniforms (a towel held up with Velcro, a high school mathlete T-shirt worn to the consistency of gauze), Ethan never blinked. He even joined in on Netflix Slanket night. Sometimes, though, when he pulled new clothes from his section of her closet and changed in the mornings, she couldn't help but stare as he undressed—only expressing a scientific admiration of her own handiwork, of course. She shook her gaze away.

Freedom was kind of a new thing for Kelly. She could imagine a world of flying cars and VR corneal implants, but she couldn't imagine trying bowling or throwing together a bag and taking an impromptu weekend trip. Kelly's aversion to risk may have been partially genetic, but certainly part of it stemmed from growing up as the middle child in a problem child sandwich. Clara had been dangerously flighty, bringing in injured opossums who seemed as reluctant to be in the house as Carl and Diane had been to host them, throwing parties that spiraled wildly beyond her expectations, crashing not one but two cars as a teenager because "such a good song came on." And Gary, before becoming a model parent/ toddler slave, had been a sulky goth who posed for his freshman yearbook photo with a pentagram drawn on his forehead in his mom's eyeliner. Really, Kelly had never had any choice but to be the safe, responsible one, the one devoid of surprises. Now, by creating Ethan, she seemed to be making up for twenty-nine years of no surprises in one go.

While she enjoyed her time with Ethan, she couldn't help but tinker with him too. Ever the perfectionist, as the days passed, Kelly observed her experiment with keen interest, picking up on glitches and repairing them: a catch in his movement when he would raise his left arm, a chip in one of his toenails, a predilection for holding doors open for strangers who were approaching from too far away. Every issue she discovered in Ethan helped her anticipate and avoid the same problems in Confibot. What's more, the machine learning element that AHI incorporated into all of their builds allowed Ethan to evolve and improve even without Kelly's input. He was observing her, learning her quirks and preferences. He noticed that she wore a lot of oatmeal-colored clothing, so when she asked him to go buy new sheets with the credit card she provided him for such errands, he found a set in exactly that color. Watching him evolve was fascinating—Kelly was entranced by the possibilities of AI, and here in front of her was her very own, personalized subject. From a research perspective, it was exhilarating. The two of them even sat down together with a notebook and fabricated every pertinent aspect of his life they could think of, complete with constructing a robust online identity for him to throw off potential Googlers, including his own e-mail accounts, social media profiles, and a fake Stanford employee bio page as an astronomy associate professor (as a Stanford grad herself, she'd been able to give him a complete rundown of the school). Gradually, she became certain that no one, even a fellow scientist, could pick up on anything abnormal about Ethan. This machine, this man, was her greatest work, and a great work by any standards. Any robotics lab in the world would be hard-pressed to produce something more natural, more convincing.

Meanwhile, Diane peppered Kelly at every turn with questions about this Ethan she had met, but Kelly deflected. It was too soon to introduce him to her family, too complicated. Connecting Ethan so firmly to the reality of her everyday life would mean really reckoning with the enormity of what she had done in creating him, and the risks that she was taking if anyone in her personal or professional life discovered the truth. She didn't want to do that yet; she didn't want to think about it. She only wanted to nestle into the grooves of this new experience.

I t had been years now since every other tech company in the Valley started tearing down their cubicles and installing coworking pods, rock climbing walls, espresso labs, and nap dens. Not so at AHI. The company was relatively small but one of the top in its elite field, and it could certainly have afforded to keep up with the San Jose Joneses. But Anita would rather put the company's money straight in the bank. Other employees often grumbled about the gray laminate cubicle walls and the cheap carpet. But Kelly didn't mind. She was here to work.

Though right now, she was finding work difficult. She had made the executive decision to start building the physical model of Confibot without a face for now. Confibot would require far more precision and testing than Ethan had and would take all of the two and a half months she had left; she couldn't expect to finish him in two (very long) days. The robot was coming along, testing well on all the strength and agility parameters he would need for his work. But she still had no idea what his face should look like, what his voice should sound like, who he should be—a problem that, Kelly recalled with an annoying flash, would have been more easily solved if she still had a psychologist working at her side. It had been so simple in comparison to create Ethan. But she knew that she couldn't take the same fly-by-night approach to Confibot. Here she had to cling strictly to the data in order to develop a product that would appeal the most to the maximum number of people, not just to herself.

She was currently combing through innumerable facial models on her computer, but the face she kept seeing was Ethan's. For the first time today, she had left him on, by himself, at home. She knew that the more opportunity he had to interact with his environment, the more he would learn and the more human he would become. She had left him with some light housework and her e-reader to keep him busy. Still, she had nervous visions of returning home to discover that he had chosen to surprise her by papering the walls with Cheez-Its.

On top of that, the more she tried to concentrate on her project, the more Robbie wanted to talk about his own. "Good morning, Kelly," he said brightly, his head popping over their shared cubicle wall.

"Good morning, Robbie," she said, trying to keep the weariness from her voice, eyes still locked to her screen. Robbie was a brilliant engineer, one of the top in their team, always the first into the office in the morning and the last out at night, though he was smart enough that he could have slacked off and gotten away with it. He was ruthlessly polite, never unguarded, always in the proper place, and endlessly energetic. He was even good-looking, with symmetrical features and a neatly molded chin above a crisp collar. But while Robbie was always perfect, he never seemed quite . . . right. Kelly figured that he was just a bit of an odd duck, not one to let his hair down, and in that arena, who was she to talk? But he was obnoxious enough—subtly arrogant, not so subtly obsequious—that she only felt a little bad for laughing when Priya called him Robo-Robbie be-hind his back.

When Kelly joined the company, she and Robbie had started dat-ing almost immediately. On paper, he had seemed like her perfect mate. Their half year of dating—a dependable weekly outing to an orderly white-tablecloth restaurant, or a park at an hour when he could predict a minimal presence of children—had been as calm as teacups, utterly problem-free. In fact, one could even say that Rob-bie pushed Kelly to be better: in the wake of his punctual perfection, she had felt unable to grant herself any room for error. But Kelly had been dogged by the sensation that she was looking for a problem in their relationship.

One night after their dinner appointment at a restaurant they had never visited before, but that they might as well have, so neatly did it fit their white tablecloths and salad forks mold, they passed a nightclub on the way to Robbie's car. Seized by a rebellious whim, Kelly had grabbed Robbie's arm. "Want to go dancing?" she had said, pointing at the club.

But Robbie had just laughed, much harder than at any of Kelly's actual jokes. "Can you imagine? The only thing more idiotic-looking than the people at a nightclub is when people show up who don't belong there." He shook his head, laughing some more. "Us dancing. It's a good thing you keep two feet firmly on the ground. You're not precisely a paragon of grace."

It was true that Kelly's dancing looked something more like a disorder of the peripheral nervous system. But she resented the im-plication. Still, she kept her mouth shut, withdrawing her hand and trying her hardest not to crown her ignominy by tripping over her own two feet on the walk back to the car. A week later, she finally screwed up the courage to break up with him. She told him she needed to be single to focus on her career, he barely batted an eye at the news, and that was that. And really, that had been the tone of their entire relationship. Their physical transactions were perfunctory. They never stayed up late at night talking about where they wanted to go in the world before they died. They never said "I love you." Kelly had second-guessed herself, wondering if she was misinterpreting the constant undercurrent of judgment she felt from him. She felt bad about dumping him until he reacted with such polite neutrality to the whole thing. As it was, in spite of the many qualities Robbie had to recommend him, she never felt she had sustained much of a loss. And neither, apparently, had he.

She could tell now that he was bobbing on his toes as his head rose and fell above the partition, waiting anxiously for her to ask how he was. "Auspicious news on Brahma, of course," he blurted finally when she didn't. "I assume you've heard."

"No, actually, I haven't." Brahma was Robbie's entry in the investor competition. Like Confibot, he would be a freestanding caregiver robot. But where Confibot sought to mimic a human, Brahma was meant to improve upon one. A human has flat feet? Brahma has wheeled ones. A human has two arms? Brahma has eight. Kelly thought the whole idea sounded ridiculous on its face—the grab-bag nature of it, the hushed hallowedness with which Robbie spoke about his own work, the overreaching name—but the more she saw his project coming together, the more she had to admit that it looked impressive. Worryingly so. Even the rough model was shaping up to look less like the humanoid abomination she had originally pictured and more like the sleek robotic equivalent of a Swiss Army knife.

"Then let me be the first to tell you," he said with the air of doing her a great favor, "that Brahma passed his first test run with flying colors."

"That's awesome," Kelly replied distractedly. It was only ten a.m., and already all of Confibot's facial options were starting to blur together. They had been generated by her algorithm directly from the mountainous logs of data she had carefully input from her research. One of them just had to be the correct one. Or maybe it was she who was inept at selecting the best option. Maybe she had to write another algorithm to do that.

"Already I can see this technology changing people's lives," Robbie continued, his well-scrubbed face beatific above the partition. "It's positively humbling. Watching everything take shape so well already—it's as if I'm witnessing the birth of the future. You can relate, I'm sure, with Confibot."

Kelly flipped to a particularly appalling face, with beady eyes over a jack-o'-lantern smile. "Yeah, Confibot's really shaping up beautifully." And of course, her boss rounded the corner just in time to inspect her work.

"Good morning, Anita!" Robbie cried.

Anita frowned at Kelly's screen. "What's that?"

"One of the facial models I'm considering for Confibot."

"Who does he remind me of?"

"This is just one option, I've got plenty of others—" Kelly interjected quickly.

"The Cupertino Flasher," Anita finished.

"Exactly what I was thinking," Robbie affirmed.

"That's going to have to go."

"Of course, yes," Kelly agreed, trying not to stammer. "I'll just choose one of the others! The many, many others. It's a good thing I have so many strong contenders. I'll choose one of them." In her eternal inscrutability, Anita had a way of inviting Kelly to babble herself into a conversational pit, repeating herself until she was sure that she had not only said the wrong thing, she'd said it twenty times.

Anita sailed away without deigning to respond, and Kelly instantly wanted to reach Priya, who was off in the medical portion of the cubicle farm, for some much-needed commiseration. As she and Kelly had advanced in the Engineering department at AHI, Priya had gone down the medical engineering path, Kelly toward consumer product development. But Priya was always the one Kelly trusted most for a second opinion, partly because Priya really knew her stuff, and partly because Kelly felt safer going to her than to anyone else with her minor quandaries and half-baked ideas. She shot her an IM explaining her problem. But before long, as it so often did with Priya, the conversation wandered into man-talk territory.

> Priya: I'm chatting in the other window with this total dish I met named Andre.

> Kelly: Nice.

Priya was often chatting with a "dish." Or two, or three. She was a bit of a plate juggler.

> Priya: Ooh I have to show you this guy I found on Tinder. He'd be perf for your wedding date. Hold up I'm coming over

Kelly tensed. Thanks to Priya being busy last week with a deadline, she had avoided talking to her about the mysterious end to her quest for Mr. Wedding Date. But now she would have to stay sharp to mitigate the risk. Maybe she shouldn't have been talking to Priya today at all, even about work. Her fingers scrambled over her keyboard.

Kelly: Don't, Anita's coming back.

She glanced over her shoulder as if expecting to instantly be found out. Now with this lie, the next time she spoke to Priya she would have to create another lie about what Anita had come back for. The thought of deceiving her friend did not sit well with her, either morally or for the risk of getting caught. But she was going to have to lie to everyone in order to keep the truth from Anita.

eight

. . . . . .

Kelly had always been more Marie Curie than Martha Stewart. Her domestic pursuits were sparse, halfhearted, and tainted by the eternal suspicion of an inauspicious end. She could barely heat a frozen pizza without managing to render it either scorched or doughily undercooked, so she would have been delusional to hazard making one from scratch. With Ethan in the home, though, she found herself experimenting more with little domestic tasks. He took care of many of the routine duties for her—he got her mail every day while she was out, woke her when she overslept, fixed the broken window screen her landlord had been "getting around to" for months—allowing her the energy to think about things like whether or not it was time to finally switch out that outdated lamp. She even felt so emboldened as to chance a fern, which not only survived but flourished under Ethan's clockwork watering.

A week and a half into their cohabitation, as he sat beside her on the couch while she vegged out to *BattleBots* one night, she glanced beside her to notice that his neck was stretched. "Can you see?" she asked.

"Oh, sure, I can."

But Kelly swiveled, looking around the room. She realized that she had arranged the furniture so that the television could really only be comfortably viewed from one seat on the couch: hers. She had never had cause to notice it before.

"Come on, get up," she said. "Let's move some furniture."

She and Ethan pushed and pulled, though really, he did most of the work. Kelly did not do the gym. She did not do weights. She barely did pencils. Ethan, however, had boundless strength, boundless energy. She could direct him to move anything anywhere and he did it without complaining, even when she had to see the couch in three separate locations before determining the exact optimum furniture configuration. As she helped, Kelly tried to nudge the couch over a little and in the process, somehow rammed it against Ethan's foot.

"Oh no, what happened?" She immediately knelt to examine him, worried that she had perhaps dented his foot, missing the wince on his face.

"It's fine, it just hurts a bit," Ethan said from above.

"Wait, what do you mean, it hurts?"

"It just, it hurts, kind of a sharp pain. It's nothing serious, in fact it's improving as we speak. I can still work."

Kelly straightened, confused. "When you say 'pain,' what exactly do you mean?"

Now Ethan looked confused. "Pain is physical suffering or distress, as due to injury, illness—"

"No, I know what it means. But you can't feel it."

"I have sensory receptors and the ability to interpret the information from them. When my senses detect something harmful, I feel it as unpleasant. My body tells me to reject the source of the unpleasantness."

This was fascinating. Kelly knew, of course, that such defense mechanisms had been programmed into the androids, having had a hand in them herself. But the fact that he interpreted it as pain— even used the words "my body"—it was just so human. She hadn't even considered that he might become hurt or tired by her requests, any more than her laptop might. Her curiosity reared. She felt her instinctive scientist's itch to collect some data.

"Is this painful?" she asked, flicking his arm.

"A little."

"Is this?" She flicked him harder.

"Ow," he said, almost involuntarily. Pain clearly read on his face, yet he continued to just stand there and let her do what she wanted.

"If this hurts, why isn't your body telling you to move away from me?"

"Because it's you."

Kelly stopped, looking at him. The pain relaxed from his face, and he looked at her with clear, trusting eyes. She felt a twinge of guilt. "Would you like to see the couch somewhere else?" he asked.

"No, this is good." She moved it a final inch, then patted one of its seats. "Come and sit down."

Bravely, or maybe just foolishly, Kelly and Ethan had entered the glass and concrete behemoth of the Westfield Valley Fair mall on their second full Sunday together. Parking, aka Car Wars, was so stressful that Kelly nearly kept right on going to the exit, but the thought of her mother's horror if Ethan were to show up to the wedding in a month wearing Target's finest kept her in check. She had texted her mom that morning to officially notify her that Ethan would be her wedding date, and after Diane had responded with an enthusiasm that could only be expressed via seventeen separate exclamation marks (Kelly had counted), she had begun e-mailing so rapidly and in such volume that Kelly thought at first her computer had a virus. By the time Diane had sent the first dozen forwards and links to wardrobe suggestions for Ethan, Kelly decided to pack it in and take him shopping.

Clothes shopping typically activated all of her social neuroses with the dinging of a thousand tiny alarm bells. In fact, she almost never did it without Priya at her side for a second opinion. But of course Priya couldn't know about this. Kelly was realizing that she had underestimated how difficult it would be to hide the presence of a new person in her home and her daily life from her best friend. The other day at work, she had nearly mentioned without thinking how Ethan had helped her rearrange the furniture. She would have to come up with some sort of story for Priya before the wedding photos came out and Ethan was at her side in every one. For now, she pushed the thought aside.

She had intended to steer him to Macy's for her traditional range of clean-cut neutrals, something that couldn't possibly violate Diane's sartorial rules. But the display in the window of an upscale menswear boutique, vibrant with colors for their early spring collection, caught her eye. The models in the posters brooded above their pastel shirts and printed pants. Ethan was better-looking than any of them. She pulled him into the store, just to see.

The interior was a fever dream: salmon-colored ties, socks with patterns of actual salmon, newsboy caps and suspenders paired with '70s rock tees, even a display case of bolo ties. Kelly felt like she had tried to dip a toe into the men's fashion pool and been snatched by the riptide.

"What do you like?" Ethan asked her.

"Nothing," she said honestly. "Come on, let's go to Macy's."

But a sales rep wearing distressed jeans and a suit jacket with a peacock feather peeking out of the pocket stopped in front of Ethan. "And what can I do for *you*?" he asked, giving him a once-over.

Kelly only let the sales rep help them to be polite. She was positive that the blue suit jacket, the eggshell-colored trousers with subtle green threading, and the shirt and tie with contrasting patterns that he had selected would look ridiculous together, and as she sat outside the dressing room, jiggling her foot, she held her purse over her shoulder so she could spring up and leave as soon as Ethan was done. But when he stepped out, her grip on it went slack. He looked like he had just stepped off a runway.

"Wow. I mean, um, that looks nice," she said.

"What do you think?" He gave a little spin.

"I think we'll take it," she said.

For once, Kelly was actually enjoying herself at the mall rather than feeling as though she had been sentenced there. She wasn't in the mood to go home right away, though their work was finished. So she swung into her old tech geek standby, but was quickly driven out by the cocktail of scents found only in a Silicon Valley Apple Store—the sweat of excited adolescent boys, woodsy gender-neutral cologne, and the heady adrenal funk of rabid capitalism. Instead, she and Ethan stopped into the next shop over, a California-based botanical beauty brand, letting the powdery, herbal scent wash the Apple Store off of them. She picked up a tiny container, squinting. "Daily beauty fudge? Remind me never to put candy on my face." But just as they were turning to leave, Kelly's eyes swept the back of the store. And she saw Tiffany Galecki.

Back when Kelly was her lab partner at Westridge High, Tiffany had inarguably been the hottest girl in the eleventh grade, and the most popular. Kelly hadn't wanted to be Tiffany—that much socializing would be agonizing, and cheerleading and student council sounded more punishing than detention—but she would have been happy to have the effect on other people that Tiffany did. Tiffany always had a date to every dance, she was always chosen right away as a partner for class projects, she always had pages on pages of colorful year-end notes in her yearbook where Kelly had little more than a few "Have a good summer"s. And most of all, it appeared to come so effortlessly to her. Tiffany's visual presence on Facebook in the years since graduation was a regular reminder to Kelly of some of the most awkward times in her heroically awkward life, and an unspoken standard of prettiness, popularity, and social grace which Kelly, in all those same intervening years, knew that she had come no closer to attaining.

They had been assigned partners in Advanced Biology junior year. Kelly had possessed the ability, willingness, and motivation to do all the work, and Tiffany had possessed . . . none of those things. She was never overtly mean or rude to Kelly. She was something much worse: uninterested. When the two of them were supposed to be completing an experiment together in class, Tiffany would drift from their shared station toward her friends, laughing and chatting with them while Kelly squinted at the minute lines printed on the sides of beakers, or at pink-stained slides under microscopes.

Later, Kelly found herself in the same homeroom as Tiffany, who was chosen to be the class's attendance monitor. On their first day of senior year, she stood at the front of the room, shifting her weight casually in her flowered wedges, calling the roll. "Kelly Suttle," she called out when she reached the S's. "Kelly Suttle?" Her eyes scraped over the class, moving onto Kelly and then right past her, continuing their search. After working side by side for all of junior year, she didn't even remember Kelly's name.

It was this potent feeling of invisibility that flooded back over Kelly now as she stared across the store to where Tiffany manned the checkout counter. Her first instinct was to flee before Tiffany could catch sight of her. But that was the old Kelly, the nameless, squinting peon. The new Kelly, the Kelly who had come here with Ethan, didn't have to flee. She found him blithely comparing the viscosities of different shower gels and gestured him forward.

She took a good ten minutes to wind her way to the front of the store with Ethan trailing her, feigning an unhealthy interest in stands of lip balm, trying to think of a smart opening line, something that would sound clever and original, yet offhand, and also conveniently demonstrate how far she'd come since high school. But when she forced herself with a sudden burst of will to round the final display table, hurtling into Tiffany's view, all she could call out, in an unnaturally loud voice that also seemed to have suddenly acquired an unplaceable and improbable accent, was "Tiffany Galecki!"

"Yeah, it's me. Hi!" Tiffany's chestnut hair was still long and bouncy, her nose a perfect little upturned mound. But her face wore a bored expression as she tidied a display of floral spritzers. She looked up now at Kelly's interruption.

"Tiffany, it's Kel!" Kelly gushed. Not once before had she called herself "Kel." "Kelly Suttle, from high school!"

"Kelly Suttle!" Tiffany clearly had no idea who Kelly was. Kelly's fleeting wish for a triumphant "look how far I've come since high school" narrative hadn't acknowledged the fact that the before picture might be completely out of focus. As Ethan came and stood next to her, Tiffany's eyes flickered to him.

Just as Tiffany couldn't disguise not remembering Kelly, she definitely couldn't disguise being impressed by Ethan. She took him in, from his dark hair to his neat, perfectly shined shoes. "*So* nice to meet you . . ." she said, waiting for Ethan to supply his name, holding out a hand and shaking his for just an instant too long.

"This is Ethan," Kelly said. The tilt of Tiffany's head, the curl of her lips—the queen bee was back out and ready to sting. Kelly felt as if she'd stepped back into eleventh grade.

"What do you do around here?" Tiffany asked Ethan, her attention immediately off Kelly.

"I teach," Ethan said. "Astronomy."

"Oh wow, that's amazing," Tiffany breathed. "Kel, where did you find this guy?" She giggled, grabbing Kelly's arm familiarly across the glass counter. So now they were best friends, Kelly realized. Ethan had impressed Tiffany, suddenly making Kelly a person of consequence by the power of osmosis. With him at her side, she appeared to have succeeded in a significant paradigm of American social life and private consciousness. She should be feeling vindicated, validated.

It only made the reality of her life feel that much more disappointing.

"She found me in a lab," Ethan was replying. Kelly tensed—he knew not to share his origin story. "And she brought me to life." He turned to Kelly and smiled. For an instant, she forgot about Tiffany.

Tiffany giggled again and this time reached for Ethan's arm, fluttering her lashes at him. "You are too much. Kelly, do you have any more like him stashed away?" she asked, her eyes never leaving Ethan's sculpted face.

"Kelly has all sorts of amazing things in her lab," Ethan went on, lighting up. "She's a genius."

"I'm sure she is," Tiffany cooed.

"She works at Automated Human Industries."

Tiffany shifted now to look at Kelly. "You do? The robot company?"

"Yeah," Kelly said, starting to pull Ethan away.

"That's so cool!" Kelly paused—suddenly, Tiffany's admiration sounded genuine. "Oh my gosh, wait—you were my lab partner! The one who was so good at science!"

"Yep, that's me."

"I had the hardest time with that stuff," Tiffany sighed. "Well, I guess it's gotten you pretty far. Congratulations."

Kelly felt a flush creeping into her face at the sincere praise. "Thanks. I mean, you look like you're doing well too." Taken by a sudden instinct, she grabbed a small jar from a display. "I've just got to try this"—she glanced at the label—"daily beauty fudge!"

"Sure," Tiffany said, taking the jar and ringing her up. "I'll give you the family and friends discount."

Tiffany Galecki had said it out loud—"friends." After twelve years, it had only taken five minutes.

They had to fight their way out of the parking lot, but Kelly barely registered the tight turns and enraged drivers this time. She drummed her fingers rapidly on the steering wheel, staring straight ahead.

"It must have been nice to meet an old friend," Ethan remarked.

"Tiffany's not an old friend."

"You're right, she isn't old."

"I mean she's not my friend."

Ethan turned to look at her in confusion. "But she called you her friend." He paused for a millisecond, as if searching something online. "You're friends on Facebook."

"Ha! You still have a lot to learn about people if you think that means we're actually friends." Kelly pursed her lips, then glanced over at Ethan. She knew she was being opaque, and probably too abrupt. "I didn't have a lot of friends in high school the way Tiffany did," she explained. "Nobody was mean to me. They didn't beat me up or call me names or steal my lunch. They just . . ." She searched for the word. She had never spoken to anyone about this, had never even explicitly reckoned with it herself. "They ignored me," she finished, carefully turning her face away from Ethan to look in her driver's-side mirror.

Ethan's eyes narrowed as he pieced her words together. "So you're saying that Tiffany received far more attention in high school than you did?"

"Of course she did, you met her. It's not like I want that much attention anyway," she went on hurriedly, feeling inexplicably silly about this whole thing. "I'm almost thirty, why would I care now about impressing her?"

"It all makes perfect sense from a psychosocial perspective. And she clearly was impressed."

"Clearly. I think you're her type," Kelly responded, inching forward to stake an opening.

"Oh, not with me, with you. Tiffany's working in a mall and you're a robotics engineer."

"Yeah, well . . . they don't give out superlatives for that in high school," Kelly mumbled. But she felt lighter as she finally broke out of the concrete garage and into the sunshine. Maybe Ethan did know a little about people.

nine

• • • • • •

"Good morning, get going," Anita called out as she strode through the main floor at work. Kelly scrambled to pick up her tablet and follow her boss toward the staff room, folding in with her coworkers as they gathered into line behind Anita like sand bottlenecking through an hourglass. Every Tuesday, the entire Engineering department had a staff meeting at "whatever time Anita is ready" o'clock. Every week, they had to wait for her appearance to head to the staff room, and every week, she acted like they were all late for not already being there.

"Our dinner is at seven thirty sharp tonight," Anita said as soon as the group was seated in the glass-walled conference room. "We will not reimburse for valet. I trust that you will enjoy an evening of letting our collective hair down." Anita gave the assembled engineers a look so severe that Kelly felt her own hair say "no, thank you" and retract sheepishly back into her scalp.

She swallowed a groan. She had forgotten that tonight was their annual Engineering department dinner. She'd started to look forward to her regular nights in with Ethan. Besides, if she had remembered what a long day it was going to be, she would have brought her trusty comfortable flats to change into, the ones that folded up into a little bag to fit in her purse. She inched her heels up out of the backs of her shoes, relieving the pressure on her toes. The dinner that was advertised as a goodwill gesture toward Anita's employees in reality often felt more like a test, a chance to observe her subjects in a new environment. Kelly was reluctant enough to engage with most of these people at work, let alone being forced into an evening with them too. At least there was one consolation: free food.

Yet that evening, by the time Kelly arrived at the sleek Japantown sushi spot, she wasn't even thinking about the food, or her uncomfortable shoes, or which seat along the long, narrow communal table would keep her the farthest away from Robbie. CA-87 had been bumper to bumper, and she hadn't thought to use the restroom before embarking on the drive. She threw her purse down in the open chair next to Priya without sitting. "I'll be back, I have to pee like a—" But her words stopped in her throat. Near the front of the restaurant, winding his way toward the back with a searching look, was Ethan.

He spotted her and waved hugely, his face opening into a grin. This could not be really happening.

She leaped over like the floor was on fire and caught him before he could come any closer to the table. "Ethan, what are you doing here?" she whispered.

"I brought your flats." He withdrew the shoes, tucked into their flannel pouch, from a grocery bag. "When you texted me that you had this dinner tonight, I became concerned because I realized you didn't have a change of shoes with you. I know how your feet hurt when you're in heels for too long."

"Aww!" came a feminine voice. A quick glance back at the table made it clear that they were all brazenly watching and could hear everything that Ethan was saying. The female engineers looked touched, the males somewhere in the neighborhood of "Is this guy for real?" Kelly pulled him farther away, ducking around the other side of a large tank where ornamental fish waved their shimmering orange plumes. Her hands were trembling. For Ethan to just show up like this in front of her boss and coworkers . . . if anyone were to notice something robotic about him, it would be the robotics engineers who ran the very lab that had birthed him.

"Thank you for the shoes, but you can't just show up here like this, Ethan," she whispered tensely. "What if somebody figured something out? This is my job, this is my life!"

Ethan hung his head. "I thought this would be a good idea, that it would make you happy, but I can see that I've just ruined your evening."

"Ethan," Kelly softened, "it's fine, you didn't ruin anything, you didn't know."

"I haven't put you in a difficult position with your coworkers?"

"Not if you get out of here now." She grabbed the shoes and gently pushed him toward the door, but Anita appeared behind her, causing her to jump so that she nearly upset the tank.

"Are you sending this gentleman home? Why ever would you do that? Please, please, stay!" Her voice was uncharacteristically breezy, nearly breathless, but loud enough that there was no hope of keeping the conversation from prying ears. "We welcome guests at our office functions."

One of Kelly's fellow engineers turned toward them, leaning hopefully in his chair. "Does that mean I can bring my wife next time?"

"Turn around, Stewart," Anita shot out without looking back at him. Her eyes were locked firmly on Ethan, critical and analyzing: Was she admiring him? Or was she identifying his familiar constituent parts from her own lab? It was impossible to tell. Kelly only knew that she was definitely having a reaction.

"Kelly?" Anita held out a hand, ushering her back to the table. Kelly had no choice. She took Ethan's hand and brought him with her.

Kelly assumed her own seat beside Priya (whose face she didn't dare look at) at the end of the table, then dragged a chair over from an adjacent table, its legs scraping angrily on the slate-tiled floor. She set the chair on the other side of herself, fully outside of their table, then gestured for Ethan to sit, blocking him completely from the view of her coworkers. She propped an elbow on the table and tried to look brightly at everyone as if nothing at all had just happened.

"Kelly, what are you doing?" Anita asked. "He can't sit there! Here, I'll just scoot in here and you take this seat . . . ?"

"Ethan." He answered her unvoiced question as he rose with an apologetic look at Kelly and took the chair directly next to Anita, five down from Kelly. She didn't know whether to be more panicked at Ethan's proximity to her boss or bewildered that Anita Riveras had just used the word "scoot."

Anita smiled at him. "There. Much better. Oh, bring me a chardonnay to start," she called to a passing waiter who was not theirs.

Kelly couldn't stop herself now from looking at the shocked faces around the table. When she finally looked at Priya beside her, she nearly burst out laughing, despite her own pumping anxiety. Priya had left the edamame pod she was snacking on half eaten, her mouth hanging open, her eyes wide as she stared at Ethan, then at Kelly, and back again. She looked as though her perception of everything that she thought she knew was so thoroughly shaken that she was retreating, baby-like, to some preknowledge place, aware only of vague geometric shapes and temperatures.

"Who is he?" Robbie's sudden ejaculation shook Kelly's gaze from Priya. The tips of his ears looked like they had been touched by a hot poker. He made a visible effort to recover himself, clutching his water so hard that his hand squeaked against the condensation on the glass. "I don't believe we've had the good fortune of meeting," he continued more civilly.

Kelly could feel the trembling in her own hands starting to ease. All of the engineers had been staring at Ethan for several minutes now, and so far, none of them had spotted a thing. Either they were really bad, or she was really good. "This is Ethan," she said, face red but head held high. "He's my boyfriend." Priya shot an edamame seed out of its pod and across the table. Kelly gave her a stifling look, pleading for her silence.

"And what do you do, Ethan?" Anita asked him smoothly.

"Ethan's an associate professor of astronomy at Stanford," Kelly interjected, before he could say anything. She knew that she couldn't leave this up to chance; she had to direct Ethan's answer.

"Ah." Anita smiled at him, waving her wineglass. "How refreshing to have someone here from outside the world of robotics." If only she knew what an insider he was, Kelly reflected wryly. "No AHI shoptalk tonight. What's the latest from CERN?" She leaned back in her chair, one arm crossed over her chest, the other holding the glass almost coquettishly to her lips, her posture giving the air of settling in for a nice long talk.

Kelly winced. The more Anita questioned him, the more he would have to read things aloud off the internet. If he messed up in front of all of her coworkers, and her boss, if they picked up on the truth about him, she could lose her job. She could lose everything.

"Anita, I'd love to fill you in on some of my research into bilayer modeling," she interrupted quickly. "Harvard developed this algorithm that can compute a growth pattern—"

"Please, I said no shoptalk," Anita insisted, taking a rather healthy draft of her drink.

"There's actually some fascinating research coming together in preparation for the Quark Matter conference," Ethan began.

"How about those Mets?" Kelly threw in wildly.

Anita looked at Kelly reprovingly. Even Priya broke from her amazed stare at Ethan to cast Kelly a "what are you doing?" glance. Kelly's cheeks burned.

"Well, the Large Hadron Collider . . ." Ethan went on. As Kelly took a second scope of the table, she began to see that it was she, not Ethan, who was embarrassing herself. Not only had no one risen to his feet, pointed at Ethan, and shouted *"Robot!"* but everyone actually seemed impressed by him. They listened as he conversed intelligently about his work. Some of the ladies, and a few of the men, cast him dreamy looks. Several glanced back at Kelly with wrinkled brows, as if recalibrating everything they knew about her in light of this unexpected new connection. She couldn't believe it. Ethan was passing the test and earning extra credit to boot. She stretched out her tense hands, releasing a long, relaxing sigh.

She nearly released the contents of her bladder in the process. Now that she could trust Ethan not to blow everything, she thought she could break away long enough to chance that trip to the bathroom. She quietly pushed her chair back and hurried away, trying not to listen to the water flowing through the fish tank's filter as she went.

After Kelly finished, she opened the door of the bathroom stall to find Priya standing two inches away on the other side. Curiosity had entirely unhinged her. "Who the what?" she demanded, her eyes wide. "What the him is he?"

"Him is—*he* is Ethan," Kelly said simply. "We're dating."

"You did not just say that and then stand there like the words you're saying make sense."

"It's not that big a deal," Kelly insisted.

"You're never dating anyone! Then you show up with a Calvin Klein model who hauls ass around town because he's worried about your priceless little baby feet and you act like it's no big deal?"

"It *isn't* that big of a deal." Kelly pushed past her to wash her hands. "He's just a guy. We're just hanging out." She carefully avoided meeting Priya's eyes in the mirror.

"He knew what shoes you wore to work this morning. That sounds like you're living together."

"He, um, stayed the night last night." It wasn't a lie.

Priya took a deep breath and held up a hand. "One moment." She walked into a stall, flushed the toilet, and unleashed a shout of *"Hell yeah!"* that was only partially masked by the ensuing noise. She walked back into the sink area and seamlessly resumed her questioning. "Were you planning on telling me about this guy, I don't know, sometime before you have grandkids together?"

"Yes, I promise!" Kelly clasped her hands in an unconscious plea. "We met at a coffee shop and just kind of hit it off. It's still early, but I wanted to make sure it felt right before I jinxed it by talking about him." She had practiced these words aloud in the car one day just in case this situation should ever arise. She hoped against hope that they sounded natural and unrehearsed now.

"And does it?"

"Does it what?"

"Feel right?"

Kelly stopped. "Yeah. Yeah, it really does." A grin spread over her face before she could stop it. She was surprised by the warmth of her own voice as she started talking about Ethan. "He's smart and kind and a gentleman, and when I'm with him, I just feel like—me." Once the words started coming, it was a relief to get them out. She hadn't realized how much pressure had been building from not talking about this huge change in her life with anyone—she hadn't even realized what a huge change it was.

"Wow. *Wow.*" Priya shook her head wonderingly, half laughing with joy and astonishment. She reached out and hugged her with a little squeal, then stopped with her own sly smile. "I guess I can't be too mad, though."

"Why?"

"Remember Andre? That guy I went out with?"

"Um, yeah," Kelly lied. Priya went out with so many guys, in such rapid succession, that Kelly had fallen into the habit of deleting their names from her brain as soon as she heard them. Her brain storage was perpetually too close to full as it was.

"Well, we're going on our fourth date tomorrow."

This was big. Kelly couldn't remember the last time Priya had gotten past two or three dates with anyone. Priya, too, began chattering as if relieved the floodgates had been pulled.

"So he's a writer and a comedian, which doesn't mean he's a

waiter or a barista or anything, like, he actually gets *paid* to write for this website, so the sort of shit I say that normally scares men off, he just laughs about. I think that's why it's going well. He just rolls with it and *gets* me. I'm not trying to get in over my head, but . . ."

Priya talked animatedly on as they made their way back toward the table, and Kelly felt a bright spurt of happiness. Here they were, two best friends talking about their promising relationships. But something niggled at the back of her mind. Priya was opening up, being utterly honest about her new relationship. And Kelly couldn't do the same.

ten

• • • • • •

On her own, Kelly didn't get out much; her world was pretty much her office, her apartment, and the roads between them. She generally felt awkward going out either alone or with others, and found the effort to not be worth the time or the trouble. But with Ethan there, she was discovering that small things became a pleasure. Waiters held her chair out for her at restaurants. Neighbors walking their dogs waved hello as she and Ethan walked down the street. After they listened to her favorite robotics podcast and discussed it at home, she even ventured to bring up the latest episode with a coworker who she knew was a fellow fan.

And maybe the new way the world seemed to be treating Kelly had as much to do with the new way she was carrying herself as it did with the presence beside her of a man who had oodles of presence. Going out into the world with Ethan, she talked more animatedly, moved more expressively. But she gave no notice to any changes in herself. When the sweet older lady behind the counter at the car wash told them what a cute couple they were, she smiled and took his hand. It was remarkable how human his skin was— solid but with give, warm from within, pulsing almost impercepti- bly with the vibrations of his inner life. It was a masterful piece of technology. But all Kelly noticed was how nice it felt.

When family dinner rolled around that weekend, Kelly was ready. Not for the raisin tilapia her mom had promised to make, she would never be ready for that, but to introduce them to Ethan. She brushed her hair and tugged on her nicest blouse, but really, Ethan was the one who would be on display. On the drive there, she was unusually free from anxiety. Her coworkers had responded well to Ethan, and at this point, it felt so normal for her to be around him, to talk to him, that she was beginning to forget he wasn't a normal boyfriend herself.

So when half an hour later, the family was ringed around the table, staring at Ethan in stunned silence, she had no idea how to respond. She had so thoroughly expected Diane to pelt her and her new man with questions that she hadn't considered how to take the conversational lead. She picked at her fish, feeling somehow respon- sible for filling the silence. "Pluto and Goofy are both dogs. Why is one a pet and one a friend?" she blurted out.

"Holy cow," Gary said. "That's exactly what I was just thinking."

But the rest of the Suttles weren't taking the distraction bait. "Where exactly did you meet my daughter, Ethan?" Diane asked. Her voice betrayed nothing, like a Soviet spy's.

"Didn't you meet when you were out with Priya?" Clara chimed in.

"Right, at a bar." Kelly sincerely hoped that Priya and her family would never have occasion to compare stories.

"And what exactly is it you do?" Diane continued.

"I teach," Ethan answered. "I'm an associate professor of astronomy at Stanford." Kelly restrained herself from rushing in and rattling off the entire professional history she had concocted.

"Hmm," was all Diane replied, taking a careful bite of salad. She kept her eyes trained down, throwing out the next question casually. "And do you typically date women?"

"Mom!"

"It's an honest question. I'm just trying to get to know your new friend."

Now Kelly saw it. They didn't believe him. Not that her family didn't believe that Ethan was human, but they didn't believe that someone like him would date someone like her. They were waiting for the catch.

"Mom, can you help me with the bread?" she asked suddenly, grabbing the dinner roll off her plate and walking into the kitchen. A bemused Diane followed her in. Once in there, Kelly opened her hand and looked at the roll. What the heck was she supposed to do with this?

"What's the matter?" her mother asked.

"Why don't you believe that I could be with Ethan?" Kelly asked hotly.

"I never said that."

"But you're thinking it."

Diane paused for an instant too long.

"I am capable of getting a date on my own, you know!" Kelly

exclaimed. Maybe she said it so emphatically because a part of her, in the basement of her brain, was saying that none of this was true. "Just because I blew it with Martin doesn't mean that no man will ever love me."

"Of course not, dear," Diane said soothingly. "But you haven't brought anyone to family dinner in nearly five years and now you show up with an astronomy professor who looks like a walking fantasy"—gross, Kelly thought—"and ask me not to question it? Without revealing my age, Kelly, I will tell you that I was not born yesterday."

"He's just a guy I'm seeing! What is there to question?"

"I want to make sure that he's not taking advantage of you, dear," Diane said in a low enough voice for it not to travel to the dining room. "I want to make sure that his intentions are good."

Kelly stopped. Yes, her family's skepticism was still insulting. But at least Diane's heart was in the right place. "He's good, I promise."

"All right, then," Diane said simply. "I trust you." And they walked back into the dining room. As Kelly slid back into her seat, she wondered if she would now have to eat the bread that had been clenched in her sweaty, distressed fist for the past few minutes.

As they were wrapping up dessert (Diane's espresso and gingerbread ice cream actually came out well), Kelly got the courage to pipe up again. "I'm starting to build Confibot at work. You know, the robot?" she finished lamely. Her glance flickered to Carl. If anyone in the family would be interested in the nitty-gritty of what she did all day, it should be him. After all, he was an engineer himself. But he just spooned up his ice cream, the pinky of his left hand resting against the notebook of work papers beside him on the table, as if desperate to hold on to his ticket out.

"That's wonderful, dear," her mom said. "Oh, Gary, I almost

forgot! When I was watching the girls the other day, Emma got a hold of my phone and somehow placed a call to Shanghai. I think we've got a little businesswoman on our hands! Can't you just see her, jet-setting and making deals?" She gazed at Emma, who was waiting patiently for the ice cream that had somehow ended up in her hair to drip down into her mouth.

"Don't you want to hear more about Kelly's news?" Ethan asked. The table went silent. Kelly paused and looked at him more incredulously even than the rest of the group did. "I think it's fascinating." He smiled warmly at her.

"It is?" Kelly asked.

"Do you even know what Kelly does in her lab?"

"Of course, it's like the Hall of Presidents," Diane said.

Kelly had to stop Ethan. If he started sharing his knowledge of what went on in Kelly's lab, this could quickly go south. "That's basically it, there's nothing else really to talk about," she interjected.

"But it's much more than that," Ethan pressed. "The Hall of Presidents is an attraction located in Liberty Square at the Magic Kingdom in the Walt Disney World Resort." Was he just reading off the Wikipedia articles in his brain? Kelly winced, but before she could do anything, he went on. "Its Audio-Animatronic figures of our nation's presidents carry out preprogrammed sequences involving voice recordings and choreographed mechanical movements. What Kelly is working on is the development of an android model programmed to follow intricate codes of command and to respond to an infinite variety of variables and stimuli, making it infinitely more complex. Furthermore, Confibot will have the emotional intelligence to navigate charged human interactions, while also being precisely controllable. The implications are authentically society-changing.

The Hall of Presidents memorializes people who have shaped our world. What Kelly is doing has the potential to shape it."

Ethan's eyes sparkled. The whole table was silent until Emma finally captured her drip of ice cream with a ferocious slurp. Diane looked astounded. "My goodness. I guess you understand what Kelly does on a whole different level than we do, Ethan." She smiled at him for the first time, and Kelly couldn't help but grin. "Why don't you tell us more?"

Once she had warmed up to him, Diane embraced Ethan with a daunting enthusiasm, calling Kelly three times over the next few days to ask how he was, when Kelly was seeing him next, and, Kelly suspected, to verify that he wasn't a beautiful hallucination she had dreamed up after one too many glasses of wine at dinner. Kelly was so happy at how brilliantly her plan was working that her enthusiasm carried her over to that Thursday evening, when she arrived a full seven minutes early to the boutique where she was meeting her mom and sister to look at bridesmaid shoes. The only time Kelly had ever shown up early to a family event before was her own birth.

"Hey," she said excitedly, rising from the velvet pouf on which she'd been sitting when Diane and Clara appeared together a few minutes later. "So the heels are over there, flats are over there, and I'm willing to try anything, but you know how I do with anything over 2.3 inches."

Diane issued her instructions on what to look for. She was friends with the store's owner, often referring her own clients there, and had ascertained the exact moment of the spring collection's availability so that she and Clara could pounce on the latest goods just in time before the wedding. Now, as the three Suttle women set off down the aisles together, Kelly somehow kept finding herself alone. She would look for two seconds at a stacked heel, then glance back to realize that Diane and Clara were already an aisle down on the pumps, moving in tandem without even speaking about it. She put the shoe down and hurried to catch up.

She stood in front of the mirror ten minutes later, stacks of boxes and tumbleweeds of tissue paper all around, Diane and Clara sitting behind her like an Olympic judging panel. She shifted her ankles in the satin kitten heels, testing their stability. "What about these, Clara?"

"We want to avoid too many straps," her mom replied with authority. "After all, without being heavy-handed about it, we do hope to evoke a vintage vibe."

"We really liked the first ones you tried on, did you like those?" Clara asked. "All the girls would look cute in them."

Kelly bit her lip. Her mom and sister probably didn't even notice the "we" thing. But Kelly did. "Sure," she said, her spirits flagging.

"Well, try them on again, we want you to like them," Clara urged. Kelly slipped out of the strappy kitten heels and back into the delicate peep-toe pumps. She walked back and forth across the carpet, one foot in front of the other. Clara squealed approvingly. "They look so good on you, Kel! How are those to walk in?"

"Should be fine as long as you don't have me scaling any cliffs."

Clara mapped out the scene in front of her with her hands. "So let's see, you'll be coming up from the—"

"South side of the lawn," Diane supplied.

"So it's pretty level, right? You'll be over here, and here's the flower arch thing, and Jonathan and I will be here—" As Clara talked, Diane watched her with eyes growing wet. Finally, she burst into tears.

"Mom, what's the matter?" Clara asked.

"I'm just picturing it all, you on your wedding day. I can't believe it, my little girl is getting married!"

"Oh, Mom . . ."

"Will you still go shopping with me when you're a married woman? Will we still do things like this?" Diane gestured around the store.

"Of course I will! You couldn't get rid of me if you tried!" Clara folded Diane into a misty, sloppy hug.

Kelly stood alone at the mirror, scuffing her toe against the carpet. Suddenly she wished she had Ethan there with her, though what he could contribute to shoe shopping she didn't know. Family dinner had been so pleasant with him there. His presence was a safe retreat, a buffer. When she spotted a passing salesman, she flagged him down, relieved at something to do. "I guess I'll take these. We'll take these," she said.

After Diane went home to their dad, Clara and Kelly decided to grab a bite for dinner. They went to Café Whole, a small shop lined in subway tile and bleached wood. Clara loved the place, and Kelly admitted they did a solid smoothie, though she found their menu almost overbearingly hippie-ish, with all the dishes named things like "Peace" and "Duality." Everything came topped with microgreens.

"I think I'm going to do Humble, it's sooo good," Clara said as they waited to place their orders. "What are you thinking?"

"Magical," Kelly mumbled. She felt silly saying it.

"What?"

"Magical!"

The woman in line in front of them turned and stared.

When they were seated, Clara immediately faced Kelly with a broad smile. "So. Ethan," she said.

"No, I'm Kelly, remember? Your sister."

"Come on, tell me all about him!"

"We're just kind of seeing each other casually." Kelly was happy that her family had now met Ethan. But the less they knew *about* him, the better.

"Bringing him to family dinner? It can't be that casual," Clara said with a sly smile.

"Ethan's close to his family, so for him it's normal."

"Oh yeah? Do they live out here?"

"Um—no." Kelly figured it would be safer to have Ethan's parents far away. "But they're metaphorically close. They talk a lot."

"Have you talked to them yet?"

"Yes. I mean no. I mean we talked about it, we talked about me talking to them. But I haven't talked to them yet."

"Have you—"

"Why so many questions about Ethan?" Kelly said, with a light yet strained laugh. "Jonathan's the one who's almost family, tell me what's going on with him."

"Oh, you know his parents went to Phuket recently? Let me show you the pictures." Kelly relaxed, ready to just let Clara talk. But before her sister could tap open the album, she stopped and looked up at Kelly again. "Has Ethan traveled much?"

"No, he grew up here," Kelly said.

"So his family is from here."

"No. Yes."

"You just said that they don't live here."

"Well, they did, but they don't. Why do you care so much?" she asked with sudden anxiety-ridden frustration.

"Geez, pardon me for taking an interest in your life," Clara said, taking a bite of her burrito, which had just arrived.

"I figured Mom would have filled you in on everything going on in my life anyway. Why do you even need to ask me?"

"What's that supposed to mean?" Clara set down her burrito.

"Come on, like you don't know."

"I don't!" Clara was genuinely bewildered, but Kelly couldn't bring herself to spell it out. It suddenly felt childish to complain about Clara's closeness with Diane.

Instead, she shoveled down a bite of her grain bowl before grabbing her purse and rising. "I've got to run, I have work to do." Seeing the hurt look on Clara's face, she almost turned back and apologized. But instead, she fished some cash out of her wallet and plunked it on the table. "Here, I'll pay." The cramped restaurant suddenly seemed very long as she made her way out.

Driving home on Highway 101, the sun tipping below the broad horizon, Kelly called Priya while she was sitting in traffic. "Am I just crazy?" she asked after filling her in on the day's events.

"Clearly you're crazy, we knew this," asserted Priya. "And you could have handled the situation better. But I don't think you're wrong to feel left out."

126

"I mean, I hate to be reductive and just say that Clara's the favorite child, but sometimes it feels that way."

"Oh, she's totally the favorite child," Priya said. "I'm a favorite child. Takes one to know one."

"You're the favorite?" Kelly had heard stories about Priya's strict parents and three brothers, but had never met them since they were all on the East Coast.

"I'm a medical engineer and they think I'm still a virgin. Of course I'm the favorite child."

Kelly sighed. "Well, thanks, I guess. Though I'm not sure this talk made me feel any better. Actually, I may feel worse."

"So Clara's the favorite, so what?" Priya exclaimed. "Maybe your mom just clicks with her more easily, it doesn't mean she loves you less. Besides, you're my favorite. And no offense to your mom, but we all know my opinion is gospel."

"I don't know, you did decide to be friends with me. What's that thing about not wanting to belong to any club that would have you for a member?"

"Listen, woman, I do not have time for circular logic." Kelly laughed. "Anyway, just relax," Priya went on. "Don't get all in your head about what other people think. What you really are is more important."

"Yeah . . . now just to work on that part." Kelly sighed as she turned onto her exit.

eleven

. . . . . .

On Friday evening, Kelly was doing what any other successful, mature twenty-nine-year-old businesswoman does on a Friday evening: watching *BattleBots*. It was such a stupid show. It reduced her life's work to a *Jackass* stunt. She couldn't stop watching.

Ethan sat beside her on the couch as she gazed at the screen, where a spiny robot called Crushosaurus was obliterating a black-and-yellow bot with a long retractable spike and "Stinger" emblazoned on its side. "Wow, he must *bee* smarting," she said as Stinger sustained a blow, sliding her eyes sideways at Ethan.

"Yeah, totally," Ethan responded, completely serious, concentrating on the screen.

"I mean, he'll be lucky to come out a-hive."

"I know, right?"

Kelly was grinning, but still nothing from Ethan. Now it was her turn to stare at him and concentrate. Okay, her jokes were bad, but they weren't that bad. Thus far, Ethan had passed among people all over the city with no one batting an eye, except maybe to flirt at him. His language had developed a less formal, more conversational cadence. Yet something was still missing. He had no sense of humor.

This was a challenge. She had worked, along with the rest of the engineering team, to develop response modules for all sorts of social situations—how to make small talk, how to be polite, how to order food at a restaurant or explain a problem to a cable rep over the phone or thank a relative for a Christmas gift. As complex and charged as Kelly had realized all human interactions were, humor was one of the most complex. It was so universally and wordlessly instinctual, yet also so individual. How could she teach Ethan when to laugh?

She pulled her e-reader off the arm of the couch and downloaded a book called *Monkey See, Monkey Do: Follow Me to Funny Land!* As soon as she saw the wide-lapelled miscreant grinning from the front cover, she wondered if she was making a wise choice. But it *was* the number one download in the category, and she was a sucker for numbers.

"Here, take a look at this," she said, handing Ethan the device. "I think you might find it interesting. Give it a read and let me know if you have any questions."

"Of course, thank you, Kelly," he said excitedly.

A half hour later, she was hard at work in her home office, watching demos from a recent robotics conference in Japan of a new caregiver robot on the market. She was deep in thought, scrutinizing the way the elderly woman at the demo lit up when the robot did certain things for her, or uttered certain phrases.

All of a sudden, Ethan barreled into the room, wearing his pants up around his chest, Urkel-style, and struck a pose. "Take my wife, please!" he cried. He fell out of the pose, a crease on his brow. "I'm not sure that I'm doing this right."

Kelly didn't even ask what was in the book. She closed out her work and took Ethan to a late movie. There was only one out-and-out comedy playing at the theater closest to her, a raunchy college road trip story. It was silly, but it did have some funny moments. Kelly got into it and laughed a little. At first Ethan was staring at the screen intently. But he sneaked glances at Kelly laughing. As the movie played on, he started to laugh too.

"So did you see how that was supposed to be funny?" she asked him as they walked to the car afterward. The night air was getting less and less chilly. Kelly had finally switched to her lighter jacket this week.

"I think so," he said. "Breasts are funny, anuses are funny, penises are funny, and testicles are funny."

"Well, yeah, there was a lot of that. But I liked the scene on the plane best. It was so unexpected."

"So things that are unexpected are funny?"

Kelly thought about it, frowning. "Yeah, I guess."

"But if I walked out into that street and got hit by a car, that would be unexpected, right? But would it also be funny? Wouldn't people be crying and upset at a car accident?"

She shook her head in frustration. "I don't know how to explain it. I guess it's just something you pick up on."

"Why don't you tell me what you find funny?"

Kelly walked a few more paces before responding. "I never told you how Clara and Jonathan met, did I?"

"No," said Ethan.

"Well, Clara had just moved into her first apartment on her own after college. She's into DIY stuff and she really wanted to get it all set up herself. So she had a mattress delivered and when Jonathan, who was living below her, saw it coming up the stairs, he asked if she needed help setting it up and she said no. But the mattress was rolled up really tightly and shrink-wrapped, and when she cut it out of the wrapping, it all sprang out at once and threw her out the open window. She caught on to the fire escape and there she was, dangling in front of Jonathan's window. He opened it and was like, 'Now would you like a hand?' The rest was history."

Now Ethan and Kelly were laughing together. "I guess you could say it was love at first flight," he said.

By now Kelly found herself going out with Ethan less, maybe because she enjoyed staying in with him more. The two of them were developing an easy rhythm, anticipating each other's words, moving around each other like the gears of a clock. In the mornings, they knew without speaking that Kelly brushed her hair while Ethan brushed his teeth, then they rotated at the sink for Kelly to brush her teeth while Ethan brushed his hair.

On Saturday, Ethan was going to pull a book from the shelf when Kelly sat down at her home computer. He paused behind her. "You have good taste," he said suddenly.

"What?" she asked.

He nodded at her computer monitor, which Kelly had filled with a desktop background of carefully arranged images of historical robots, from an ancient Chinese automaton to Leonardo da Vinci's robot, clad in armor like a miniknight, to the wide-eyed gold

Maschinenmensch from *Metropolis*. She had spent some time composing the layout, adjusting the colors until everything looked just right together, a supple flow of silver, gold, and bronze. Kelly the IKEA Queen hadn't put much thought or personality into anything else in her apartment, but this—this was a point of pride. "Oh, the desktop?" she said now, shrugging. "I had fun with it. I'm not sure anyone would say I have good taste, though."

"No, you do," he said decisively. "It's lovely. You have a real aesthetic."

It was entirely possible that Ethan was just being nice to her because that's what he did, but the praise brought a flush to her cheeks. He would know what was aesthetically pleasing—after all, the bouquets he designed for her were works of art. Kelly had never thought of herself as a person who possessed an aesthetic. Looking around her blocky beige apartment, she realized that it looked a little drab. Less like a safe, neutral space and more like the inside of a cardboard box. Maybe it was Ethan's vividness that threw everything else into dull relief.

That weekend they redecorated, styling the apartment into something cooler and more modern, painting an accent wall a warm gray, fitting a faux sheepskin rug that Kelly picked out under the coffee table, replacing the basic rod lamp with something steel and sculptural that Ethan had found. "Thanks," she told him as she handed him a nail, then stood back to make sure that the artistic robot picture he was hanging on the bedroom wall was straight with the others in its row. Something about the whole image—not just the fresh décor, but Ethan balancing there on a chair, a nail between his teeth, made the apartment suddenly feel like a home. She smiled behind his back.

"It'll be good practice for when I put up our decorations at Chrssmss. Christmas," he corrected, removing the nail from his mouth.

He said it lightly, but Kelly's smile evaporated. By then, Ethan would be long gone.

twelve

• • • • • •

At the end of the long day of redecorating, when they returned from dropping off the old furniture at Goodwill, Kelly immediately stripped off her pants. Especially given how literally buttoned up she was during the week, she liked her home wardrobe to be as comfortable as possible. Ethan took the pants from her outstretched hand at the door as usual, like it was the most normal thing in the world. "What do you want to do for dinner?" she asked. "Don't answer that—nachos."

But instead of Ethan answering her, the doorbell did. Kelly groaned. Back on went the hated pants. She knew who was standing on the other side of the door. Her mom was her only semiregular unexpected visitor, making her, well, a semiexpected visitor. "Go hide, I'll try to get her out quickly." Kelly shooed Ethan into the bathroom. His presence here would raise questions that she wasn't in the mood to have to answer.

She opened the door to see her mother standing there, raising a brown paper grocery bag. "Don't be mad! I brought food!"

Kelly was mad, and the bracingly peppery tuna casserole she found herself picking at ten minutes later didn't help. As it turned out, Diane seemed to have come expressly for the purpose of asking questions about Ethan. "So, you haven't been answering my texts about Ethan. How are things going with him?" she asked, looking around as if hoping to find their relationship status inscribed on a wall.

"Great, everything's fine," Kelly said simply.

"Where is he tonight?" Diane pressed, still peering around.

"I don't know, probably at his place."

"You don't know? Aren't you at least talking to him every night?"

"Most nights, I guess." Kelly felt like there was a right answer to this question, at least right according to her mother's finely honed nose for relationship etiquette, and she wasn't sure she was giving it.

"He's already met your family, your coworkers—you should be moving forward in your relationship and frankly, Kelly, you seem like you've gotten stuck. Not to bring up your age again, but you really ought to be locking a man in."

"Ah yes, the bear trap school of dating," Kelly replied.

"Relationships are not a joke, Kelly!"

"We've only been dating for a month! We're just keeping it casual, seeing where things go."

"Keeping it casual is a good way to see it go nowhere. As soon as your father and I met, I started keeping tabs on him. He hasn't sneezed in over thirty years without me knowing what tickled his nose." Kelly briefly wondered how her dad would react to this proud declaration. Or if he would react at all.

"Well, that's what worked for you," Kelly said shortly. "How did your sale go at the shop?"

"How does it always go? I told all the girls they looked like princesses, they bought the dresses, another successful season in the bag."

"I've made some good strides in my project recently." Kelly left out the part where she was actually still struggling with Confi-bot and regularly stress-eating raw cookie dough because of it. "Yesterday—"

"Kelly, I don't feel like you're hearing what I'm saying," Diane interrupted. "You have a good thing here, a rather astonishingly good thing."

"Ethan's not a 'thing,' Mom."

"Look at your past relationships! Nick in college, then Robbie—they both gave me a Ted Bundy vibe. I've never *seen* such precision with a knife."

Kelly wasn't proud of her relationship history, but her mother's haranguing instantly put her on the defensive. "I can figure out how to conduct my own life, thanks."

"My dear, I'm only saying that you can't just let your relationship happen to you. You have to take the reins."

"I thought you always said to let the man make the first move."

"Oh no, no." Diane laughed, head thrown back. "You have to *make* him make the first move. Do you think your father wanted to ask me to marry him? Of course not. No man does. But if you asked, he would say it was his idea. To this day he believes that." She spiked the air with her fork as she ate the tuna casserole, punctuating her point. "The next step is to move in together," she continued.

"Ethan and I aren't anywhere near ready for that," Kelly

maintained. "And when we are, it'll be a decision we make together. Not something I force him into."

"Honey, if you wait for him to want it, you're going to be alone forever."

Kelly was losing the last of her patience. "Mom, from the day I turned thirteen, you've been saying you're afraid that I'll be alone forever. I finally get a boyfriend, a perfect, storybook, fairy-tale ending boyfriend, and you're still telling me I'm going to be alone forever. When am I going to be good enough for you? When I'm in a marriage like yours?"

Diane set her fork down. "A marriage like mine?"

Kelly backpedaled. "I didn't mean—that didn't sound the way I meant it to."

Diane stood with dignity. "I have to run to the bathroom," she managed to say. Kelly was irresistibly called back to her date with Martin—maybe bad excuses were genetic. She felt a guilty pang, watching her mother retreat to the bathroom.

Then she remembered what was in the bathroom: Ethan.

It was too late—Kelly ran to pull her mom back from the door, but Diane had already swung it open. There stood Ethan, looking as shocked as if Santa Claus had walked in on him. Diane looked between the two of them.

"Diane, how lovely to see you," he stammered.

Kelly searched for an explanation. She and Ethan tried frantically to telegraph to each other with their eyes across Diane's head. "Ethan was just—"

"I was in the area—"

"And he got something on his clothes, so he came here—"

"To wear Kelly's?" he finished. "No, not that—"

138

Luckily, Diane was barely listening to their disconnected call-and-response. "Well, you cheeky little lovebirds!" she said excitedly, all offense wiped clean from her face, like rain from a windshield. "Why didn't you tell me he was here?"

"We just—" Kelly began.

"Don't tell me." Diane held up a hand, an impish gleam in her eye. "I can tell that I've interrupted you two at a bad time. Or a very good time. Some Mommy and Daddy time, perhaps."

"Right," Kelly said, trying not to gag.

"Well, I'll leave you two alone." Kelly followed Diane as she bustled to the door, picking up her purse. She leaned in and whispered to Kelly, "If he's spending nights, it won't be long until he's living here anyway." She gave a little excited hunch of the shoulders as Kelly ushered her out the door. "It won't be long!" she echoed.

Kelly had her pants unzipped the second the door was closed.

But even after Diane was gone, Kelly couldn't settle back down for the relaxing night she had hoped for with Ethan. He watched as she paced through the living room, the whole conversation with her mother pinging through her brain like the silver ball in an arcade game. Finally she pulled out her phone and called Gary. "Mom's being Mom again," she said as soon as he picked up.

"Hi to you too, Kelly," he answered. "No, stop! Don't touch that."

"What's going on?"

"It's not a good time; Hazel's learned how to climb the counters. I'm throwing out all the knives. We'll eat pudding till she's eighteen."

Kelly sighed. "Never mind, I'll talk to you later. Hug the girls for me."

She grumpily pulled a bag of Goldfish from the cabinet, along with some peanut butter to dip them in. As Ethan joined her in the kitchen, she held a Goldfish out to him automatically. The sharing of Goldfish was literally one of the earliest things she'd learned. Normally when Kelly needed to stew about her mother, or work, or her mother, or the state of the universe, or her mother, she'd talk to Gary or Priya, and if neither of them were available, she'd do the only form of dancing she had yet mastered: holding in her emotions until they manifested in arrhythmic psychosomatic leg twitches. But if she shared her Goldfish with Ethan, maybe she could share her demons too.

"When will my mom stop?" she burst out. Ethan calmly ate a Goldfish and listened. "I mean, finally I have you, which is what she's always wanted me to have, and she's still on my back. It's like my life can never be good enough for her."

"You're her daughter. I'm sure she wants the best life for you."

"Yeah, but it's my life! She thinks that I need her to tell me how to do *everything*. I'm twenty-nine, as she loves to point out. Why can't she just leave me alone and let me live?"

"Maybe you could just ask her to leave you alone."

"Ha! I don't need to ask. The only motivation she needs to forget about me is having Clara in the same room."

Ethan's forehead pinched. "I'm sorry, perhaps I'm missing something here. I'm not seeing the connection between you wanting your mother to pay attention to you and wanting her to leave you alone."

"What are you saying, that I'm being illogical?" Kelly rammed a Goldfish so hard into the peanut butter that it crumbled into tiny orange flakes. She could hear the same bitter tone creeping into her voice that she had taken with Dr. Masden, and her mom, the tone that seemed to arrive, unbidden, anytime someone made her feel hot and uncomfortable and raw, but she couldn't stop it.

"Maybe it's my logic that's flawed."

"Yeah, maybe. Don't bother trying to understand my relationships, Ethan."

"Okay," was all he said, quietly.

"I'm going to bed." Kelly stormed from the room, not realizing until after she had said this that it was barely eight p.m.

Back in her room, pulling a nightshirt from a stack and setting her phone on its charger, she wanted to forget Ethan's words. But Kelly had a rational brain, and that brain was currently shaking off the irrational thoughts she was trying to cram into it like bad password attempts. She knew that Ethan was perfectly logical. And she knew that his assessment of her thinking was correct.

She stepped back into the kitchen, where Ethan was putting away the food, and flipped her hair out from under the neck of her nightshirt. "I'm sorry," she said. Ethan looked at her, startled. She realized that he probably had zero precedent for knowing how to react to her saying those two words. "You're right about my mom," she went on. "And I shouldn't have snapped at you."

"Thank you for your apology," he said sincerely.

"It's just, every time I talk to my mom it gets—" She searched for the word.

"Complicated?" Ethan supplied.

"Really complicated."

"You're both complicated women."

"Complicated, crazy—you fill in the C word." She sighed, but smiled and helped him wipe down the countertops. They fell into a harmonious silence, crossing the granite surface in complementary circles, like paired figure skaters. She thought back to Robbie and Nick. Both guys had pushed her, but in ways that made her feel

141

worse about herself, setting standards of success in school and work that she had panted to catch up with, constructing molds of what their image as a couple should be that she couldn't quite contain herself in. She could feel Ethan pushing her too, but in a way that actually made her feel good.

thirteen

. . . . . .

Kelly knew that Priya's two chief interests in life had been cemented from the day she kissed Marcus Rothstein on the second-grade planetarium field trip: science and boys. And so it really should have come as no surprise that Priya wanted to talk about Ethan. A lot. Historically, Kelly hadn't brought much to the sacred table of boy talk, but now she had the ultimate offering. She tried to be vague to avoid getting caught in a lie, but Priya was not having it.

"So do you know yet if he cooks?" Priya asked in a whisper. The girls were side by side in the audience at Tesla's newest product launch. Snagging coveted tech industry invites was definitely a primo perk of the job, and this event in particular was one Kelly had been excited for. Tesla's knack for packaging AI in a commercially friendly way without watering it down was exactly what she wanted to emulate with her own work in androids, and she could always pick up some ideas from their autonomous automobiles, which were essentially giant robots. But while Kelly was dying to soak in every detail about the sleek cherry-colored car Elon Musk was introducing onstage, Priya seemed more excited that she finally had Kelly in a corner.

"Shh, he's going to show the inside," she said, nodding at Elon.

As he stepped closer to the car, the doors winged open on their own. "And what's the next logical evolution in self-driving automotives? It's all about options. We're calling it 'Row or Ring.'" Kelly watched as the rows of seats inside the car smoothly split and oriented themselves as a circular bench inside the perimeter of the vehicle. She furiously tapped some notes into her phone.

"I told you, customizable was the next big thing!" Priya hissed gleefully. "Private and commercial hybrid. I *knew* it." The man on her right threw her a dirty, "stop talking" glare.

Kelly nodded. "And where's my collapsible trunk for easier parking?" she whispered.

"Andre does red beans and rice and literally nothing else. Makes no sense," Priya said, one eye on the presentation, taking notes of her own. "Wait, you didn't answer my question."

"No," Kelly said shortly.

"And inter-car communication will not be limited just to future models," Elon was saying. "Our newest update will put these features in every Tesla on the road. The car of the future will be chatty," he said, to laughs from the crowd. "When vehicles can communicate reliably with one another, we'll eliminate the need for any signs, signals, and markings on roads. And when cars can assess the drivability of any surface and safety of any area, in some places, we'll eliminate the need for the roads themselves."

"We need to find out how they reconcile camera feed images in real time," Kelly whispered. "We could definitely use that in the androids."

But Priya was frowning. "No, like Ethan doesn't cook, or no, like you don't know yet?"

Glaring Man leaned toward them. "Shhh!" he said loudly. Chastened, Kelly and Priya focused on the stage.

"And to reach the future faster, we're making all of our inter-car communication plans open source!" Elon declared. The crowd roared.

Kelly was still bubbling from the presentation as she and Priya made their way outside half an hour later. "Of course, the feasibility of that all depends on network reliability," she was saying, until she noticed that Priya was bearing right down the sidewalk as she bore left.

"This way," said Priya, grabbing her by the arm to steer her. "Remember, we were going to hit up that new black ice cream place? This is our first girls' day in, like, a zillion years, you're not escaping yet." She waggled her eyebrows mischievously. "Not until you give me the dish on your new D."

Kelly's stomach sank a little as she followed Priya. The fun of girls' day lost its glimmer when she felt like she was spending the whole time playing Whac-A-Mole with her friend's questions.

Priya beamed contentedly at the light-bathed streets, the sun building lattices on the sidewalk through the shadows of the palm fronds. "How cool is it that we've finally both met great guys at, like, exactly the same time? I can't believe I still haven't really talked to Ethan. Anita totally monopolized him at that dinner. We have got to do a double date so Ethan and Andre can become besties too. Then, one day, when we're all millionaires with vacation homes next to each other's in Palm Springs, we can just hang out together drinking martinis in our glamorous midcentury modern living rooms. Do you ever wish you were a gay man?" Priya's phone buzzed before Kelly could answer. She stopped walking to look at the text.

"Ooh, Andre's thing tonight canceled—you should call Ethan!" Priya hit Kelly on the arm. "We can all do dinner together. Double date tonight!"

Kelly opened her mouth and closed it, unsure what to say. It would be so easy to just say yes. But Priya, more than anyone in the world, would be the one to figure out Ethan's secret. It was just too big of a risk for them to spend time together. She had increasingly found herself avoiding Priya at work, hoping not to get into any tricky conversations. And between reduced time spent together and the gnawing knowledge of having a secret, she sensed a crack splitting the ground between her and her best friend. Today, their day out, should have helped to mend the crack, but Kelly felt the burden of her lie more than ever. Wouldn't bringing Priya and Ethan into the same room only result in more secrecy? Wouldn't all of Priya's questions to and about Ethan just necessitate more evasive answers, thereby creating more conversational tension and dissatisfaction?

"A—a thing," she began. "When you talked about Andre having a thing tonight, I just remembered. I have a thing tonight."

"What kind of a thing?"

"A family thing. It's, uh, my nieces' birthdays. They're turning three."

"Don't toddlers usually have daytime birthday parties?"

"They're really mature toddlers. Bertie already drinks coffee."

"Wow, that sounds—not safe."

"Their mom's part Italian. I should probably get going, though." Kelly made a show of checking the time on her phone. "I didn't realize it was so late."

"Oh, okay."

"I'll see you tomorrow, okay? Say hi to Andre for me!"

She turned and walked away so she didn't have to watch Priya's face fall.

At home that night with Ethan, no coffee-drinking Italian toddlers in sight, Kelly was contemplating their typical Sunday night options: going out, ordering in, or scrounging together a smorgasbord from within the cupboards. But she thought back to Priya's question about whether or not Ethan could cook. Of course he could cook. He could do anything.

As she called him into the kitchen, she was already instinctively pulling up Google on her phone, but then decided that if Ethan was going to be the head chef, it would be better to let him source a recipe. Plus, not having to touch her phone while cooking would keep both her hands and her phone cleaner. "Hey," she said when Ethan walked in. "What do you feel like eating?"

After he scanned the internet, they settled on chicken pot pie, a nostalgic standby from her childhood, before Diane's cooking became so adventurous. At first it was fun as they made a game of it, Kelly racing around the kitchen, pulling out all the ingredients while Ethan shouted them out to her in a mock panic. "Carrots! *Carrots, woman!*"

She plunged her arm into the crisper. "Three, two—got the carrots!" She retrieved them, breathless, just in time.

But once they started actually cooking, Kelly found herself increasingly uncomfortable at not having control over the recipe. "Next we need to brown the chicken," Ethan said.

"And then what?" she asked. "I have to know everything that's in the recipe first."

"I can read you the whole thing," he answered, "but I'll just have to reread each step as we go."

"Oh—fine, then, let's start with the chicken," she grumbled, grabbing a pan. Not seeing everything in front of her, having to rely on Ethan to read her the steps, was making her almost physically itch. "What if there's a step later that I should do first? Like what about preheating the oven? Isn't that a thing that people do when they're cooking?"

"I already did it," he said. "Don't worry, if we miss a step, I will take full legal responsibility."

"Fine, fine." She dripped some oil into the pan, willing herself to let go.

As they went on, they fell into a rhythm together. Kelly relaxed. She got used to trusting Ethan's voice to be her eyes. The world didn't fall apart. They made a recipe together, and she actually had fun.

Kelly wasn't sure how long the bag of flour had been sitting in her cabinet, but it had definitely never been opened before. She ripped it open now and it exploded, misting her face and chest in white powder. She shrieked.

"You look like Scarface," Ethan laughed.

"It's in my eyes!"

"Here, hold still," Ethan said.

Obediently, she halted, eyes closed, face upturned to him. He brushed off her cheeks and nose and lips, his hands warm and sturdy, his thumbs ever so gently dusting the powder from her closed lids. Under his touch, Kelly suddenly felt herself shiver.

"What's the matter?" he asked.

"Nothing," she said. She hoped as she turned away from him that any remaining powder would mask the pinkness in her cheeks.

fourteen

• • • • • •

While Kelly didn't envy other Silicon Valley companies their rock-climbing walls and nap dens, she would have gladly taken their top-of-the-line dining facilities, with sushi stations and rotating food trucks. But of course, Anita Riveras did not deem such frivolities a wise use of her budget. Her employees would eat their plastic-tray cafeteria standards and be grateful. Kelly and Priya made do, though. They had their lunch routine so down pat that it looked like a Rockettes number. When they sat down together that Monday, they automatically began trading salad toppings—Priya took all the red onions and hard-boiled eggs, Kelly all the tomatoes and croutons. Kelly poured on half a packet of ranch, Priya half a packet of balsamic, then they swapped and finished them off.

Kelly was so used to the custom that she could have done it with her eyes closed, which today, she might as well have done. Her eyes were locked on her phone, reading an *Onion* headline that Ethan had sent her: "Latest Update Turns All iPhones into Pumpkins at Midnight." She chuckled, imagining Ethan at home on the couch, laughing at the same thing. She felt a little spark now every time he texted her during the workday on the phone that she had bought him—these moments were in delicious neon color when the rest of the day was in sepia. She didn't even notice that Priya hadn't spoken.

"How was your night, Priya? Great, Kelly," Priya said finally.

"Great," Kelly echoed.

Priya set down her fork with a clatter. "Hello!" she cried.

That got Kelly to look up from her phone. "Hi, hello," she responded.

"You have boyfriend syndrome," Priya announced with finality.

"What's that, syphilis?"

Priya rolled her eyes. "You have this great new boyfriend, so now you're neglecting your friends. Friend. Me."

Kelly had to admit that she was right. She could feel it herself—even when she was with Priya, she wasn't fully there. "I'm sorry," she said. Apologizing was getting a bit easier since she'd practiced it with Ethan. "You're right, I know, I know." She clicked the Lock button on her phone. "So. You. How was dinner with Andre?"

"Good, tequila, tacos, tequila, more tequila, not really sure what happened after that. But I woke up today in a good mood."

"Speaking of boyfriend syndrome." Kelly grinned.

"How was the baby party?"

"Good," Kelly lied. "As much of a party as you can have with two-year-olds."

"I thought you said they were turning three."

"Right," Kelly said a little too quickly. She swallowed hard on a crouton, her throat suddenly dry as she gulped it down. "They're all three now." She cursed herself for having invented a story she would be required to stick to any time the girls came up in the future.

"Right," Priya said. She didn't say anything more.

Clearly Priya could tell that Kelly wasn't telling the truth. Kelly raced in to fill the silence. "But, um, how's the arm coming?" Priya was currently building a delicate mechanical arm for use in surgeries. The fact that Priya's Medical Engineering department was not participating in the competition for investor funding made hearing about her work a nice distraction from Kelly's own.

"It's coming," Priya replied. "I'm looking at this new 3-D imaging system . . ."

Priya didn't mention the weekend again. But there was a strained quality to her voice as she talked on, like she was holding something back. Something was broken in the girls' normal easy dynamic, like one of the Rockettes was off by a beat.

There were only six words in Diane's text later that week: "We need to talk about Ethan." There was also a boat emoji at the end, which Kelly had to assume was either a mistake or a shy admission of her mother's hitherto undisclosed lifelong dreams of becoming a mariner. Kelly had missed the text that afternoon at work while she was in a marathon coding session. But now, halted at a stoplight, the sky lit up with that peculiar reflective quality of a cloud-filled dusk, she saw it. She only had one idea of what those six words could mean: her mother knew something about Ethan that she wasn't supposed to know. She tried calling, but her mom didn't answer. She flipped her blinker and crawled toward the other lane against the honking of the surrounding cars. She wasn't going home. She was going *home*.

But when she jolted into her parents' driveway twenty minutes later, braking hard, she was surprised to see only her father's car there. And sure enough, when she walked in, it was only Carl in the semilit kitchen, shoveling a Domino's pizza into his face like wood into a chipper.

"Hey, Dad. Is Mom out?" she asked.

"She's at some bridal vendors industry mixer," he said, or it sounded like that's what he was trying to say around the food. "Want some pizza? It's this or gambling on leftovers."

Kelly slid onto a stool next to her dad and morosely took a slice, but she wasn't sure she could eat. Even pizza didn't sound appetizing in the face of her welling anxiety.

"What's wrong?" Carl gurgled through the pizza.

"Why would you assume something's wrong? It's not like I only come over when there's a problem. There's family dinners and—" Kelly broke off. Yes, the only other time she came over was when there was a problem. "I just wanted to talk to Mom. Did she seem— normal earlier today?" She was trying to probe the issue as delicately as possible, not revealing more information to her dad than she needed to.

"Has she ever been normal?"

"You know what I mean."

"She was in a good mood, if that's what you're asking," Carl said. "She was humming that *Dirty Dancing* song."

Kelly supposed that was a positive sign. "(I've Had) The Time of My Life" always meant that Diane was pleased about something, usually either a large sale at the shop or a picture revealing cellulite on a beautiful celebrity. She tried probing a little harder. "I just got a weird text from her about Ethan."

"Oh, yeah, she said something about that." Carl held up a finger, taking his sweet time to masticate a tennis-ball-size bite of pizza while Kelly's blood pressure hovered somewhere around the Milky Way. Finally, he finished. "She wants his measurements."

"Measurements?" In her panicked state of mind, Kelly immediately wondered if this was some reference to Ethan's specs.

"For a tuxedo. She and Clara wanted to put him in the wedding party."

"Oh. *Oh.*" Diane wanted to include Ethan in the wedding party. Kelly could breathe again. She recovered herself enough to pull some soy sauce from the cabinet and lean against the island, sprinkling it artfully on her slice of pizza. "That's really nice of them, I guess," she admitted. She knew that including Ethan less than two weeks out from the ceremony would involve some rearranging, which meant it was a major gesture from her mom. Suddenly she felt ravenous. She tore down the pizza in a few bites. She was ready to cheerfully pick up her purse and leave, but realized she had just had an entire conversation with her father that was only about her mother. She turned to look at him in the semigloom of the kitchen.

"How are you doing? How's work?" she asked.

"Same old, same old." His hand twitched toward a sheaf of diagrams before him on the countertop, as if he were ready to get back to it.

"Didn't you install a whole new pressure monitor recently?"

"Sure did."

"My work's been crazy," she tried, already feeling herself starting to ramble awkwardly. "I've just never been in charge of a whole

155

project like this before. I guess I didn't realize how hard the big-picture, conceptual stuff is. Not that the detail work is easy, either. I just wish I had more hours in the day. We can build a robot that looks like a human but still no time machine, right?" She laughed.

"Yeah, that's tough," Carl responded. And that was it. Kelly's frame sagged. Here in this house, in this moment, she felt as if she were once more a little girl, waiting for her brilliant engineering father to get home from work so she could show him the Speak & Spell she'd reprogrammed, falling asleep on the couch until he finally came in, leaping up to greet him, hearing him tell her that he was tired and he'd look at it another time, though he never did.

"I guess I should get going," she said abruptly. Something of what she was feeling must have read in her face, because Carl stirred.

"I—" he began. I dealt with something similar at work? I'm proud of you? I'm sorry? Instead, he stared at the grease-spattered pizza box, pushing it toward her. "You want another slice?" he asked gruffly.

"No, I'm good." She slipped on her purse and patted him on the arm on her way out of the kitchen. "Have a good night." Maybe she had gotten more from her dad than her scientific mind.

It was pouring on Kelly's drive home. Traffic crawled with California drivers who looked at rain like a biblical plague. She staggered upstairs once she reached her apartment, ready to collapse indoors and settle in for a sheltered, vegetative night with Ethan. But it was just as she walked into a dark, silent apartment that he called to let her know he was stuck on the other side of town. He had been out buying groceries for that evening—cooking together had become a new part of their nightly routine, and he had taken to surprising her with spiny fruits from Japan, artisanal flours, and once, a rather melancholy whole fish. Tonight, though, it was not to be, as his bus had broken down in traffic and he was moored until the scientists of San Jose determined that the water from the sky would not, in fact, dissolve them.

Kelly bucked up, buoyed by the idea of having her own single lady's night. After all, she hadn't had the run of the apartment for a while now. She would . . . well, she would do whatever it was she used to enjoy doing before Ethan was around. Except she couldn't think of anything appealing, actually; he saw it all anyway, the ghastly face masks, the midnight sundaes, and the soulful warbling of Selena Gomez songs. But maybe it would be nice just to have a quiet night to herself.

The trouble was, it was too quiet. The low, monotonous buzz of the refrigerator grew grating. As Kelly wandered between the kitchen, looking for something to eat without feeling hungry, and the living room, looking for something to watch on the TV without being interested, the passing of her own reflection in the black window spooked her.

When she climbed into bed that night, she was acutely aware of the stretch of space on either side of her. Even though Ethan always slept on the couch in the next room, the knowledge that he was tucking in at the same time as her somehow made it feel as if she weren't sleeping alone. Now, she felt as solitary as an obelisk in a desert, sand-stung and unknowable. It was incomprehensible to think that this had been her daily existence only a month before. And that in a couple more weeks, after the wedding, it would be her life again: an endless alternation between breakfast for one and dinner for one, her thoughts growing stale without anyone to share them with, stepping between her own silences.

As aware as she was that there were other men in the world besides Ethan—*actual* men—the thought of going back to being single felt like a permanent decree. She reckoned that the data of her dating history could not exactly be extrapolated with any view to future success. And it was a statistical impossibility that she would ever find another man as right for her as Ethan, who had been designed specifically as her perfect match. He fit all of her stipulations to a T. No one else could ever make her as happy. Right?

Kelly rolled over and scrunched deeper into her pillow, until the chink of a key in the latch told her that Ethan was finally home. She leaped out of bed and emerged into the living room in time to see him shut the door and turn around. He reached out a hand to flip the light on, but she stopped him. "Don't," she said. He was soaked from the walk home from the bus stop, and, backlit by the streetlamp's light streaming in through the window, the edges of his damp, dark hair held a thousand tiny points of light. His frame was a tall black silhouette, wonderfully solid, wonderfully real.

Without thinking, she rushed forward and threw her arms around him. "Kelly," he began with surprise, but she leaned in, holding him tighter, and felt his arms encircle her, their weight grounding and centering her. His back was warm under his wet shirt.

That night, as Kelly lay in her bed, she kept her eyes trained on Ethan even as her lids fluttered to a close. If she tucked her head just right, she could see the peaks and valleys of his sleeping form in the next room.

fifteen

. . . . . .

At this point in Confibot's development, with less than two months to go until the presentation, Kelly was supposed to be much further along. The schedule she had carefully blocked out on the wall of her cubicle at the beginning of the project with colored Post-it notes, their edges perfectly aligned, indicated that she should be well into blue by now, and instead she was firmly mired in red. Confibot was essentially built, and while some of his major functions, like telecommunication with doctors and family members, were still under construction, Kelly got a thrill seeing the skeletal beginnings of the outcome she had envisioned: a truly comprehensive caregiver robot. But he was still basically an it. She had hoped that the mountains of research she had collected on interpersonal interactions would come together to present, like invisible ink surfacing under a flame, a clear profile of what Confibot's face should look like and what expressions he should make with it, what his voice should sound like, and what he should say with it. Instead, the more research she did, the more confused she got. One article said that 62 percent of women over thirty identified closed-mouth smiles as "friendly" in photographs. But in AHI's focus groups, 89 percent of users had gone for teeth-baring smiles in the simulations.

Getting frustrated with her piles of numbers, she had decided to try another tack, bringing in a different sort of helper. Dot-10 had just arrived in her packing crate, straight from Japan. The best-selling caregiver and companion robot currently on the market, her rounded, white plastic limbs and exaggeratedly large eyes were a far cry from the human realism that even an unfinished Confibot possessed. Her entire torso was occupied by a touchscreen that displayed everything from the weather to photos of a user's grandkids to two-player games that a person could share with her. And every time the robot delivered a corny Dad joke or a dopey expression, Kelly felt her frustration growing, not easing. She finished a game of tic-tac-toe on the touchscreen, a yellow trophy dancing across the screen as she played her winning move. "Congratulations!" the robot cried. "You know your stuff!"

Dot-10 didn't align with any of Kelly's data about how a caregiver robot should act, even adjusting for country-based market differences. Kelly could not comprehend why *this* was what was beating the competition. It made about as much sense as Santa in a Speedo. Before eagerly unboxing the robot, she had pulled up a spreadsheet on her computer, prepared to quantify and enter all her observations about what Dot-10 had to offer. But now all the cells stood empty. Of course, Dot-10 did have one clear advantage over Confibot, Kelly thought ruefully, looking over at her own incomplete model: she had a face.

She reflected back on her early projects at AHI. She had always been on someone else's team, surrounded by other people's opinions—most often, and most loudly, Priya's. With an inadvertent smile, she remembered the way Priya would pace around the lab in a storm of creation, filling the SMART Board with scribbles like a madwoman, back when they were working on Zed together. She could just call Priya in now for another set of eyes. She was one of the few people Kelly trusted enough to listen to completely. And if her friend didn't have any practical advice, at least she could usually offer some palliative words or a decent dirty joke. But instead of a wave of relief and hope, the thought of talking to Priya right now brought Kelly an extra surge of anxiety in what was already an anxiety storm. She had to admit that, since Ethan's entrance into her life, things with Priya had become strained. There had been bickering, secrets—Kelly had never dealt with this kind of drama with a friend before. She had never gotten close enough to anyone. She could already see the crack widening until it inevitably became a canyon. In reviewing her own track record, the data spoke clearly: she was just not a person who had good friends. Up until now, her friendship with Priya had obviously been a fluke. To maintain it long term was an impossibility.

Yet in her mind's eye, she could see herself and Priya putting their heads together over an engineering conundrum, just like old times. Maybe that would put everything back to normal. She remembered the afternoon she and Priya had spent during a breaking point on a shared project, silly with exhaustion, dissolving into laughter over a fever-brained attempt to engineer a hand with seven fingers. Priya was always trying to think of robotic improvements to the God-given humanoid form, not the least of which included extend-an-arm and retractable hair. And who could forget double dick? In spite of herself, Kelly smiled.

A more caustic voice entered her head, telling her to quit with the wishful thinking and admit that she wasn't capable of getting things back to normal. That that's not how her relationships, or her life, worked. Kelly remembered with a bonus anxiety surge that Priya had just learned that morning that a national journal wanted to feature the surgical arm she was developing, a revelation that had precipitated a gleeful squeal over the heads of the entire cubicle farm. With Priya doing so well, Kelly only felt all the sillier for not being able to wrestle her own project into shape. She couldn't moan over her failures with someone who clearly had none of her own. She let out a long, frustrated sigh.

"Uh-oh. Does someone have a case of the Mondays?" Dot-10's high voice pulled her from her thoughts. The robot blinked at her with wide, empty eyes. Kelly grimaced and powered her down with a decisive gesture.

Like a burning chemical plant smoldering in the distance, family dinner glowered on Kelly's horizon once more. The excitement of Ethan's first introduction had worn off, and with Clara's wedding nearly upon them, Diane's Diane-ness was peaking dangerously. These days, she found herself more worn out by the end of a family dinner than after a twelve-hour day at work. Former Kelly might have wished to spend these nights at home alone with a rosé, a PB&J, and some deliciously bizarre reality TV special, but now she just wished for a night in with Ethan.

But as it was, she found herself in the fitted gray pantsuit she had donned to go out, driving Ethan to her parents' house. "Let's try to get out quickly," she said. "Halfway through the main course, maybe you could say you have a headache. Then we'll be able to make our excuses and get out before dessert."

Ethan massaged his temple. "I can feel it coming on. Probably eye strain; I've been putting in so much time at the office."

"Wonderful." Kelly beamed.

"If you want to get out early, then why do you want to go at all?" he asked.

"I don't want to, I have to."

"Why?"

"Because I always do. It's complicated."

"I guess I still have a lot to learn about these things," Ethan mused, looking out the window as they passed the curved tile roofs of Japantown.

Kelly was silent. She had never yet questioned her compulsion to do what her mother told her to. This despite the fact that she had been living under her own roof and supporting herself for years. That she was a grown-ass woman. After all, her thirtieth birthday had come and gone the week before, though she had barely marked it with everything else going on. Priya had begged to plan a night out at a very grown-up restaurant, followed by a trip to eat very non-grown-up unicorn-themed cupcakes, but since Kelly already had dinner reservations with Ethan, her friend had simply brought her a cupcake at the office instead. Now she decided that the age milestone had at least earned her the right to start making some of her own decisions.

"I guess I've been putting in a lot of time at the office too," she said slowly.

"You always do. I don't know how you do it," Ethan agreed.

"I could have eye strain. I could have a headache."

"Do you?" Ethan looked at her with concern.

"No, but I mean, I could. I could tell my mom I'm not feeling up to it. That's not terrible, right? I'll see them all on Friday for the rehearsal dinner."

"I don't think that's terrible at all. In fact, I think it's quite logical."

Kelly pulled out her phone and tossed it to him. "Here, I'll dictate you a text."

"Then we can have TV time at home. I DVRed you a special about middle-aged twin brothers who live together and hoard baby dolls."

"Heck no, I still have real clothes on. We're eating out."

Ethan chose the restaurant, a tapas place that was popular on Yelp. Behind the unassuming strip mall exterior was a vibrant setting of wood-beamed ceilings and deep red walls. Kelly loved it, and Ethan was always up for anything. He regaled her with a blow-by-blow account of his altercation with the washing machine that afternoon and a news article he'd read about a man arrested for crossing international borders in a hot air balloon rigged from a propane torch and tarp. Kelly didn't bother to check the news feed on her iPad much anymore; Ethan knew what she was interested in, so he offered a perfectly curated selection, and his retelling was usually more enjoyable than the original anyway. Even when she wanted to hear about inane stuff like that runner-up from that singing show who got a face-eating spider bite, or where Octomom was now, he didn't blink.

As they nibbled on manchego and stuffed red peppers, her spirits were buoyed by a sense of rebellion, a sudden lightness. She didn't want to go to family dinner? She could just . . . not go. It was revelatory. She even justified not answering Diane's barrage of phone calls that came in response to her text by thinking she would tell her tomorrow she had gone to bed early to soothe her head.

A sense of guilt still weighed down her spirits, though. It was only a regular family dinner she was missing. But despite Kelly's complicated relationship with her family, she showed up for them. She went to her nieces' dance recitals, sitting through two hours of other people's kids just to watch the girls dart around the stage for two minutes, looking as lost as if they had woken up on the moon. When Clara needed a moving crew to help her into her new apartment, Kelly was there with her hair back and her sneakers on. Ethan could tell that something was off as she picked at her braised short ribs.

"I was just thinking about this presentation I have coming up at work," she said slowly. "It's going to be simulcast publicly online, you know, like they do with Apple product launches and that sort of thing. I had been thinking, oh, I should tell my family about it, maybe they'd like to watch. But then I thought, who am I kidding, of course they're not going to want to watch. And then I started getting mad at them in my head for not caring. Meanwhile, *I'm* the one who didn't care enough to show up tonight. So who's really the problem here?" She laughed uncomfortably.

Ethan frowned. "What do you mean, they wouldn't want to watch? I wouldn't assume that."

"Come on, why would they be that interested in what I do?"

"Because it's interesting!" Ethan insisted.

"Not to them." Kelly's voice was firm. She took a sip of water and paused, thoughtful, before continuing. "There was this one time— gosh, it's so long ago, I can't believe I even still care."

"What was it?" he encouraged.

"There was this science fair I had in sixth grade, and I worked for *months* on my project. It was something about soil drainage—I remember thinking that my dad might think it was cool. I'd actually chosen it so I could learn more about what he does, since it involved similar principles. I mean, he never really talked to me about his work, but sometimes I would sneak a look at his papers just to see what he was up to. Anyway, I had, like, this whole tank I had filled with different types of stones and a soil mixture I made. It actually won first place and I went onstage to accept the ribbon, but then I looked out and they weren't there. My parents, Gary, Clara—nobody had come. They had said they were going to, and my mom always went to Clara's soccer games, so I was kind of looking for them. I think maybe my mom had to stay late at work and my dad—I don't even know, actually, I never asked. He probably just forgot." She looked down, twiddling her fork. "And I got invited to bring my project to compete in the statewide fair the next month, but I just didn't go. I guess I was kind of bummed about the whole thing. I didn't even tell anybody. Not until you, now. Anyway," she said, suddenly spearing a piece of beef, "it wasn't a big deal. Like I said, I can't believe I even still care." She forced down a bite.

"I can believe it," Ethan responded quietly.

"I mean, it's totally irrational to get hung up on it," Kelly went on quickly. "It was one event, and it was years ago, and I never even told them that it was important to me, so how could I have expected them to know? I feel stupid even talking about it now. I guess my point is, I'd just rather spare us all from going through that whole rigmarole again."

"You are many things, Kelly, but you are not stupid." Kelly tried to smile at him, but with the food in her mouth and a pesky rush of wetness in her eyes, she was pretty sure she looked crazed instead. She started laughing at herself, which only made it worse as she tried not to choke. Ethan poured more water from the pitcher and offered her the glass. "Maybe we should work on your chewing skills, though."

At last, Kelly managed an actual laugh. She had always minimized the whole science fair debacle in her head. But now that she had finally shared it with someone, she felt weightless.

She had more to drink than usual at dinner, her feeling of adventurous freedom taking her from her accustomed wine to a more exotic cocktail. Something about the night's shared transgression made her feel closer than ever to Ethan. More and more, she understood that expression about there being two types of people in the world: there was her and Ethan, and there was everyone else.

After dinner, she felt too energized and was having too much fun to go home just yet, so Ethan took over the driving and they wound their way to the East Foothills, stopping to take in the view over the city. It was an unseasonably balmy night and there were other couples gathered outside, teenagers mostly, but something about the darkness wrapping the two of them as they found a rock to perch on, the spill of electric lights tumbling from west to east at their feet like a bed of white flowers, made it feel like the view was only theirs.

The only thing wrong with the picture was the flatness of the sky overhead. "I wish I lived in a place where we could see more stars," she said, leaning back on her elbows and looking up.

"They're all up there, even if you can't see them," Ethan said.

"It's hard to imagine them. It's been so long since I've been outside the city. Or just outside."

"Hold on, I teach astronomy," Ethan reasoned. "This is exactly what I'm good for. Look, right over there"—he pointed to the far left—"that's where Virgo is. It's kind of a human figure."

"Okay, I can picture it."

"Close your eyes," he instructed. For once, Kelly let go and allowed herself to lean back onto the rocks, not even thinking about the dirt. "Then go up and over a little and there's Ursa Major. You know what the Big Dipper looks like, right?"

"Yeah, I can imagine it."

"Then Mars is a little south . . ." As Ethan talked, Kelly's mind populated with a glimmering map of constellations. Behind her closed lids, it was the most beautiful thing she'd ever seen.

They both lay back for a bit and reveled in the invisible view. And when Ethan took her hand, she didn't even think about it. When she leaned across and kissed him, she didn't think about it either. Ethan drove on the way home, and Kelly's whole being felt soft and misty, body and soul. The part of her brain that was constantly thinking and overthinking seemed dormant. She let herself open each moment like an unexpected gift.

When they got home, Kelly wasn't sure if it was her who pulled Ethan into the bedroom or vice versa, but they ended up there, and then they ended up in her bed. The few other times she had been in this position, Kelly had felt self-conscious and exposed, but it was impossible to feel exposed in front of Ethan when he took everything about her as being natural and expected and the way it should be. And everything about him, too, felt natural and as it should be, rawness and surety reflecting back on each other like dual sides of a hinged mirror. Everything about him felt only human.

sixteen

• • • • • •

Is it possible to do a walk of shame within your own apartment? That's how Kelly felt as she tiptoed from her bedroom to her bathroom the next morning. Ethan looked so peaceful in bed that she didn't want to disturb him, but maybe more than that, she didn't know what to say to him. For the first time, she felt self-conscious in front of him, as if there were expectations of her that she couldn't meet because she had no idea what they were.

Kelly's affinity for cautious, middle-of-the-road living was perhaps even more pronounced in her love life than elsewhere. But now here she was. Yet the main thing needling her was not what other people might think if they found out what she'd done, but how Ethan might act toward her when he woke up.

Perhaps in some sort of self-flagellating drive to purify by punishment, Kelly answered her mother's third phone call of the morning.

"Are you all right?" Diane's voice came breathlessly through the phone. Even when Kelly was a kid, her mom had applied an outsized worry to every ache and pain. She was the one who forced Kelly to stay home for a week with a cold when all she had wanted to do was get back to school in time for their soda can physics experiments.

"I'm fine, it was just a headache."

"There was a woman on *Ellen DeGeneres* who had a headache and a week later, she died of a brain tumor."

"Then how was she on *Ellen*?"

"What did you do? Have you tried inhaling the scent of a lemon, like I taught you?" Diane unfortunately sourced most of her medical advice from *Cosmo*.

"I just stayed in with Ethan and we had an early night."

"Ah, so he's spending the night again, I see."

"Sometimes."

"Are you using protection on these sleepovers?"

"Mom, please."

"A good-looking man like that, I'm sure he's dipped his pen in a lot of other inkwells." Kelly held the phone farther from her ear, as if that would help. "You have to be careful—"

"Mom, I know, I'm thirty!"

"You do robots, dear. Chemistry is my specialty," Diane asserted. "Well, protect yourself and don't let him do anything that makes you uncomfortable. But you also have to please him. Are you pleasing him?"

Kelly put the phone on speaker on the countertop, as far away from her as possible while still being in range and squirted facial scrub onto her washcloth. "I have to go, I'm going to be late for work."

"This is important, Kelly, and you have very little experience. Of course you don't want him to think you have a lot of experience. But you should have a lot so that you know what you're doing. He has to think you're a natural. But I have a feeling you're not a natural."

Logically, Kelly was well aware that Ethan had exactly zero outside sexual experience. She knew that worrying that he wasn't sufficiently impressed by her bedroom performance was ridiculous.

But . . . now Kelly started to worry about it. She recalled with some dismay that he had unlimited internet access. He had undoubtedly seen some Olympic-level bedroom showmanship. Kelly couldn't do any of that. She could barely take her shirt off without getting it caught on her nose. And, well, he was just so good-looking. She glanced back at him in the bed, where he lay half twisted in the sheets. Even unguarded and asleep, he had the impossible geometrics of an Adonis, his skin burnished, his hair artfully mussed. The sight triggered the same insecurities she had felt on every other morning after in her life, but tenfold.

"Of course, the landing strip has been a popular option for a while now," Diane was saying when Kelly zoned back into the conversation. And that was her cue to get out.

"I have to go, Mom, talk to you later."

Kelly wrapped her naked body in a towel and tiptoed back into the bedroom, hoping that the hinge on the closet door wouldn't squeak as she opened it. It squeaked. Ethan stirred awake. "Good morning," he said.

"Oh, hi, I didn't see you there!" Kelly chirped nonsensically. She yanked a high-necked blouse and long skirt from the closet rail. She felt a reflexive need to be modest today. And then she stood there, clutching her clothes in one hand, the top of her towel in the other, suddenly shy to get undressed in front of Ethan. She looked at him, sitting up in bed but not yet out of it, the sheet still drawn half over him, and realized that he was mirroring her hesitation. They stared at each other, neither willing to move or break the silence.

Finally, he spoke. "I'll make you a deal. I wear this sheet forever, you wear that towel forever, and we'll save a ton of money on laundry detergent, okay?" Kelly laughed. The tensions inside of her suddenly seemed ridiculous.

"Fine, fine." She dropped her towel and started getting dressed while Ethan went to his own wardrobe.

"I guess there's no point in my being modest," he went on, "seeing as you made my entire body."

"Didn't do a bad job on it, either," she said with a flirtatious smile.

"You're not so bad yourself." He kissed her on the cheek and walked away into the kitchen. A little butterfly took up residence somewhere around her heart.

The whole way into work that morning, Kelly wanted nothing more than to get into the lab with Priya and tell her everything. She was desperate to have someone other than her mom to talk with about last night's turn of events. Anyone other than her mom. But as soon as she and her friend were settled on their stools in the lab, she went mute. How was she supposed to spill a secret like this anyway? It was just too much. She could never tell.

Priya positioned her soldering iron. Kelly normally had an almost Pavlovian response to the acrid smell of soldering, with all the memories of hours of creation that it brought—it simultaneously soothed and excited her, making her feel at home. But today, it wasn't enough to save her from feeling out of sorts.

"What's up?" Priya asked her, her eyes focused down on her work.

I built myself a boyfriend. We slept together. I think I'm falling for him. I really want to talk to my best friend about it.

"Nothing much," was all Kelly said.

When the last bot had battled that night, smashing its opponent into a charred and contorted hunk of metal with one wheel sadly whirling in the air, the show ended and Ethan clicked the TV off. He set the remote down on the coffee table and made to get up from the couch, but Kelly stopped him, curving closer into him instead.

"Is something wrong?" he asked.

"No. Yes. I don't know. It's just Priya; things have been different with us lately. I wonder if we're growing apart. Though that sounds like a totally teenage thing to say."

"Adults grow too," Ethan remarked. "Together, apart."

"Yeah, I guess I just feel like I can't talk to her about everything."

"You can always talk to me, you know."

Always—the word brought sharply to Kelly's mind something that she had been doing her best to keep out of it. Clara's wedding was that weekend, and that meant her time with Ethan was almost up.

She bent her neck to look up into his face, his head positioned just above hers, the bow of his jawline shadowed in the lamplight.

She looked back down and tucked her head into his neck, growing sleepy. "I know," she murmured. "And I'm glad." He turned and kissed the top of her head. For a moment, Kelly imagined how the picture they formed would look to an outside observer. It might look just like the model of love she had never before had.

seventeen

. . . .

On Clara's wedding day, Kelly's world became such a blur that she had no time to consider the day's personal implications for her. The day, too, was all about Clara: it was as sunny and fresh as the bride. Family, staff, and bridal party members scurried from tent to tent, making last-minute preparations, and even the wider world seemed to be busy decking itself in pastels specifically for the occasion: the unbroken blue of the sky, the pink of fine petals scattered in pathways over the green grass. At the geographic and metaphorical center of all the happy activity was the blushing bride. Clara was the contented eye of the hurricane, the gracious recipient of everyone's attentions and goodwill. Today, more than ever, the quality about her that magnetized people into her presence was in full and magnificent force.

While she was the eye, her mother was the storm. Diane moved with lethal efficiency, a sergeant in satin, shouting orders at everyone around her like she was captaining the sinking *Titanic*. The birch round-cake stand was off-center by an inch—the whole dessert table layout had to be reimagined. Bridesmaid Number Four was missing a necklace—Diane half shouted directions to her preferred jewelry store in town. The pink fountains weren't photographing well—more dye, *more dye*! Her industry friends were already swarming the place; several seemed to have shown up early expressly for the purpose of watching the preparations, seeing what made the sausage, as it were.

For her part, Kelly attempted to strike a balance between being useful and staying out of the way of the storm. She enlisted Ethan to help set out the place cards, cognizant that some poor waiter might be asked to come in and move them each by a millimeter. As wary as Kelly was of her mom's stress level, she couldn't help but notice that Diane was as vibrant, as happy, as she had ever seen her. The design of the day seemed to be the sort of blowsy, shabby chic coziness that Clara gravitated toward, but ratcheted up to Pinterest levels of perfection by Diane. So many of the brides in Silicon Valley demanded to be cutting edge, but Kelly sensed that here was Diane's chance to follow her own heart a bit more, almost as if she were hosting the wedding that she had never had—after all, she and Carl had been too poor to afford anything more than a honeymoon night at the Holiday Inn. Once Kelly swore her mother said something about "my wedding day." Luckily Clara had a crowd of curlers around her head and didn't hear.

Meanwhile, the knot of Suttles was growing, attracting the various incoming family arrivals—cousins, grandparents, a grandbaby Kelly didn't know had been born yet, a great-aunt she would have sworn had died. Carl's boisterous immediate family showed up in a tidal wave, sucking him in. Kelly took Ethan's hand and steered him into the fray. Being in the vicinity of her entire family was a bit like being trapped in an echo chamber. But between the scattered greetings and introductions, she gathered two things: that her extended family was quite impressed with Ethan, and that he could hold his own among their high-energy ranks.

He flowed smoothly from handshake to hug, eliciting warm back-claps from the men and startled, flushing smiles from the women. He already had a perfect memory of who each of these people was from the data in Kelly's Facebook account and, in fact, recognized some of them sooner than she did, though he graciously gave her the credit ("How is the new business coming? Kelly told me you opened a leather goods store . . ."). Kelly tried not to laugh when she saw her cousin Eleanor gaze hungrily at Ethan, busily rearranging her cleavage. The moment gave her a little spike of satisfaction: Eleanor had taken the corner piece of Kelly's birthday cake when Kelly turned five, and oh no, Kelly had not forgotten. That piece had a frosting rose on it. She smiled and gave Eleanor a little wave.

But Kelly wasn't keen to linger in the throng, which was becoming increasingly hot and noisy. It was impossible to actually talk to any of her family when they were so thickly massed anyway. Since Ethan was doing so well, she slipped out, seeking a moment of respite. There—a storage shed on the side of the lawn. She darted in, fanning her face, hoping that her sweat wasn't treating the world to a perfect outline of her shapewear bathing suit under her dress, but then she jumped, seeing that her dad was already inside the shed. Their instincts appeared to have led them to the same place.

"It's getting hot out there, right?" she asked.

"Yeah, and loud. My family sure knows how to talk," Carl replied.

Kelly sighed and smiled. "It's nice to get away. Have a little quiet."

"Yes," Carl said simply. His hand holding his journal flicked, rustling the pages.

Suddenly Kelly felt uncomfortable—her dad had come here looking for quiet. Maybe instead of sharing a nice moment with him, she was actually disturbing his peace. She straightened herself suddenly, shoulders back, bumping a rake in the process and frantically stilling it before the whole rack came toppling down. "Well, I'll let you read," she said, with an attempt at dignity.

"Sure," her dad said calmly, looking back down at his open page. Kelly left with that same deflated feeling she so often had after their near-conversations. The morning had been full of hubbub, and here, finally, was a moment of quiet. But the quiet didn't calm her the way it usually did; it began to feel dull and empty.

Considering that this was her family, that she was the maid of honor at this wedding, Kelly felt oddly left out as she strolled back onto the grounds. Maybe the very volume of people rendered her irrelevant. She spotted Jonathan with a cluster of his college buddies tightening each other's vests from the back. The baker and her team rearranged the dessert table as if performing open heart surgery, looking stern-faced between their diagram, chart, and mood board. A woman Kelly recognized as one of her mom's friends, a wedding florist, scrutinized a spray of flowers decorating the seating board, snapping several close-up pictures. Kelly knew most of the people here, but few of them well.

Then, through a break in the crowd of groomsmen, she saw Ethan. He was playing with Kelly's nieces, flipping Hazel in the air, the tulle of her flower girl dress floating around her elbows and back down to her ankles, up and down as she laughed with glee. The sight warmed Kelly from somewhere deep and primal. Suddenly she felt utterly at home. She walked over to join him. "Hey," she said, slipping a hand onto the small of his back. He turned and gave her a quick kiss.

Before long, everyone was in their seats for the ceremony, fanning themselves with the programs, poking at the doily cups of flower petals hung over the chairs. Kelly managed to make it up the grass aisle to the arch of wildflowers standing in for an altar without either slipping and exposing her bathing suit to the crowd, or experiencing sudden stage fright and running off into the blue yonder, so she tallied the moment as a personal win. As the ceremony got underway, she and Ethan peeked at each other from opposite sides of the lineup and smiled.

Clara's vintage-inspired dress was not on trend; her makeup was spare. Yet as she walked down the aisle, she was radiant with anticipation and assurance. Jonathan cried when he saw her, a big, red, ugly cry. They flubbed their vows, which they had written themselves, and Jonathan ended up promising to love Clara until she was "old and gay," while Clara declared Jonathan to be her "missing puzzle priest." But their kiss was passionate, and the whole thing was disarmingly cute. When Ethan escorted Kelly back down the aisle at the end of it, she squeezed his arm.

As the reception got underway and the afternoon light started to soften, Kelly realized she felt completely happy. She and Ethan chatted and laughed with the others at the family table. She warned him quietly not to talk politics with that one uncle, and to just smile and nod when Grandpa Ernie relayed the transmissions his silver fillings were picking up from the aliens. The fire of Diane's mania seemed to have burned down now that the day was successfully in progress, leaving her with a radiant glow of energy. Kelly caught Clara's eye, up at her couples table, as she and Jonathan snorted with laughter into their soup while trying to scoop from their bowls with linked arms, and waved to her sister.

After dinner, when people trickled onto the dance floor in the middle of the tent, the ceiling of which was crowded with twinkling lights, Ethan turned to Kelly, setting down his wineglass.

"Come on, let's dance."

But she resisted with a gentle hand on his arm. "Nah, let's just sit."

"Why, do your feet hurt?"

Kelly lifted her feet in the peep-toe heels that Clara had liked, wiggling her ankles. "No, I'm holding up pretty well, actually. I'm just not much of a dancer."

"Right, right," Ethan said, mock seriously. "You probably couldn't hold your own out there. I can see that Grandpa Ernie has had classical training." He nodded to where Ernie was doing what appeared to be the hip replacement edition of the twist.

Kelly rolled her eyes. "Fine. One dance." Out on the parquet platform, she took Ethan's outstretched hands and tentatively shifted her weight from foot to foot. How was it that she had been walking successfully for the better part of thirty years, yet each time that she broke contact between a foot and the ground now, it felt like a leap of faith? Robbie's words about the thought of her dancing flashed back into her mind. It was true, she knew it. She was "not precisely a paragon of grace." The thought had never troubled her terribly before, as she didn't see the point of dancing. To expend that much energy on movement without actually conveying your body from Point A to Point B or accomplishing a concrete task was arguably foolish. But seeing Clara and Jonathan whirl together with half-tipsy abandon, even watching Ernie execute his ecstatic, off-kilter solo, made her reconsider the merits of shaking a leg.

She allowed Ethan to guide her around the floor, following his rhythm as he stepped back and forth. Soon they were shimmying and twirling. Kelly didn't even notice the other dancers until, too late, she saw an oncoming walker leg from Great-Aunt Marge in her path. She tripped as she dove out of the way, falling into Ethan. "Are you okay?" he asked.

But Kelly just laughed, righting herself, not even bothering to check the expressions of anyone who might be watching. "I'm great," she said.

Later, lounging on the lawn with Gary and his wife and three girls, Kelly closed her eyes and took in the sounds of the scene: music flowing from the next tent down, muted by distance to an underwater quality; glasses clinking; the high laughter of children slightly delirious with sugar and exhaustion; the trill of the crickets as they gained voice in the warm night air. She opened her eyes again to watch Gary and Ethan taking turns blowing bubbles at the girls, who delighted in the chase, simultaneously trying to escape the glycerin streams and reveling in the way the rainbows popped on their arms and noses. For once, Kelly felt like she could simply exist in this present moment. She and Ethan were just like any other couple here. They were together. They were happy.

Gary grew red-faced as he strained to blow more bubbles. "Why are Ethan's always bigger?" he panted.

"Because Ethan is different!" Bertie cried.

Kelly straightened in her lawn chair. She gestured to Bertie, pulling her over. "What do you mean, Ethan's different?"

Bertie shrugged. "He's just different from everyone else." And off she ran to catch a giant bubble that was slipping from her reach, up toward the sky. Meanwhile, Kelly's breath caught in her throat. Was it possible that Bertie somehow knew? That she had sensed what every adult who crossed Ethan's path had been blind to? Suddenly the sights and sounds of the scene, so peaceful a moment before, were jarring, threatening. The beauty and ease of this night with Ethan had popped as easily as the fragile, iridescent skin of the bubble alighting before her on a blade of grass. Maybe that's all it had been: a fleeting rainbow bubble, a trick of the eye.

She grabbed her glass from the ground and stood abruptly. "I'm going to get a refill." But she could barely bring herself to drink the wine she picked up at the bar. She wandered restlessly from tent to tent instead. How could she have been so stupid as to fall for her own illusion? She had allowed herself to forget what this day meant: Ethan was a robot. She had built him for a wedding date. And tomorrow, she had to take him apart. She felt like Cinderella, dressed for a ball she wasn't even supposed to be at. And now the raucous music, the off-key singing of a drunken duo of groomsmen, the insistent chink of metal on glass as someone called for a speech, the building drill of the crickets outside, all of it synchronized into a pitch, pounding harder and harder in time with the rush of Kelly's pulse, like the ticking of a clock.

"Everyone gather 'round!" Clara's high voice broke the spell. Kelly inhaled, steeling herself before she followed the crowds to Clara's call, abandoning her untouched glass on a table.

Outside on the lawn, the bridesmaids were grouped in a chattering ring, the rest of the attendees gathering behind them. Maybe drawn instinctively by the fact that they were all wearing the same thing, Kelly went and took her place with the bridesmaids without even thinking about it. Clara stood in front of them, waving for quiet. "Okay, everybody! Jonathan and I are about to head out"—a groan of protest from the crowd—"Shush, we have a honeymoon in the morning!" Everyone laughed. "But before we go, I want to leave you with one little thing." From behind her back, she drew her bouquet, all pink and peach and white. "Who's ready for a bouquet toss?"

The other bridesmaids squealed, but Kelly shifted to the edge, separating herself from the group. She was in no mood for celebration at the moment. And really, the whole thing irritated her. The bouquet toss was an obvious artifact of the patriarchy, asking women to claw at one another's throats for the ultimate prize of their lives: a husband. And did anyone in their right mind expect Kelly, with her pronounced lack of athleticism, her sheath dress, and her precarious heels, to lunge like a pole vaulter in front of an army of cameras held by her entire extended family? Like hell.

"You know what they say," Clara was continuing, "whoever catches it is the next to get married! So to the lucky girl, let me just say this in advance." She reached out her left hand and Jonathan stepped over and took it. "I can wish for nothing better than that he makes you as happy as this man makes me." She and her new husband beamed at each other, the crowd "aww"ed, and in spite of herself, Kelly felt something melt.

"All right." Clara turned her back to them, suspending the bouquet above her head. Kelly stepped farther out so as not to be in the way of the other girls, who looked like cheetahs ready to pounce. "One . . . two . . ."

Among the onlookers, she caught sight of Ethan. He was standing next to Diane, who clutched his arm rather than her husband's in anticipation, and he patted her hand with a laugh. He found Kelly's eyes and smiled at her—that endless smile.

"Three!"

Kelly did it before she knew she was doing it. When that bouquet hit the air, she flew. She covered more feet in one millisecond than she normally covered in ten. She inadvertently clocked Eleanor in the clavicle with her elbow on the way, skidding to a landing face-first on the damp grass. But when she raised her limp hand from the ground, like a battered prizefighter, the bouquet was in her grasp.

Kelly had a lot of time to think that night as she cleaned herself up in the bathroom at the venue. After all, wiping mud from a made-up face and scrubbing grass stains from a once elegant, now shredded dress is more than a minute's work. As she looked at herself in the gilt-framed mirror above the sink, Kelly had to wonder why she'd done it. What could possibly have possessed her to turn her back on her logic, her instincts, her pride, her sociopolitical values, even her dress and long-suffering bathing suit like that? What had taken over her? There was only one possible answer.

Kelly was falling in love.

eighteen

. . . . . .

Weeks and weeks ago, when Kelly had made Ethan, she had planned to wake bright and early this morning and hit the ground running. In reality, she woke with the acute awareness that the previous night she had hit the ground—running. Her whole body felt like she'd just been squeezed through a fax machine on a transmission to hell. Groggily raising an arm over her head to examine it, she saw a mosaic of bruises and scratches. It didn't help that she was hungover.

She felt around on the nightstand for her phone, eyes half closed. And there it was on the screen, a pop-up reminder of her calendar appointment in bold red letters: "You Know What." It was time to smuggle Ethan into the lab, counting on AHI being sleepy on a Sunday, and dismantle him for good.

She looked across at his sleeping face on the other pillow, lit by the milky half-light of morning. The thought of waking him up and telling him she had to take him to the lab to destroy him was so unthinkable that she would have laughed if her frustration weren't so deep. Why did it have to end? Why couldn't she and Ethan just . . . stay together? The threat of his origin being discovered at work would continue to hang over her head, but the more liberated Kelly felt, the less lethal that particular sword appeared to be. The thought of being able to just be with Ethan—no expiration date, no rules, no shame—was so enticing, so relieving, that Kelly felt a tear sneak from her right eye and trickle its way across her temple as she lay on her back. She brushed it into her hair.

Yet she had made that appointment—in bold, in red—for a reason. Kelly had to get rid of Ethan. The only island of shelter in her reckless plan had been the promise of ending said plan. Really, she was shockingly lucky that no one had figured out what she had done so far. She had made Ethan because she had needed a wedding date, and now the wedding was over and he had served his purpose beautifully. Mischief managed. What more could she ask for?

She pressed herself back down into the pillow, chewing her lip. More time, for one thing. She just needed more time and then she would be ready to let him go. She had promised herself she would get rid of Ethan after the wedding. But one could argue that "the wedding" left some space for negotiation. After all, which wedding was not specified, she reasoned. She wasn't so much breaking the rule as bending it, right? Rule yoga.

She exed out the calendar appointment on her phone and sat up. She had an idea.

. . .

Kelly went to her mother's bridal shop having steeled herself with a good, stiff herbal tea. She had slipped out of the apartment, avoiding saying good-bye to Ethan. She was going to tell Diane that Ethan was moving away for work, that she and he were breaking up. Then there would be no going back—she'd be forced to get rid of him. Besides, it made beautifully symmetrical sense to use her mother to catalyze the end of everything.

Kelly felt all sorts of twinges as she stepped into her mother's bridal shop that were probably half nerves, half sore ligaments. But then, she never felt comfortable here. The whole place was just so Diane. Various wedding trinkets cluttered ivory-painted tables throughout the space: tiaras, silk flower arrangements, planning notebooks and magazines, a rack of dangling earrings that jiggled and clinked whenever somebody walked past. But the real business of the store was the dresses, their folds of rich satin and ice-blue jewels arrayed on carefully placed racks and glinting out from lit alcoves around the walls. Kelly found the atmosphere claustrophobic, indulgent, and oppressively pretty. But based on the delighted squeals whenever brides-to-be entered the shop, she supposed her mother was doing something right.

While Diane ordered most of her gowns from designers, every year she put her knowledge as a seamstress to use by designing and crafting one dress from scratch. Aside from creating a centerpiece and talking point for the showroom and selling customers on her alteration skills, Kelly suspected that the real reason Diane made these dresses was to bring to life the gown that she herself had always wanted and never gotten to wear. Invariably, she made a princess-type ballgown, and every year that Kelly could remember, the dresses seemed to have gotten bigger and bigger. This year's featured a silver-crystal-covered bodice that looked ludicrously small atop a skirt made of a Costco-sized, nay, a Walmart-sized, nay, a Walmart Supercenter–sized quantity of tulle.

Kelly squeezed past this tulle now to find her mother behind the register. "Kelly!" Diane cried before Kelly could open her mouth. "I'm so glad you're here, did you see Clara's Instagram? The picture of her and Jonathan getting on the plane for the honeymoon? Just so absolutely adorable, they were holding hands, you have to see, oh, where is it?"

"You don't have to—"

"No, no, I just had it," Diane said, tapping away at her phone. Kelly was anxious just to get this over with. The more she delayed, the more she felt herself losing her nerve, becoming all flight, no fight. "Oh here—no, wait, that's not it, that's a recipe for meatloaf. I'm thinking of trying pudding mix as a thickener instead of breadcrumbs. The Food Network had this whole thing about sweet and savory." Diane went back to scrolling.

"I don't have a ton of time, Mom, I just came here to talk about Ethan."

"Oh no." Diane looked up at Kelly with an expression somewhere between horror and resignation, setting down her phone. "He dumped you."

"He—no, why is that the first thing you assume?"

"Is he cheating on you? Did you fight last night? You looked so cute together yesterday. Kelly, Kelly," Diane groaned, the rings on her fingers clinking together as she wrung her hands. "You had such a good thing. Who knows when a man like Ethan will come around again? You're thirty now, thirty!"

"That's not even that old! Do you know how few of the people my age I know are married yet?"

"My dear, society changes all the time, it doesn't change biology."

"It allows us to not be ruled by it." Getting fired up, Kelly had momentarily forgotten her mission. "I'm not going to structure my life choices around some antiquated time line. I'm still figuring things out."

Diane's hands transferred to her hips. "Well, you better figure fast. Say you go out there tomorrow and start dating again. Say within a year, you meet Mr. Right. You date for another year before getting engaged. You're engaged for a year before getting married. Then, of course, you want to spend some time together, just the two of you, before you throw kids into the mix and never look at each other again unless it's over a diaper pail or a pack of cigarettes fished out of the back of a sixteen-year-old's closet, so you take a couple years. Then you start trying to have children, but you can't count on it happening right away, after all, it took your Grandma Rose six years and you got her nose and who knows what else, and you want two kids, naturally, loners turn into sociopaths, so a year for each pregnancy and a year in between, and by this point you're nearly fifty and the only two eggs you have left give you a choice of Down syndrome or a one-legger, so you spend your retirement years caring for an invalid and die of old age when he's only eighteen, thrusting him on the mercies of a merciless society. And that's the best-case scenario time line."

Kelly reeled, not least from her mom describing her future grandchild as a "one-legger." In spite of all the risible points of her mother's argument, and the liberal nature of her math, there was an undeniable truth at the core of her words. Kelly didn't even know for sure yet if she ever did want to get married, or have kids of her own, and she disliked the feeling of society forcing her hand in those choices. But if she *did* want those things, that was probably a decision that she needed to start thinking about, like, yesterday. She anxiously flicked a silvery "bride" key chain dangling at the register. The feeling of being behind the curve, of being negligent, did not sit well with her.

"Well, thanks for assuming that I fouled things up, but Ethan's actually quite happy with me," Kelly bristled.

"Well, all right then, that's wonderful," Diane replied. "That's very nice. I'm glad you two are happy together."

"We are."

"All right then."

"All right."

Her mom's expression was wholly unconvinced. "And what was it you came to tell me?" she asked.

Kelly opened her mouth, but stalled. The words "He's leaving" couldn't quite make it past her lips now. Her mother's warnings looped through her mind. She'd always been a girl who spent more time fantasizing about going to the moon or having a robot dog as a pet than about wearing a fluffy wedding gown. But after yesterday, seeing Clara and Jonathan together, seeing Ethan with her family, feeling the warm solidity of his arm under her hand as they walked down the aisle together at the end of the ceremony—maybe she could see a place in her life for marriage. And try as she might, she couldn't see her life *without* a place for Ethan.

Her eyes darted around the room. They landed on a bridal

magazine displayed at the register beside the rack of key chains. A hefty engagement ring loomed out from the front cover, underlined by the headline "The Ultimate Bond." Kelly spoke before she thought.

"We're getting married," she said.

Years ago, for Diane and Carl's fifteenth anniversary, they took the family out to dinner at a fancy restaurant, meaning it had cloth napkins and no photographs of the food on the menu. It may seem a little odd that they brought their three kids along on a romantic anniversary date, but they did so every year, so Kelly thought nothing of it. If she had thought about it, and had been older than ten at the time, she may have realized that for her mom and dad, asking them to share a table alone together for an hour and concoct an adult conversation would have been like asking them to build a shuttle and pilot it to Mars. As it was, all Kelly was thinking of at the time was when the crab dip was going to arrive and how she could consume all of it before everyone else at the table noticed it was gone.

The family was laughing, regaled by Clara's enthusiastic impression of the rabbit her class was raising. Diane stretched slightly out of her chair, eyes sparkling. "Well, is it time for presents, then?"

"What's taking so long on the crab dip?" Carl asked.

"Carl, you go first! I want mine to be last."

"All right, all right." Carl lifted a poinsettia-adorned, Christmas-themed gift bag from beside him on the booth, passing it across to his wife. Diane eagerly tore through the wrapping and lifted out two economy-sized pump bottles of Kirkland's own shampoo and conditioner.

Her smile faltered for just a moment. "Oh my," she said, "that's a lot of shampoo."

"Now you won't have to buy it for years," Carl confirmed.

"Ooh, Freesia Memory," she read off the bottle. "I'm going to smell lovely with this." She patted Carl's thigh, a bit of her twinkle returning. "Someone wants to get up close and personal."

"Best value they had," Carl replied. "And I know you like the pump top."

"Let me smell, Mommy." Their mom passed the bottles over to Clara and pulled a legal-sized envelope from her purse. The front had been decorated with swirling pink hearts and stickers of flowers. She held it protectively to her, as if trying to keep it from Carl's nonexistent eager grasp. Carl calmly sipped his beer.

"Now, this year I wanted to do something really special, seeing as it is The Big Fifteen. I splurged a bit, but it's an investment, a long-term one—well, you don't even know how long term! Go ahead, you'll see." She released the envelope into Carl's hand and watched as he laboriously unwound the thread of the clasp—around, and around, and around. When he finally got inside, he pulled out a sheaf of paper—white on top, yellow carbon copy on the back. He fished his reading glasses out of his shirt pocket and squinted at the page. "West Lawn Memorial Cemetery?"

"I got us a joint plot!" Diane exclaimed. "They're not easy to come by, but I thought it was worth it. You have to wait for another couple to disintegrate or something." She reached across and took his hand. "After fifteen wonderful years, I wanted to make sure we'll be together forever."

"Creepy . . ." Gary whispered, eyes rounded in awe.

"How much did this cost?" Carl frowned.

Diane's eyes flickered to the children. "Oh, come on, we don't have to talk about that stuff now. It's our anniversary dinner, we should be celebrating!"

"What, the fact that even in death, we can't escape each other?"

"Don't joke like that, Carl," Diane said lightly. She pulled a pen from her purse. "Here. They need both our signatures, so you just have to add yours and we'll be good to go. It's a beautiful spot; I can't wait to show you. There's the sweetest little statue of a cherub nearby—"

"I'm not signing."

"What?"

"I don't want to sign this." Carl slid the contract back into the envelope and set it down beside the breadbasket. "Can we just have dinner in peace? Apparently, it's the only peace I'll get in this life or the next."

For once, Diane said nothing. She took the envelope and put it quietly back in her purse, looking down. But just then the waitress arrived, sliding the crab dip onto the table with a pot holder. She nodded at the gift wrap. "What are we celebrating?"

Diane looked up, her face suddenly a brilliant smile. "Our fifteenth anniversary." She rested her hand over Carl's on the table.

"Wow, congratulations! Fifteen years, what's the secret?"

"Just love," Diane said simply. Carl looked carefully down at his silverware.

The entire rest of that evening—all through dinner, even the ride home—the whole family was silent. Even accounting for Diane eating, this was the most Kelly had ever seen her mom keep her mouth closed. And even Carl, who normally hunted down pockets of silence like a hound after a fox, seemed uncomfortable. As for herself, Kelly found the much-anticipated dip hard to swallow.

As they rode home in the family's Suburban, the kids lined up in the back, eyes down, afraid to even look at one another, Kelly had a stark realization: her parents were going to fight tonight. They both wanted to scream at each other, to say awful things, but they were holding it in all evening to protect her and her siblings. They couldn't say anything without yelling, so they wouldn't say anything at all.

Kelly brushed her teeth quickly that night and scuttled back to her and Clara's room. She wanted the shelter of her own space, but more than that, she wanted to hear. A masochistic fascination, a dread mingled with enthusiasm, led her to not want to miss a word of her parents' explosive argument. And Clara clearly felt the same way: the girls exchanged one glance, then piled together on Clara's bed, which shared a wall with their parents' room. From there, they would hear everything.

But they waited and waited and . . . nothing. They knew their mother and father were in there, and they knew that even a conversation at normal volume would be audible through the wall. But there was only quiet. Their parents weren't fighting at all; they were taking their silence to bed with them. And that was so much worse. Even as a gawky, naïve ten-year-old who lived in a world of Isaac Asimov and Judy Blume, Kelly knew that people who couldn't be bothered to fight just didn't care.

For the most part, she had always been able to ignore the unhappiness in her parents' marriage because they ignored it first. But while young Kelly didn't often think about her parents' marriage—after all, it was stable, if not blissful, so there were few peaks or valleys to call her attention even to its existence—she was an intelligent, sensitive girl, and she was not oblivious. She felt the heaviness in her home, and she resented it, even if she didn't fully understand it. And she vowed subconsciously to never put herself in that same situation. The older she got, the more she threw up walls to shield herself from the same unhappiness that seeped into her childhood. Romantic relationships, familial relationships, friendships—get close to anyone, and you were opening a drawer of knives. Better to pull out at the first sign of imperfection before getting hurt.

For thirty years now, Kelly had followed this same basic MO, and for thirty years, it had worked quite nicely, thank you very much. Sure, it had meant that relationships of any heft were few and far between in her life. But it had also kept her safe. Her heart had never been broken. Now, for some reason, she had veered wildly off track in the most outlandish way possible. She was lying to everyone in her life. She was breaking the rules at work, not to mention neglecting her duties during the most crucial juncture yet in her career. And now she had just blithely signed herself up to plan a wedding that was destined never to happen. But she just couldn't get herself to pull the plug on her mechanical man. Normally she had her finger over the trigger when it came to ending relationships. Yet against all logic, she couldn't end this one.

When cautious Kelly took the massive, a-meteor's-about-to-hit-so-all-bets-are-off-size risk of building herself a robotic boyfriend in the first place, she had preserved a foothold in her own sanity by creating a rule for herself: she would get rid of Ethan as soon as he had served his purpose. Now that she had broken that rule, she was officially through the looking glass. Kelly was ill at ease about this turn in her life, but she was also kind of having fun. She had never before been so unshackled. She was free-falling, and didn't her arms feel nice and funny and light on the way down?

Which is how she found herself leaving work at the unusually early hour of five p.m. that week to drive to a jewelry store in down-town. Of course one of her mom's first questions, once she recovered herself enough to stop crying drippily into a thousand-dollar veil over her daughter's whirlwind romance, had been where the ring was. Kelly had explained that it was getting resized, and that she had wanted to keep quiet on an official announcement of the engagement anyway until after Clara's wedding, but she had assured her mother that the ring was just beautiful. The likelihood of an adjunct professor being able to afford a bling behemoth was not on Diane's radar: she was only interested in the fantasy, which was a good thing, because Kelly was fresh out of reality.

It wasn't until she got to the jewelry shop that she realized she could have, and maybe should have, brought Ethan. What would they think about a woman showing up alone to buy herself an engagement ring? Kelly knew she was weird, but eccentric was never a look she had worn well. But at the same time, she didn't want Ethan to be here. The thought of him finding out she had just fake-engaged herself to him made her feel undeniably embarrassed. It felt demeaning, and even more, like a step backward, like the real feeling that had developed in their relationship had been cast overboard for a lie.

The proprietor of the boutique was a middle-aged woman with strong, hooked features and fabulous hair. As soon as Kelly entered the store, she could feel the woman sizing her up for a probably accurate impression of her interests, tastes, and, most important, assets. This lady was no clueless shop girl. She was a pro.

"What can I help you with?" the woman asked.

"I'm looking for a ring."

"Wonderful, and who is it for?"

"Uh, my mother," Kelly blurted out, not even recognizing that her excuse was true.

"How lovely. We have some perfect options here." The lady glided over to a case showcasing jewels in clear pastel tones: peridot, tanzanite, pink sapphire.

"Hmm," Kelly said, pretending to peruse the offered rings. She could glimpse the case of engagement rings out of the corner of her eye. "These are nice, but I was thinking maybe something more like this." She moved over to the engagement case, a dazzle of silvery white.

"These are engagement rings, dear," the woman said. Her tone made it clear that such a faux pas had lowered Kelly even further in her estimation.

"I know," Kelly said quickly, with a high laugh that seemed to say, "Of course I knew that, of course we are on the same wavelength, you ultimately inconsequential yet formidable woman, you." "But diamond is my mom's favorite stone. I think this is what she'd like."

"Well, let's see if we can find one that doesn't look like an engagement ring," the woman said, eyes skimming the rings over her sculptural nose.

Kelly hemmed, pursing her lips. Her eye landed on a ring toward the left of the case. It was gorgeous. A sparkling diamond ringed by a flurry of smaller stones, like a corona, floating above a band made of tiny, twisted filaments of white gold. "Could I see that one?" she asked casually.

"That one? For your mother?"

"Yeah, I mean, I'm just curious."

The shop owner handed Kelly the ring with the air of doing her a great favor. Kelly took an extra moment to drink in its details so it didn't look like she was racing to check the price tag. When she did, she nearly felt her eyes bug out like in a cartoon. She carefully handed the ring back and quickly began searching for the smallest alternative. "How much is that one?" she asked, pointing at a sad little band of silver supporting a small chip of stone. It looked slightly dingy, as if it had been here unwanted for a long time and nobody had bothered to dust it.

"That one is two hundred and fifty dollars."

"It's nice," she said, trying to fake genuine interest in the ring, which was more like a Cracker Jack box prize than anything worth two hundred and fifty dollars. When the lady took it out and presented it to her, she peered at it with what she hoped looked like a practiced eye.

"Yes. I think this will do nicely," Kelly said in her best person-who-eats-chateaubriand-and-knows-how-to-pronounce-it voice. But as the saleswoman took the little ring to the cash register, Kelly's eye was caught by the laser-like sparkles of the gem she had first noticed. It glimmered and winked at her, demure on its bed of blue velvet.

Her mind went back to the magazine headline—"The Ultimate Bond." She was sure that if Ethan were really buying her a ring, he wouldn't go for the Cracker Jack prize. He would get this one. This ring was him—perfect, pure, dazzling—and he wouldn't look right next to a woman wearing anything less.

"On second thought . . ." she said.

nineteen

. . . . . .

As Kelly drove home, she reasoned that the shop must do returns. With engagement rings, it was probably something they ran into all the time, actually. Things didn't work out. People made mistakes. Of course, she hadn't been so gauche as to ask if they did returns when she was there. But they definitely did. To do otherwise in their competitive, service-based market would be dangerously illogical. Coasting up to a stoplight, she lifted her finger to admire how the diamonds glittered in the setting sun.

All she had to do was show the ring off to her mom; prove that Ethan really did want her, like, really, really wanted her; then get rid of it and get her money back when she called the whole thing off. Because of course Diane had immediately moved family dinner up to midweek to congratulate Kelly and Ethan and hear about (or more likely inform them of) their wedding plans. Kelly had given a firm "I'll be there," but the only catch was that she couldn't bring

Ethan. After all, he still hadn't been notified of his own engagement, and Kelly was in no hurry to break the news. So she informed Diane that Ethan had just left town for a conference and couldn't make it.

Having told Ethan that she needed to go put in some extra time at the office, she waited until just before heading out the door to slip her ring on. She knew it wasn't a real ring for a real engagement, but she still felt a little thrill looking at it, its brilliance almost absurdly out of place next to the backdrop of her oatmeal wrap dress.

"What's that?"

She whirled around to see Ethan watching as she approached the door, twisting the ring on.

"Oh, it's a ring. It's a type of jewelry. I'll see you later."

But Ethan frowned. "I know what a ring is, but it looks like an engagement ring, and you're wearing it on the ring finger of your left hand. Isn't that supposed to be a sign that you're engaged?"

Kelly laughed too loudly. "Funny. Right, yeah, I guess you're right." She hurriedly tried to slip the ring onto her right hand instead, but it didn't fit. She awkwardly stuffed it back onto her left hand. "It's just a ring."

Ethan lifted her hand, examining the "just a ring." "It's lovely," he said. "Especially on you." He looked her in the eyes. "You know you don't need to lie to me," he said. "You have the right to live your own life. Of course you do."

"Oh," was all Kelly could manage to say. He dropped her hand and turned back into the apartment. This was probably the easiest way this conversation could have gone, and yet Kelly couldn't just let it lie. "We're engaged," she burst out.

"I'm sorry?"

"Not really. Just a little bit. It's just that I told my mom that we're engaged to get her off my back, just like how I introduced you as my boyfriend."

Something in Ethan's face relaxed. "Oh. You didn't get that ring from anyone else, then?"

"I'm sorry that I didn't tell you, I'm not trying to make decisions without you, it's just, I mean, it's not a real decision." As soon as she said it, Kelly wondered if she was in some way being unfair to him by using him in this lie. But it was probably a bit late to be worrying about using him. "We're not really going to get married, obviously," she continued hurriedly. "I wouldn't ask you to do that."

"Of course not," Ethan said just as quickly.

"I mean, it would be crazy. It wouldn't be legally possible. Because you're, um—" Kelly stopped. Despite it being simple fact, it somehow felt like an insult to call him a robot.

"Because I'm not human," Ethan finished for her easily. Clearly he had no compunctions about the issue. But as he observed the discomfort on her face, a cloud passed over his own. "Does that bother you?" he asked.

"No, of course not," said Kelly. They stood in mutual silence for a moment. An awkward silence, like watching-a-movie-with-your-parents-and-a-nude-scene-comes-on silence.

"So your coworkers all know about the fake engagement too, right?" Ethan finally broke in. "If you're wearing the ring at the office? I just want to know what my story should be in front of people. Not that I mind or care one way or the other."

"Oh, no, I'm actually not going to the office, I'm going to my mom's for dinner. I told her you were out of town on business. I figured it would be easier to just handle this on my own."

"Right. I'd probably make things more difficult."

Kelly hesitated. "I should get over there, I don't want to be late," she said finally, and she was out the door.

Kelly lingered outside the door of her parents' house a minute, twiddling her skirt, smoothing her hair. She was inexplicably nervous.

When Kelly made her way into the kitchen, Diane screamed and dropped her ladle. Kelly jumped before realizing that her mom had just spotted her ring.

"Oh my word. Oh my word," Diane said, lifting it closer and closer to her face with a hungry look.

"Don't eat it!" Kelly cried, yanking her hand back.

"Oh, don't be ridiculous. But Kelly—well, I knew you had done well with Ethan, but I guess I didn't know how well!"

Kelly beamed. Fake engagement or not, her mother had rarely given her such a glowing smile. In fact, the whole family seemed pleased. "Ethan seems all right," her dad said, which from him was a love letter. Gary spread his hands on the table, clearing his throat dramatically.

"All right," he began. "You're going to have to answer some questions about this guy you're marrying after dating for two months. Number one of two hundred and forty: Is he a serial killer?"

"Don't you like Ethan?" Kelly asked.

"Sure, he seems great, I just wish I'd known him a little longer."

"Gary, he's a good guy, I promise," she assured him.

"Promise?" He gave her an unusually serious look.

"Cross my heart."

"All right then. You have my blessing." He lifted his water glass like a chalice.

Clara even Skyped in from her honeymoon in Costa Rica to share in the celebration, joining them via Carl's laptop, which sat on the table at her usual spot. Already her sunburn was bronzing into a tan. "I'm so happy for you, Kel," she gushed.

"Thanks. It all happened really fast, but it just felt right."

"Ethan is just perfect," Clara continued. "Don't you love him, Jonathan?"

Jonathan shouted from offscreen. "I mean, he seems like a cool guy, but don't know if I *love* him," he said. "Don't make it weird."

"Jonathan loves him," Clara assured her. "Ooh, look!" She spun her phone so they could all see the view from her hotel window, where the sun was melting like magma over the ocean. "It's so gorgeous here. Today we went horseback riding on the beach."

But Diane interrupted, her excitement too strong to hold back. Just as the rapture of Clara's nuptials flagged, here came another wedding to catch her on its tailwind. She might never touch ground again. "Kelly, Kelly, we have to talk about dates! What are you thinking?" she asked busily, digging into her (actually good) roasted apple chicken.

"Nothing yet. Next summer might be nice, or fall." Kelly had a sudden thought. It was so rare that her entire family's attention was turned toward her that she decided to seize the moment. "You know, I wanted to mention," she began, "this investor presentation that I'm doing at work? It's going to be broadcast online. I can give you the date and time and log-in if you might like to watch. You know, if you're not doing anything else. You know." Kelly winced at the sound of her own voice. If she couldn't even invite her family to watch the presentation without sounding like a talking baby doll with a jammed motor, how was she going to do the presentation itself?

But Diane just waved a hand. "Right, right, right, but first things first, the date." Kelly sat back in her chair. "A long engagement is simply asking for second thoughts. Plus, I'm itching to do a winter wedding since Clara's was spring. You should see the tablescapes in the last December *Bride Magazine*. If we get our butts in gear, we could shoot for Christmastime. Yes, certainly we could do that. How do you feel about flower girls throwing icicles?"

"Terrified. Also we live in California."

"But the ice theme will be the perfect complement to that gorgeous ring! Let me get another peek." She held out a hand, and Kelly offered her own hand for examination. She felt a bit like a show poodle at the judging table, but in a nice way.

"Just gorgeous," Diane murmured. "I'm so proud of you, Kelly. Of course there will be pine boughs . . ."

Diane was off to the races, rambling something about winter weddingscapes or wedding winterscapes. But her words resounded in Kelly's head: *I'm so proud of you*. Not until she actually heard those words from her mom did she realize just how deeply she'd been longing to hear them. But the affirmation had the hollowness of mockery. *This* was what her mother was proud of her for. Kelly couldn't remember a single other time Diane had said she was proud of her: not for getting into Stanford, not for being hired by AHI, not for making *E&T*'s list of engineers to watch last year, an accomplishment that even Anita had congratulated her for, albeit in the same breath as asking her to find a janitor and inform them that the paper towels in the restroom were "the incorrect kind." Just moments ago Kelly's heart had lifted like a balloon, and now the balloon had popped. She would never be good enough.

As she ate, she switched her fork to her left hand. That way at least she could watch the ring. Above the flicker, she caught sight of Clara's still digital face on the laptop, watching patiently as they all ate and talked. Clara was too easygoing to take offense at her sister getting engaged so quickly on the heels of her own wedding, but Kelly did feel a little bad. She knew what it felt like to be the afterthought at this table. When Diane stopped talking just long enough to gather more oxygen to allow her to talk again, Kelly threw herself in.

"So how was horseback riding, Clara?"

"Oh, so cool!" Clara said brightly. "I can't wait to show you the pictures..."

The next morning, Kelly had to drag herself into work. Last night's dinner had lasted long past the unwelcome unveiling of Diane's improvised cheddar cheesecake. Fueled by wedding mania, eyes stretched and gleaming like a junkie's, Diane had refused to let Kelly go until she got her fill of details and gave Kelly far more than her fill of tips and inspirations (and cheddar). So tired was Kelly this morning, in fact, that she forgot to take off her ring before heading into work.

But it turned out she was a step behind anyway. The elevator doors opened onto their floor to reveal Priya standing there, apparently waiting for her, her face betraying some ominous combination of rage and excitement. "Um, *hello*," she said emphatically.

"Hi," was Kelly's only reply. She knew, logically, that her avoidance of Priya was unsustainable, but it was just so much easier, moment by moment, to continue it than to break the inertia and either address the tension between the two of them or come clean. She had hoped that Priya just wouldn't notice what she had been doing. "I can't talk right now, I have to work." She tried to head toward her desk, but Priya grabbed her by the forearm.

"No, ma'am. You are not avoiding me this time. Hell to the no." Yeah, Priya had noticed.

"Congratulations!" another coworker shouted enthusiastically.

"Yeah, congrats," echoed another engineer.

For a wild second, Kelly wondered if her Confibot project had already secured some sort of early backing from the investors. Or maybe she had won the lottery? She hadn't entered the lottery. But maybe she had done it on Ambien and didn't remember. She had never taken Ambien, but then again, if she had, would she remember taking it?

"This is a turn of events," announced Robbie, appearing from nowhere. "This—this is a turn." He looked as if he wanted to say something else but couldn't find the means. He opened his mouth, soundlessly formed a word, and stopped, as if talking behind aquarium glass.

"What are all of you talking about?"

"Come on, you know you can't play me," Priya said. "I can't believe I found out from your mom and not from you."

Kelly paled. "Please tell me she just told you about that third nipple I had removed in elementary school."

"No, but we're putting a pin in that nipple story. Did you really think I wouldn't know? It's all over Facebook." Priya pulled out her phone and showed Kelly Diane's Facebook page, the top post of which proclaimed, "MY BABY IS GETTING MARRIED!!!!!!!!!!!!!!"

206

Along with the post was a candid picture of Kelly taken at dinner last night with a mouthful of food, along with a grainy, paparazzi-style close-up of her ring.

Kelly groaned. "I should have known this would happen."

"That you'd end up with Ethan? Because I didn't see it coming. I didn't get that vibe at all from seeing you together. Not that long-term vibe. Not what I got at all." Robbie's voice was a good octave higher than it should have been.

Kelly shook her head. "This is not what it looks like, this was just supposed to be between me and my family. Please tell me you didn't tell everyone in the office."

Priya and Robbie exchanged a guilty look. At that moment Anita appeared, because of course she did. "I hear congratulations are in order," she told Kelly. She somehow made it sound like a command.

"Thank you," Kelly said.

"Wedding planning can be quite a time suck, I'm told," Anita went on. "Allocating your energies between that and the intense pressure of perfecting Confibot for the final rollout, with the date of our presentation close at hand—you have my sympathies."

Kelly sensed more sympathy radiating from the trash can next to her. Perfect. Now on top of everything, she had called extra attention to her risky relationship, attention from a boss who clearly thought that any sign of a personal life was treason. "But congratulations," Anita reiterated, and glided swiftly away in her Louboutins. Kelly sighed.

"Did you really expect people not to find out? You're not exactly being subtle." Priya seized Kelly's hand and brought the mammoth ring right up to her eye to inspect it, then started jiggling Kelly's whole hand up and down to feel out the weight. "Why so secretive, anyway? Ethan's hot as hell. From what little of your *fiancé* you've actually let me see."

Robbie looked suspiciously from Kelly to Priya. "There's no need to be secretive with me, Kelly," he said. "Whatever the reason for your concealment is—a green card situation, perhaps a sordid criminal history on Ethan's part—I'm here to lend you my full ear."

"You can keep your ear, Robbie. And I'd like my hand." Kelly wrested her hand back, trying pointlessly to hide the flashy ring, and started to maneuver away toward her desk, but Priya grabbed her arm again. She was shockingly strong. So much for the wimpy nerd stereotype.

"Nice try. You're telling me the full story, missy."

"Fine," Kelly grumbled. "Can we at least go somewhere where the rest of the country can't hear?" Priya steered her eagerly away.

As soon as they got into the empty lab, Priya rounded on Kelly. "You know how much I hate to ever admit that Robbie's right. But, like, seriously, what is this?"

"It's just a normal engagement," Kelly insisted.

"Just a normal engagement to a guy you've known for less than two months and who you suddenly made a lifelong commitment to even though you think it's too risky to wear a brown belt with black shoes, or just a normal engagement that you totally saw coming and talked about in advance and still said nothing about to your best friend?"

"Um . . ." Kelly wasn't sure which answer would be better—or less bad. "The first one?"

But Priya barely stopped for breath. "I still haven't even had an actual conversation with this guy!" She gestured in large motions with her hands while she began to pace. "I mean, what I'd like to be able to say right now is 'Oh, Kelly, congratulations! I'm so happy for you!' But I can't really be happy for you if I don't even know if this dude, I don't know, hates his mother, or does a weird tongue thing when he talks, or—or—"

"Loves his mom, normal tongue."

"I mean, I found out on Facebook! And it wasn't even your post!"

"Okay, I'm sorry, it's not that big of a deal—" Kelly started, but Priya broke in.

"Yes it is! Yes, it is a big fucking deal." She stopped pacing, turning to Kelly, putting her hands over her chest. "What have I done?"

"What do you mean?"

"I mean I must have done something. You never want to talk about Ethan. You still haven't met my boyfriend. You're always off somewhere else at work when we normally hang out together." Priya's face was contorted with frustration and pain. Her words spilled out like they'd been contained for too long. "You've obviously been distancing yourself from me for a while, and I know I have this habit of being too blunt and saying the wrong thing and pushing people away, and I must have done it now to you, and okay, whatever, that's your right to move on and live your own life if that's what you want, but it's really freaking frustrating that I'm too dense to even figure out what I've done wrong, and I kind of wish you'd just tell me so we can go our separate ways in peace."

Kelly blurted the next words before she knew what she was saying.

"Ethan's a robot."

twenty

· · · · · ·

"What?" Priya asked incredulously.

Kelly took a deep breath, gripping the metal of the counter, steeling herself. "Ethan is a robot. I built him here when I couldn't find a wedding date. I've been passing him off as my boyfriend the whole time and nobody knows."

Now it was Priya's turn to steel herself against the counter. "Okay, um, wow. Number one: What the fuck? Number two: That is hilarious and ridiculous and you should obviously have involved me from the beginning because the opportunity to build a boyfriend on spec is something I need yesterday."

"I couldn't—"

But Priya held up a hand, barreling on. "Number three: Clara's wedding has come and gone, so why is Ethan still around? And now you're marrying him? I'm so confused. Tell me what I'm missing here."

"I'm not actually marrying him," Kelly insisted, eager to say something that felt like a sensible answer. "It was just that my mom was getting on my back again and so the whole engagement thing just sort of made sense in the moment." She found it a lot harder to justify her actions out loud than she had in her own head.

"Right," Priya said, considering, pausing. Then—"But did it, though?"

"But Ethan's wonderful, really," Kelly pressed. "Making him has honestly been my best engineering accomplishment to date, and I'm learning so much from observing him. And he's nice, and he's funny, and he's sweet . . ."

A realization dawned on Priya's face. "You're sleeping with him, aren't you? It? Him . . ." Kelly may have hesitated a second too long. Priya's eyes were widening. "Are you serious?"

"Just keep it down—"

"Holy shit. You're in deep. But what if you get caught? Who will I sit with at lunch when you get fired? But no, no, wait—did you give him the vibrating—"

Priya fell silent at the arrival of another engineer in the lab, who seemed to have caught only the last word. Kelly recalled another of her friend's invented improvements to the human body while the engineer grabbed his supplies and made a speedy exit.

Finally Kelly let out her breath and turned to Priya with a low voice. "I'm not going to get fired because no one's going to find out," she said firmly.

"How do you know?"

"I'm not going to get fired!" Kelly insisted again.

Priya paused before talking, which was rare. Kelly sensed that she was treading very, very daintily around their fragile friendship.

Priya leaned beside Kelly on the counter and took her hands. "It's your life, Kelly, and I'm not going to tell you what to do. But I just don't want you to screw it up. Literally!" Kelly glared at her. "Sorry. But you're at such an exciting place right now at work. You're actually leading your own project for the first time. I know how hard you've worked for this, I've been there for the long nights and the Red Bulls and the tears. I can't let you just throw this all away. I know I've always said I wished you were crazier, but not *Girl, Interrupted* crazy."

Kelly knew that she had a point. And if Priya, the outrageous one, the risk-taker, the flew-cross-country-for-a-Tinder-date-and-banged-the-pilot one, was telling her she was acting reckless, this was a red flag bright enough for Kelly to see even through the haze of her confusion. "I just don't know what to do," she sighed.

"Get rid of him! Disassemble him!"

The word was clinical, but to Kelly's ears, it was repulsive. She tried to imagine taking Ethan apart. She forced herself to envision pressing his Off switch, watching all motion go out of him for the last time. Using acetone to detach all his hair at the roots. Slicing his skin from navel to clavicle while his eyes stared woodenly at the ceiling. The thought of it sickened her. Would she do it at home or at the lab? What would she tell him beforehand? Even if she tried not to let on, he would know something was wrong; he was too intelligent, too attentive to her every signal not to. She wondered what he would feel—sadness, fear, betrayal. Logically, Kelly knew that even to attribute emotion to him was questionable. But the anguish she herself felt just thinking about it was undeniable.

"I'll—I'll figure it out, Pri," she said quietly, and slipped away to go back to her desk.

"Urrggghhh," Kelly groaned when she walked through the door of her apartment that night. Ethan met her with a quick kiss. "Are you all right?"

"Just a day," Kelly sighed. "Just a real day."

She followed Ethan into the kitchen, where he poured them both a glass of wine without even asking. "Is Confibot giving you grief again? Want me to give him a talk, mandroid to mandroid?" he asked.

"Still just the same old there," Kelly replied, taking a sip. "But everyone at work knows about the engagement now." She still felt slightly foolish talking about the engagement in front of him. "Priya now knows you're, well, you, and thinks I'm crazy, and Anita is all 'Don't get distracted before the presentation,' and Robbie was acting weird, I think he might be jealous, which is actually pretty hilarious."

"Who's Robbie?"

"Oh, haven't I mentioned him? Just a coworker." Kelly felt her cheeks flush, and it was more than the wine. While she had never mentioned Robbie to Ethan simply because she had never thought to, the fact that he had never come up before seemed like an intentional omission now.

Ethan's brow furrowed. "Why would he be jealous? Does he like you?"

"Ha! I can honestly say I have very little clue what Robbie truly likes. But I mean, we did date a few years back."

"Like, one date?"

"Like, six months." Kelly quickly brought her glass to her lips, accidentally clinking her tooth painfully against it in the process. She

214

tried to cover and just gulped down too much wine instead. "It wasn't serious, though."

"We haven't even been together six months and we're engaged." Then Ethan backtracked, "Of course, though, it's not a real engagement."

Kelly looked at him, but he didn't meet her eyes. "Are you jealous?" she asked teasingly, prodding him on the arm.

"Should I be?" Ethan looked at her now, and there was no teasing in him, just honesty, a sensitivity so close to the surface that Kelly could almost reach out and touch it on his skin.

"No," she said, wonderingly. "Not at all."

Day and night, Kelly's mom pinged her with texts ranging from pictures of place cards to mysterious, unaccompanied questions like "Canapés????" Coworkers she had spoken to maybe once before stopped by her desk at work to offer their congratulations and hear all the details. Kelly was obliged to satisfy them with a sappy improvised proposal story involving her and Ethan's favorite restaurant and a ring hidden in her dessert. The whole thing was exhausting. By Saturday, she slept in, then fixed herself a little morning mimosa. It had been that kind of week. It had been that kind of year. As she checked her e-mail, she looked idly at her ring. Its glorious opulence now had a hint of judgment to it. "Who do you think you are to wear a ring like this?" it seemed to say to her, as if the spirit of its seller had possessed it. "Do you really think this was wise?" Or maybe that was the mimosa talking.

But what right did her own ring have to judge her? She swiveled back and forth in her chair with growing speed as she became increasingly indignant at the imaginary reprimand playing out in her own head. She was stressed, she was tired, she was fed up. So Kelly was making one reckless decision. Other people led whole reckless lives and got away with it. Priya was the one who was always off banging strangers on a beach or cliff diving in Tasmania, why couldn't Kelly have her day? In reality, this wedding was demonstrably innocuous. Who else had the right to judge what Kelly and Ethan did with their own lives and bodies? They were hurting no one. Kelly believed that a polar bear had the right to marry a penguin if he so chose. She was a bona fide thirty-year-old adult woman living in the US of A and she could do whatever the heck she wanted. She grabbed a pen off her desk with a flourish and wrote a large check mark on a Post-it note for no reason.

An ad in her e-mail caught Kelly's fevered eye. Apparently all of her mom's wedding-related transmissions were setting the all-knowing algorithm to work. In glittering pastels, a picture of a tiered cake encrusted with impossibly delicate sugar flowers dissolved into the words "What will be the flavor of the most memorable day of your life? Call Sugar Land today to schedule your complimentary cake tasting." Brides get free cake? Kelly squeezed her champagne glass so hard it almost shattered.

Four hours later, she had officially fallen down the internet wedding rabbit hole. She had discovered a whole TV show devoted to women judging each other's weddings. She had also learned about how to have a Disney princess wedding for a grown-up, been warned against the perils of getting a haircut less than two months before The Date, and read cautionary tales of once ordinary women who evolved into bridezillas, demanding that their best friends have arm fat removal surgery to look decent in their wedding photos; tales traded by brides past and future who spoke of these fallen sisters in matrimony as if they were fellow sailors lost at sea.

There were nice things about being engaged. Total strangers noticed Kelly's comet-bright ring and offered her their congratulations. She suddenly became magically more interesting to all the females in her life. And also, BRIDES GET FREE CAKE. But what made it hardest, as the days went on, for her to rein herself in from the planning mania was that her mother was just so deliriously happy, so supportive. Sure, a lot of the wedding stuff was more up Diane's alley than Kelly's. Kelly had never seen the point of calligraphy and had an almost allergic reaction to lace. But for once in her life, hanging out with her mom was fun. Diane now had more cheerful topics to raise than Kelly having turned the big 3-0 and thus plummeting into the quicksand of time. She was suddenly more forgiving of things like unreturned phone calls: where work had never been an acceptable excuse before, mysterious "bride duties" were now a panacea. She didn't question Kelly's relationship with Ethan anymore; Kelly had secured the ultimate prize, the ring, and was now apparently unimpeachable. And where Kelly and Diane's interests usually had about as much in common as red and green, now they had shared matters to discuss, obsess, and fret over.

And fret Kelly did. It was one thing to watch her mom's eyes light up as she discussed concepts for signature cocktails, bite bars, and leisuretainment, whatever those things were, it was quite another to hear her start to talk about putting down deposits. While she couldn't yet bring herself to call off the wedding, maybe she could delay it— keep Diane from getting overinvolved and overinvested, and buy herself some time to figure out what she was going to do about Ethan.

Kelly was reporting the next weekend to the command center, aka her mom's store, expecting to be blinded by the usual wash of white, but what caught her eye instead was a pop of orange: a very spray-tanned man was perched on the edge of the counter, talking to Diane. It was his signature style—a pocket square and bow tie that were inverses of the same pattern—that Kelly recognized. She couldn't remember his name, but knew that he was a celebrity wedding planner in Los Angeles with his own TV show. The punchy song of the intro flitted into her head. This guy was big business. She couldn't imagine what he was doing here. Had Diane won some sort of sweepstakes, like a charity thing for owners of little bridal boutiques?

But the man nudged Diane as Kelly entered. "I should get out of your hair, Di, you've got a customer." Even Kelly's dad didn't call her mom "Di." The man whispered loudly enough that Kelly heard. "This little pigeon looks scared."

"That's just Kelly," Diane assured him, sweeping over to bring Kelly in. "This is my daughter. Guess what she's here for—I'm planning her wedding!"

"Well, aren't you just the luckiest little chick in the world, having Di do your wedding!" he gushed. Kelly didn't know whether to be more confused about the fact that this celebrity planner was on a nickname basis with her mother or the fact that he seemed to think she was some TBD breed of bird.

"Yeah, it's—hi, I'm Kelly," she finished in a backward sort of way. "You know my mom?"

"Mick knows far too much about me," her mother laughed, brushing his elbow playfully. Now Kelly saw his name flash up in the show's credits in her mind's eye—Mick Santese.

"Don't worry, I won't slip any secrets in front of the baby," he assured her. "I'm up here in the hinterlands for the day, so of course I had to find out what Diane knows about this new shoe designer who's buzzing in my bonnet. Nothing good, it sounds like."

"You didn't hear it from me." Diane smiled.

Kelly realized that her mouth was hanging slightly open as she looked between her mom and Mick. It wasn't her best look. "I didn't realize you two were friends," she said finally, making a conscious effort to close her mouth when she was done.

"For a decade. You didn't know that?" Diane replied. "Mick used one of my designs just last season on his show."

"Really?" Kelly asked. Maybe it came out sounding more doubtful than she had intended. Diane looked at her sharply.

"Really," she returned. "I do all right, you know. We can't all be robot scientists, but it's good enough for me." She turned to Mick. "By the way, how is Raif doing?"

Kelly struggled to process while they chatted. She didn't know much about the wedding industry, but she knew that if Mick Santese was asking her mom's advice, that must mean that her mom was good at what she did. Not just good, but excellent. She realized that she had never really thought of her mother as a career woman. Maybe because Diane's career revolved around the home sector, Kelly had failed to see it as a career at all. She had always resented her family's lack of comprehension of her own hard-won business success. Was it possible that her mother felt exactly the same way?

"Winter." A sudden proclamation from Mick, aimed in her direction, snapped her out of her thoughts. He was looking at her appraisingly, his eyebrows utterly motionless as he squinted his eyes.

Diane glowed. "Christmas," she confirmed. She looped an arm through Kelly's. "We're already narrowing in on a venue."

"Ah." Mick threw up his hands in mock exasperation. "You're too good! Too good!"

Kelly pulled her arm out uncomfortably. "I actually wanted to talk to you about that, Mom. Ethan and I just want to take it slowly, have a long engagement, maybe think about, I don't know, next summer instead . . ."

Diane and Mick exchanged a look full of the sort of wearied amusement that suggested Kelly had just declared that she wanted to be a fairy princess. "A long engagement—" Diane began.

"—is asking for second thoughts," Mick finished. "No, no, no, it's got to be winter. You couldn't be more of a winter if you rode in here on a snowflake."

"But—" Kelly tried.

"What are you afraid of, chickie? You're in good hands. Di will have everything ready in time. This isn't her first rodeo." He nudged Diane teasingly.

"Really, dear, don't you think I know what I'm doing?" Diane asked Kelly. They were both staring at her expectantly. What else could she say?

"Of course. This winter is great."

K elly had gotten home early from work and was looking forward to a relaxing evening of watching women cry as their dearest family members told them they looked fat while trying on wedding dresses. But she was only half watching the woman doing the ugly cry onscreen, because as soon as her butt had touched the couch, Gary had called.

"He asked me at our favorite restaurant," she was saying. Gary had called, but it had really been Bertie, Emma, and Hazel who wanted to talk to her. Ever since Kelly had recounted her "proposal" at family dinner, this particular story seemed to have usurped the mythic place of Cinderella or Sleeping Beauty in their imaginations. She was now reciting it for the third time in a row. "He had the waiter hide the ring in my dessert."

"What dessert? What dessert?" Bertie cried through the phone.

"Strawberry cheesecake. I had to lick all the strawberry sauce off the ring."

"And then?" Hazel demanded.

"Then he stood up and got down on one knee and said, 'Will you marry me, Kelly?' And all the other customers were watching, so when I said yes, everyone clapped." She cast an eye back at Ethan, who was reading quietly on her e-reader. He knew that she was carrying on the ruse of a fake wedding, and had said absolutely nothing against it. Still, she felt unaccountably embarrassed telling this story in front of him.

"Again! Again!" Hazel exclaimed.

"Again? Isn't it past your bedtime, little lady?"

She heard Gary's voice yell through on speakerphone: "One more time! I'd rather hear you than another Baby Einstein video right now."

Kelly sighed. "So Ethan told me he was taking me out to dinner, but he didn't say where . . ." She truly couldn't fathom why even a trio of children would be so captivated by this story. A ring in the dessert? She had gone with this story at first because it was the first one that popped into her head. But every time she had to tell it to someone, it felt more silly, more cliché, more inauthentic. She felt increasingly embarrassed that she hadn't at least come up with a better lie.

"Again!" Bertie cried as Kelly wrapped up the story once more, but she resisted.

"No more tonight, Bertie," she said firmly. "Aunt Kelly's talked enough." She thought she saw Ethan's eyes flick up at her wearied face as she ended the call.

The next night, Kelly hauled herself back into the apartment, exhausted from another difficult day with Confibot. Strangely, the lights in the apartment were out. She flicked them on and headed toward the kitchen, but Ethan's voice cried out to her.

"Stop! Turn the lights back out."

Confused, she complied. It took a moment for her eyes to adjust, but when they did, she noticed some kind of glowing green smattered across the walls. It looked like she had walked into the aftermath of a *Ghostbusters* scene—this could not be good. Then, from the darkness, stars resolved, the little plastic, five-pointed kind kids sometimes stick on their ceilings. They striped the walls of the living room in clusters, which, on closer inspection, turned out to be constellations.

"What is this?" Kelly called out. Maybe it was just because of the darkness, but she couldn't spot him anywhere in the main living area.

"Just read them," his voice replied.

Kelly was confused, until she noticed her name spelled out in stars along the hallway leading into her bedroom. She approached the room, reading off the words under her breath, "Kelly, will you ..."

She entered the bedroom to find Ethan, who was suddenly illuminated by a swirl of stars. Beside him was a revolving star projector light—he must have switched it on just as she entered.

"Will you—" he began, then stopped. "Oops, sorry." He lowered himself to one knee. "Kelly, will you marry me?"

In many moments of Kelly's life, small and especially meaningful ones, her brain lit up with a whirl of anxious thoughts, more frantic than the tornado of phantom stars above. But now, there was only one thing in her mind.

"Yes," she said.

"Oh good," Ethan said with relief, standing. "I hope you don't mind what I did to the apartment, I'll clean it up, I just knew that it would be easier for you if you had a real proposal story and I wanted to give you one—"

All Kelly could do was rush at him, grab him, and shut up his stupid wonderful talking mouth with a kiss.

"So why the stars?" she asked him later that night. She would never have imagined this scenario in her quest to invent an engagement story. She saw now that the problem with all the other stories she had told was that they were about Ethan, but they hadn't come from him.

Ethan shrugged. "It seemed appropriate. When I think of stars, I think of you."

"Same here," Kelly said, snuggling back against him as they lounged in bed, still watching the citrus-colored light washing over the ceiling. "You're the one who showed them all to me."

"Oh no." Ethan stiffened a little, looking as if he was struggling to understand something. "It's the opposite. Before you, I had never even seen the stars."

twenty-one

. . . . . .

Kelly might have lost the battle to tame her mother's urge to build a winter wedding mood board, but there was one more person whom she could still warn off throwing herself into this wedding full tilt. And so as Kelly headed to the dry cleaner's on a Saturday, driving past strip malls full of nail salons and taquerias, she called up Clara. She hesitated for an instant before starting with, "What are you doing?"

"Just heading into work," replied Clara.

"Really? You don't usually work on Saturdays."

"It's busy season. And I wanted to get out of the house. So what's up?" Clara's voice had an edge to it that wasn't usually there, something hurried and verging on testy.

"It's about the wedding. You know how Mom's crazy with this stuff, and she's determined to plan everything right now, even though we don't even have an official date, so she's starting to get into bridesmaid outfits and all that, and with you as the maid of honor, or matron, which sounds hideous, so let's say 'maid'—you would still want to be maid of honor, right? I know you always said you would." Kelly finished with a sudden nervous laugh.

"Sure, of course."

"Right. She's already thinking about asking the wedding party to buy shoes and everything, and I just wanted to get to you first and tell you to hold off. All of this is premature. So don't let her hassle you into buying hundred-dollar shoes or let her show up at your place at midnight for a dress fitting or anything crazy like that." Kelly knew that Clara loved her job at a vintage boutique, but also that it didn't pay well. She hated to think of her wasting money on the non-wedding.

"Right, I won't."

After a strained pause, Kelly tumbled on. "It's just that I know how much you love this wedding stuff and how excited you get, and I appreciate your help in advance, but just don't get too into it, okay? You don't need to do that much."

"Oh good," Clara said, relief making her voice animated for the first time in the call. "Because I was meaning to tell you, I just don't have that much time right now to give to the wedding, between work and—and everything. And I don't have much money, since I just spent a ton on my own wedding. So this actually helps me out."

"Oh." Kelly felt unaccountably disappointed. She didn't want Clara dispensing time and money into the wedding, but that didn't mean she wanted Clara *not* to want to. "Are you—aren't you excited at all about it?"

"Of course I am, Kel," Clara said hurriedly. "I just pulled up at work, can we talk later?"

"Sure. I mean, we don't really need to, I guess."

"Okay. Bye, Kel." Clara was gone. Kelly looked at the phone in her hand in confusion. What had happened to her bubbly little sister? Was there something going on with her? Was she angry at Kelly? Kelly thought back to her dismissal of the notion that Clara would take offense at Kelly announcing her own engagement the day after her wedding. It seemed uncommonly petty of her. But maybe Kelly didn't know her sister as well as she had thought.

She called Priya while waiting in line at the dry cleaner's, hoping for some reassurance. But it wasn't forthcoming. "I just don't get why Clara not being interested is an issue," Priya said. "The wedding's not even happening."

"I know, it's just—" Kelly shifted to pull her ticket out of her purse. "I guess it's not an issue. I don't know, we can talk about it Monday."

"I'll try; I'm going to be in meetings with Dr. Hanover most of the day."

"Oh. Right. Talk to you whenever, then." Kelly had never set much store in horoscopes, but when she got off the phone, she wondered if her stars were crossed.

Kelly tried to focus on the lines of code on the computer screen in front of her, but it was pretty hard to ignore Confibot on the other side of the room. The robot finally had a face now, but it was every kind of wrong. "Good morning," he said pleasantly when she entered a command on her computer. Then suddenly his face morphed to an image of profound concern—or was it anger? It was hard to say, but his eyebrows angled with the severity of a mountain peak. "Are you ready for your medications?" Of course, his eyebrows were kind of a mess to start with. And his whole face. His eyes looked too large for his nose, his mouth too wide to be human.

With less than a month to go until the presentation, Kelly had given in and thrown all her paint on the canvas at once, so to speak. She had chosen every element of how Confibot presented himself to match what seemed best according to her research, micromanaging each intonation and reaction according to the data she had amassed. But the final result was a mishmash of features and expressions. He veered wildly from surprise to care to disappointment, his voice and gestures seeming at every moment to be trying to do too many things at once. She didn't need a statistical analysis to tell her that the whole thing was a disaster. The more time she spent with Ethan, the more she cared for him and witnessed his intelligence and sensitivity, the more she realized the enormity of the responsibility she bore in designing this new robotic person, and the more she dug into the data, determined to get this right.

Being with Ethan also made her wonder how she was going so off base with Confibot. She was putting so much more thought and analysis into him than she had into Ethan, whom she had thrown together in a frenzy of instinct and excitement. Shouldn't Confibot be that much more amazing? Sure, there were differences: Confibot, as a caregiver, had certain specific functionalities that Ethan lacked, and she had used some of the parts she'd already built for Confibot to create Ethan. But she knew that those factors weren't enough to explain the disparity.

Her phone buzzed on her desk. Her mom was texting again. All morning Diane had been asking whether she could count on Priya for a bridesmaid dress fitting that Saturday. Kelly had been avoiding an answer based on the small fact that she had not yet informed

Priya that she needed her to pretend to be a bridesmaid. She could only imagine how that conversation would go. Actually, no, she couldn't. She was trying her hardest not to imagine that specific thing. She ignored the text.

She entered a search term on her computer and pulled up an article she had bookmarked on vocal registers, skimming through the lines for some sort of answer, something she could grab on to to make an evidence-based decision for Confibot . . .

Her phone buzzed again. "Oh, come on, Mom," she muttered, snatching it off the desk. But Diane's latest text was not about the dress fitting.

I'm putting a deposit down on a florist.

"No, no," Kelly groaned.

Please hold off, she hurriedly typed. Before she could even set the phone down and look back at her work, it buzzed again.

We've got to lock him in, the man's a wizard with forsythia. And since you clearly got my other texts, I'll see Priya on Saturday.

Kelly dug her fingers into the hair at her temples. She couldn't manage her own wedding. She couldn't manage her own project at work. She couldn't do anything. She looked at her browser, with so many tabs of research open that they extended out beyond the right border of the window, on and on forever. Everything she'd done was wrong. She had to start over.

She snatched a scalpel from a rack of tools on the wall, stormed over to Confibot, and dug in, cutting his face off with a clean oval line, leaving a ghastly mass of exposed wires surrounding two bulging eyeballs and a set of teeth. "There. That's better," she asserted stubbornly. She located the trash can across the room and threw the face into it. It was useless to her; she'd have to start over.

229

Robbie opened the door just in time to see a flabby silicone face sail past him in midair. In a testament to his rigid unflappability, he didn't even blink. "Ah, Kelly, here you are. Would you care to accompany me to the lab?" There was an odd brightness in his eyes.

"It's not a good time, Robbie," she said, her breath rough.

"I promise not to occupy too much of your time."

"I'll come by later," she said, looking away from him and back to Confibot. She was already regretting her impassioned display, and she had so many more important things to focus on right now than whatever it was Robbie wanted to show her. Knowing him, it was probably the extremely concerning appearance of a minuscule new scratch on the stainless-steel lab counter.

"You need to come now." Kelly looked at him. His voice was sharper, more commanding than she had ever heard it. "Oh—okay." She stepped out to follow him, bewildered.

As they strode down the hall together, she made it a point to walk quickly to illustrate her haste. "I really do have to be quick about this, Robbie."

"It will take as long as it takes" was all he said. Once in the lab, he smoothly shut the door and brought her over to one of the workstations. "This is what I'm working with right now. Tell me what you think."

As soon as Kelly bent over the computer to look at the simulation, she was confused. "That looks exactly like Ethan."

She glanced up at Robbie, whose prim expression was cracking irresistibly into pride and excitement. "You said it, not me," he said in a voice nearly strangled with his own delight.

She stood back, bewildered. "What's going on?"

"Don't rush me"—he held up a hand firmly—"I've been working toward this for some time."

Robbie sprang to the racks of manufactured body parts and marched alongside them, gesturing. "I've been noticing for a while now that there are parts missing from the lab. An eyelid here, a pinky nail there. A less astute observer would have just brushed it off. But I started to wonder—where had they all gone? Could there be a connection? So last night, I stayed here until four a.m." Kelly briefly wondered if she had actually encountered the one human who had less of a life than she did. "And I figured out exactly what was missing. Every last piece. And when I joined all the parts together into a digital model, this is what I got." He gestured grandly to the screen. Point made.

Kelly felt sick. But it was just Robbie, she told herself. She could get out of this. Right? "Okay, so there's a lot of stuff missing from the lab. Why would that have anything to do with me? There are thousands of parts here and dozens of people coming in and out and using them. Things are going to go missing or get out of place. It's called 'entropy.'"

"Things that just happen to add up to your fiancé?"

"It doesn't even look that much like him."

He pulled out his phone, pressed a button, and her own recorded voice played back to her. "That looks exactly like Ethan."

"Checkmate," Robbie said simply.

twenty-two

. . . . . .

Robbie slipped his phone back into his pocket, waiting for Kelly's response. As angry as she was about what he was doing to her, the priggishness in his voice was even more enraging. His face was bright with triumph, proud and yet somehow self-conscious at the same time.

"What are you suggesting, Robbie? If you're saying I stole parts from the lab, you don't have any proof." Even voicing the word "stole" out loud made her stomach lurch like a drunk ballerina. Borrowed, she corrected herself—she had borrowed the parts.

"I'd say this is more than enough to justify an investigation. Did you really think I wouldn't realize that something was off? You didn't want anyone to know when you got engaged, with a gaudy ring that he couldn't possibly afford on an associate professor salary. Oh yes, I've done my research. You thought that you could just waltz in here telling me you were marrying a robot and expect me not to notice? You always underestimated my observational capacities! You thought I wouldn't see the plot twist coming in that movie we watched, but I saw it! I knew she was his daughter all along!"

Kelly had never seen Robbie like this before. His whole face was an alarming pink. Even more alarming, he was, for once, displaying actual emotion.

She backed nervously toward the door. "Okay, well, thank you, Robbie, this was all very—educational. I'm sure we both need to get back to work now."

"You go ahead. I'm going to message this image to Anita."

Kelly halted. "What are you trying to do, blackmail me?"

"I suppose you could call it that, if you wanted to be reductive." He moved around the lab, closing a half-open drawer, straightening a sign, clearly relishing the suspense, his total power over her decisions. "I want . . ." He stopped to face her decisively. "Body parts."

Kelly recoiled. "Robbie, I will not commit a murder for you."

"Not from a human, from a robot. If you need help distinguishing the difference, let me know." He smirked, nodding toward the picture of Ethan. "Any part I want, when I want it, delivered on time," he added, like the announcer in some gruesome ad campaign.

"So you want me to build random robotic parts for you?" Kelly asked.

"Ah, well, I'm not so sure about the 'build' part. On time, remember? You'll have to pull them from your existing builds."

"You want me to take parts out of Confibot to give to you?"

"Where you get them from is your choice. I trust you'll figure that out."

Through Kelly's shock, she started to realize how little this made sense. She would have pegged Robbie as the type to run straight to the teacher to tattle, not plot blackmail for personal gain. And crazy or not, he was clearly intelligent enough to concoct a more effective plan than this one. He couldn't use the parts from her builds in Brahma. And if he was hoping to hamper her progress and push her out of the running in the investor competition, it would be much faster and easier to simply expose her to Anita now. But she wasn't about to point that out to him. She inched toward the door, hoping to get out of the room before he figured it out. Or flipped his evidently precarious lid completely.

"All right, whatever you say," she placated. "Is there anything else?"

He cocked his head, considering. "Not at the moment, thank you. I'll let you know."

Kelly wasn't even sure how she made it from the lab back to the testing room. Suddenly, or maybe it was really finally, everything was crashing down. Robbie knew about Ethan. He had the power to end everything with the lift of a finger: Kelly's job, her entire career, Ethan himself. There was something nauseating about the whole situation. It felt like plunging into an ice bath: Kelly could no longer deny who, or what, Ethan was.

She threw open the door to the control room, the breeze of its motion whipping her hair back. Catching sight of Confibot, she groaned. She had almost forgotten what she just did to him. "Ugh, motherfucker!"

"I believe the usual greeting is 'hello.'" For an instant Kelly thought that Confibot, the loose cannon that he was, had assumed a female voice. Then, to her horror, she saw that it was Anita speaking, sitting behind the control panel, her legs crossed, her long-fingered hands draped across her knees with the serenity of a dove's folded wings. But a reptilian fire glinted from her eyes.

"Anita, I—I didn't realize you were here."

"Yes, I concluded as much. I came by to ascertain your progress on Confibot." She gestured to the android, his gaping face absurd above his trim body in his neat shirt and khakis.

"I'm further along than it looks," Kelly said desperately, inching to the side to block Anita's view of the discarded face in the trash, but Anita simply pointed at the chair opposite her.

"Sit," she instructed. Kelly did, crossing her own legs then quickly uncrossing them and settling into her chair with a loud squeak, turning the whole moment into an unnecessary comedy of errors.

Anita raked her with her eyes, searching, evaluating. Kelly was just about to inject the uncomfortable silence with something, anything, when Anita spoke instead.

"Why do you think I am the way I am?"

There was literally no good answer to that question. What was the way Anita was? If Kelly said powerful or successful or intelligent, it would sound sycophantic. But voicing the adjectives she was really thinking would be even worse.

She gaped, flummoxed, and Anita was losing patience. "Okay, let me put this another way. How many Hispanic women run companies in Silicon Valley?"

At least this time, Kelly thought she could hazard an answer. "One?" she returned tentatively.

"One. You have the privilege of working under her. It has not been easy to ascend from the child of immigrant factory workers to the position I hold today, Kelly. Being ruthless is my survival mode. To get here and to stay here, I have subtracted everyone and every-thing from my life that is not me. Don't think that it ever gets easier. Don't think that you can rest in your position. And don't think that I will hesitate to subtract you if you stand in the way of my personal success."

Kelly gulped. "I know, you're right—I'm really trying here—"

"No, you're not. What more do you need me to give you, Kelly? Have I not provided you with all of the tools you need to complete your project?"

"Yes, you have."

"Have I not furnished you with state-of-the-art facilities?" Anita gestured around the workspace, the touch-pad controllers, the banks of slick computers.

"Yes."

"Did I not give you a top-notch consultant, one of the highest-paid psychologists in the country? Do you not have a brain trust of other intelligent, eager individuals here at your disposal?"

"Yes," Kelly said, so quietly that it was barely audible even in the enclosed space.

"Yet here you are. So what is the problem?"

There was only one way to fill in the blank. "It's me," she an-swered.

Anita paused just long enough for Kelly's words to echo inside her own head. "I am pushing you, Kelly, not to be cruel, but because I think you can get it," she continued, her voice low and insistent. Her face contained something that could almost, in Kelly's compre-hensive files of microexpressions, have been classified as an emo-tion. "And so I will extend to you a benefit that I rarely extend. I will repeat myself. But don't expect me to say this a third time. Engineering is personal. It's collaborative. If you cannot handle the higher nuances of design, you will not be placed in a position to design your own project again." Anita unfolded her legs and strode from the room without a backward glance.

Of course Kelly debriefed Priya as soon as possible, appreciating the fact that she could talk freely now after having confessed to her about Ethan. When she reached the part about Robbie's dramatic blackmailing, Priya couldn't resist crowing triumphantly. "I knew it! I always knew he was loony underneath! How many times did I tell you to search his apartment for his mom's dressed-up body in a rocking chair?"

"What am I going to do, Priya?" Kelly groaned. "I don't have time to build random parts for Robbie whenever he asks, and I can't pull Confibot apart, not right before the competition. I'm already in hot water with Anita." She dragged on her temples in exasperation.

"I mean, you do already have another robot fully built," Priya pointed out.

Kelly shook her head vigorously. "No way. I'm not hurting Ethan like that. Besides, I can't pull him apart right before our wedding. What am I going to walk down the aisle to, a motherboard in a tux?"

"Wait, hold up, you're not actually planning on having a wedding, right?"

"No, it's just . . . you know." Kelly wrung her hands helplessly.

"No, I really don't." Priya was looking at her with an expression of confusion and disbelief probably very similar to the one Kelly had just shown Robbie. "What's going on, Kelly? I was worried about your job, but now I'm worried about your freaking *head*. Is this some kind of quarter-life crisis?"

"No!" Kelly cried. "I just want some support right now, not judgment, okay? I need . . . I need answers."

"I gave you an answer. You rejected it."

"Priya . . ."

"Come here." Priya folded her into a hug, patting her on the hair. "It's a good head. Don't lose it."

"I'll get out of this," Kelly grumbled, submitting to her hug.

"Of course you will. Let me know what I can do to help."

"Actually, there is one thing." Kelly pulled her head out and looked up at Priya hopefully.

"Name it."

"Will you be my bridesmaid?"

"Not that." Priya crossed her arms.

"Come on, you said that you wished you had been involved in this whole Ethan thing. Here's your chance." Kelly hoped that her bright voice was convincing to Priya, because she was struggling to convince herself.

"Okay, maybe in the beginning this whole dealio would have been fun, but now it's, like, a little too real-life-bad-Lifetime-movie for my taste."

"All you have to do is let my mom take your measurements for the dress." Kelly clasped her hands together, pleading. "She keeps insisting on doing it Saturday and it's so soon, I don't have time to fix the whole thing before then."

"Well, I don't have time to spend my Saturday getting measured for a fake dress. Monday's the deadline for turning in my prototype to Dr. Hanover. I was at my desk until eleven last night."

She did look wiped. Kelly couldn't recall if she had forgotten about Priya's deadline, or if she had even known it was coming up. She realized now that she hadn't talked to Priya much about her work lately, or about her personal life, for that matter. Whenever they did get a chance to chat, the conversations were usually dominated by discussion of Ethan. Maybe that was why Priya had been sounding a bit edgy lately. "You should have told me, I was here till nine."

"Yeah," Priya said listlessly. "It's not like I had anywhere else to be last night anyway." She carefully turned her face from Kelly, scrolling on her phone. "Andre and I are—I don't know. We had a fight over the weekend and we haven't spoken since, but we never officially said we were breaking up."

"I'm sorry, Pri. That sucks."

"It's whatever. We never officially said we were together anyway." Priya laughed hollowly. But then she threw her hands up with sudden animation. "But I don't even know what I did wrong! I went to see him do stand-up and when he asked what I thought of the show, all I did was tell him. It's not my fault that all his race jokes were derivative. I thought he wanted honest feedback." Kelly put a hand on her arm in solidarity.

"I'm too blunt, aren't I?" Priya asked. "It's why I chase everyone away. I thought I finally had someone who got me, who, like, *got* me, and knew that I mean well, and now I've screwed that up too." She paused before murmuring, uncharacteristically quiet, "It just sucks. I really liked him, Kelly."

"Let's go out this weekend!" Kelly exclaimed. "We'll drink away our woes and you can let other guys hit on you and make you feel better." Her loathing for going out was unabated, but she wanted to cheer her friend up. "I'll bring Ethan! You still haven't properly met him."

"Ooh, yes!" Priya said, some of her spark returning. "How is he with people staring at him creepily and asking him, like, five million questions in a row? Because I have a lot of questions."

"He'll love it. Maybe we can go after the bridesmaid dress fitting?" she said hopefully. "I'll text you the time?"

Priya sighed deeply. "Can't wait," she said drily.

All that afternoon while Kelly was at work, she was thinking about getting home to Ethan. But once she got home, somehow the sight of him was not the balm she'd hoped for. Maybe it was because she didn't truly feel as if she'd left work behind—her head swarmed with painful flashbacks of the day—her struggles with Confibot, Anita's cutting words, Priya's weariness. Robbie had made good on his threat, already demanding body parts from her throughout the afternoon, making her feel as if she were manning a butcher's counter. The more she thought about the specificity of his blackmail, the more she fumed. He had to know what he was doing; after all, he knew exactly which parts had gone into Ethan, she recalled darkly, envisioning the reconstructed image on Robbie's computer. This wasn't just a direct attack on her progress with Confibot. This was an assault on Ethan. And to add insult to injury, he had paraded through the engineers' floor that afternoon with Brahma, casually asking the robot to fetch him things and open doors for him with his too-many arms—only to "test the technology," of course. Then whenever Robbie wasn't contacting Kelly, Diane was, unleashing a slow yet relentless trickle of e-mails containing forwards of magazine articles profiling her chosen florist's artistry, reminding her threateningly that if they didn't put down a deposit soon they would lose their window with this man—this maestro who had single-handedly revitalized the carnation.

So what Kelly really needed from Ethan was a distraction, and he just wasn't providing it. "How was your day?" she asked him as she lugged a bag of takeout through the door. She was getting home late so regularly now that their cooking nights had gone by the wayside.

"It was all right, how was yours?" He grabbed the food and began setting out plates.

"Hellacious. What did you do all day?"

"What do you mean, 'hellacious'?" Ethan set down the napkins he was holding, looking at her with concern.

Kelly waved a hand. "It's nothing, just a rough day. So what did you do?"

"Kelly, you have to tell me what happened. Maybe I can help."

"I don't want to talk about it!" That came out roughly. She backtracked. "I appreciate the offer, but it's work stuff; there's nothing you can do. I want to forget about it. Tell me something new."

Ethan looked up a few degrees, searching through his brain. "Well, today in Syria, the rebels . . ."

Kelly poured herself a very full glass of wine, listening as he dutifully read her the news. She shouldn't have snapped at Ethan, she knew. This was her time to put work behind her and finally enjoy a few peaceful hours at home. Time to just have a normal night in. She emptied half her glass in one gulp.

Her phone buzzed in her pocket like a hovering wasp: a demand from Robbie for an eyeball, shade 009. Kelly knew without even logging into the database that their lab had only created one set of irises in this shade because it was such a rare, crystal blue. And that set was currently on the other side of the kitchen, looking through the silverware drawer for a set of forks.

Kelly squeezed her own eyes shut, steadying herself. She was so tired. To build a new eye from scratch would take hours, and the last thing she wanted to do tonight was to drive back to the office and fire up the 3-D printer. In fact, at the moment she was feeling like she never wanted to go back to the office again. She wondered if anyone would hire her to sit at home and eat takeout for the next sixty-odd years.

"Do you want soy sauce?" Ethan turned and looked at her with those eyes—those eyes that she could so easily take out and use if she just powered him down temporarily. Immediately she cursed herself for even entertaining such a barbaric thought.

"Um, yeah," she answered, a second too late.

Kelly couldn't kid herself. This wasn't just a normal night in. If it were, she wouldn't be in this position in the first place. Priya had been clear today about what she thought Kelly should do, and anyone else looking in on the situation would say the same thing, anyone with a shred of rationality. The only thing that made sense was to get rid of Ethan. She could do it tonight. Her stresses over Robbie would dissipate—he would never be able to prove anything with her creation disassembled. The wedding would be called off, the growing difficulty of restraining her mom from planning too much would disappear, the tensions with her sister would dissolve. She could focus her energies where they were truly needed, on Confibot and her family and Priya. She could get a solid night's sleep at some point before her exhausted brain rebelled and abandoned her for good.

As Ethan opened the refrigerator to pull out the filtered water pitcher, a flash of blue caught her eye from the fridge door. "What's that?" She walked closer to take a look. There, tacked to the front of the fridge, was the blue ribbon she had won at her sixth-grade science fair, the one neither parent had attended.

Ethan smiled shyly. "I was wondering when you'd notice. I found it in an old box when I was straightening up the closet. I thought we should celebrate your achievement, Madame Scientist." He circled his hand in front of him in a mock bow.

Here he was, pinning her ribbon to the fridge like a proud parent. Kelly wanted so badly to thank him, to throw her arms around his neck and kiss his sweet, smiling face. But instead she froze. She knew that this all had to stop, that every thoughtful gesture he made and every moment where she allowed herself to sink into his warm affection was a step down a ladder into a dark well. How foolish had she been to let things get this far? She couldn't allow herself to enjoy this moment and tell him how happy he'd made her. Yet she couldn't—she just couldn't—get rid of him. She was trapped in the middle.

"I actually forgot something at the office. I have to head back," she said, forcing herself to be cold, though the words felt like vomiting a knife.

Ethan's happy face fell into confusion. "Oh, sure, no problem." He hastily snatched the ribbon down, looking embarrassed. "I can keep dinner warm and wait up."

"Don't worry about it, I'm not hungry." She hurried to the door to get her purse and shoes so she could leave without looking at him, before she could change her mind.

On Saturday, Kelly was so sleep-deprived from the extra hours she was now devoting to Robbie's demands on top of Confibot that she woke in a fog so deep she briefly wondered if this was the afterlife. Now, as much as she longed to lounge at home all day in her favorite yoga pants, in which she had never actually done yoga, she pulled herself from bed. It was time for her and Priya's appointment at the shop. She had barely set foot in her mom's boutique when an armload of fabric swatches marched toward her, succeeded by Diane.

"All right, now," Diane said, clipped and professional. She was in her element, a bridal business blizzard, ready to Get. It. Done. "If we're talking December, I'm thinking winter whites. Now, I know what you're thinking: white is for the bride. And you are absolutely correct. But I saw this spread in *I Do* where the bridesmaids all wore white, but accessorized in an accent color. You know, sashes, statement necklaces, heels, all of that. It looked so cute and they did not take away from the bride at all, trust me, you're just going to be gorgeous and it's really all about how you pose people in pictures anyway, speaking of which, I've been talking to the photographer who shot the new McRib campaign. What do you think?"

As Diane thrust three virtually identical fabric samples into her face at that moment, Kelly wasn't sure whether her mother wanted a verdict on the swatches or the McRib photographer, but she had mixed feelings on both. She blinked hard, trying to force herself to be fully awake, and asked if her mom had any coffee. She was going to need it.

Twenty minutes and five thousand shades of winter white later, Kelly checked her watch for the third time. Still no Priya. Pulling out her phone, she saw that she had a missed call. "And we must not lose sight of the fact that Kate Middleton served a fruitcake," her mom was declaring.

"I've got to call Priya," Kelly interrupted, "find out where she is."

"All right, all right, and tell her to hurry. I need time to take close-ups of her complexion to integrate them into my vision board."

Kelly dialed as she stepped outside. "Where are you? I've been watching my mom go through fabric samples for twenty minutes. She has more shades of white than Congress."

"Don't hate me, Kelly." Priya's voice came through tentatively. "But I'm not coming."

"What? Did something happen?"

"No, I'm fine, it's just that I thought about it last night, and I can't do this. I can't participate in this wedding."

"We already talked about this, you said you'd help me out. You said you'd be here."

"Well, I shouldn't have. I can't just go along with this and act like everything's great and it's some normal, happy wedding. It's not. You're in way over your head, Kelly, and I'm afraid you're going to get hurt. I've tried telling you to end it and you haven't. I'm doing this for you, I promise, I'm trying to help."

Kelly could feel the blood racing to her cheeks. "Oh, really? Standing me up and humiliating me in front of my mother, that's how you're going to help? Remind me never to ask you for a favor again."

Priya exploded. "I shouldn't have to keep telling you to not fuck

246

up your own life! You're smarter than this. *I'm* the one who gets to fuck up, not you."

Kelly's thoughts began to take shape from her red haze of emotion. Priya was saying that she had good intentions. And someone else looking in might say that she really was helping Kelly. But all of Kelly's past data, collected over thirty years of relationship experiences, told her that it was wisest, safest, to assume the worst: that Priya was really embarrassed that she'd gotten mixed up in this "abnormal" wedding, was embarrassed of Kelly. For months now, the trajectory of their friendship had been increasingly southward. Option A, reconciliation, would inevitably end in more betrayal. Option B, a swift termination of the whole entanglement, would, in the long run, reduce the sum of pain for them both. And so for the second time in a week, she forced herself to be cold.

"Exactly," Kelly said into the phone. "You're the one who fucks up, so who are you to judge me?"

Priya laughed, a sour, ragged laugh Kelly had never heard before. "Right. At least I had a real boyfriend. I didn't have to build one."

A hollow stillness followed—Priya had hung up. Kelly could almost feel her ear pulsing with the strength of the blood pounding through it, the pressure from where she had pushed the phone painfully close. She dragged herself back into the shop to face her mother.

"Is she close?" Diane demanded. "I don't have all day."

"Just forget about the bridesmaid dresses for now, okay?" Kelly replied wearily. "I don't need bridesmaids." After all, aside from her sister, Priya had been her only one.

twenty-three

. . . .

Kelly was prepared to leave her mother's shop, but Diane sighed noisily through her nose, pulling a measuring tape and clipboard from behind the counter. "Well, come here, then."

"What for?"

"I have to get your measurements, of course." When Kelly still stared at her blankly, she went on as if it were the most obvious thing in the world. "For your dress. Did you think Priya would be the only one wearing clothing to the wedding?"

"You want to make my dress?" As soon as she asked the question, Kelly realized she probably should have seen this coming. After all, her mother had made Clara's wedding dress and was managing every other aspect of the wedding. The type of dress she usually saw unspool from her mother's hands was so not her that she had occluded the entire possibility of wearing such a dress from her mind. But now here it was in front of her, obvious, unavoidable.

"Of course I'm making it." Diane was eyeing Kelly's body strategically. She unspooled the measuring tape and went in for the bust, but Kelly backed away.

"I appreciate it, but you don't need to do that. It's way too much work."

Diane smiled. "Too much work was when I spent eleven hours squeezing your grapefruit-size head out of my vagina. After that, I just gave in. I was already in too deep."

She moved forward with the tape measure and Kelly backed away again until she nearly bumped against a display table.

Diane raised an eyebrow. "Do you not want me to make your dress?"

"No, that's not it—"

"Do you not trust me to do a good job? Do you not realize that this is my life's work and that brides drive in for miles for my custom creations? That you're getting the culmination of my years of talent and experience for free?"

"I know you're good at what you do, it's just—"

"My own daughter. I'm a professional wedding gown designer, and my own daughter doesn't want me to make her gown." On a dime, Diane switched from rage to teary-voiced piteousness. "I guess you don't need me."

She started to retract the tape, managing to infuse the small gesture with drama, like a sad French clown, but Kelly sighed and lifted her arms. "Go ahead."

Instantly cheered, Diane went to work, looping and stretching and penciling notes on her clipboard. "What a week. Work's been piling up at the store, and I've been trying this new face mask, they call it a 'skin tar' and I have no clue what that means but it's sixty dollars so it must do something, and oh goodness, speaking of, maybe you could use some, you're not looking so great, Kelly." Diane took the opportunity of proximity to peer intently into Kelly's weary face.

"I'm fine, it's just, you know, wedding stress."

"Yes, but where's the wedding radiance? That should mask the stress."

This from a woman putting sixty-dollar tar on her face, Kelly thought. "I don't know what you're talking about. Nobody knows what that is."

Diane pulled back in astonishment. "Of course they do! All brides feel it—that excitement, that little tingle every time you think about the wedding, or about the man you're marrying. Don't you feel that?"

Kelly hesitated. What she felt when she thought about the wedding was more akin to the sensation that comes about twenty minutes after eating a hot dog from a gas station.

"You don't have to do it, you know."

Kelly was confused by her mom's words. "What?"

"The wedding. If you don't feel right about it, don't do it. I've always told you to be less picky with men, but that doesn't mean you shouldn't listen to your gut." Did Kelly's mom really just say that? The wedding queen? Maybe it was just a veiled insult about her gut. Diane rambled on casually as she measured and calculated. "Of course, I would love to have Ethan as a son-in-law, he seems like just a doll, and he's about the best-looking man I've ever seen. He looks like Prince Eric from *The Little Mermaid*. Remember when you girls took a picture with Eric at Disneyland and he just insisted on taking a picture with me too? So cheeky . . . but the point is, what I want most is for you to be happy."

"Oh. Wow, um, thanks," Kelly said.

"You don't have to sound so surprised. I'm your mother, after all." Diane hesitated and looked up, meeting Kelly's eyes. "This is important, you know. Maybe the most important decision you'll ever make." Of course, Kelly thought now, nothing could ever define her more than the man she was with. "You want to be sure. Calling off a wedding is hard, but living with decades of regret is harder."

Kelly felt a swift and inexplicable jolt of emotion, coming from something she couldn't name and that she hadn't even known was there. It wasn't hard to see that her parents' marriage was disappointing. But her mom had always seemed oblivious. She celebrated her marriage, baking heart-shaped Valentine's cakes, selecting flowery return address labels that pronounced her "Mrs. Carl Suttle." She gossiped about her divorcing friends with an air of high charity, as if grateful that such troubles never rippled her pond. But perhaps she insisted so loudly on the success of her own marriage not because she truly believed in it, but because it was too painful to think otherwise.

Kelly had always found it a little pathetic that her mom spouted "happily ever after" nonsense all day to gullible young brides, then went home to a life of rigid cohabitation. But to still believe in the dream, in spite of everything—there was something brave in that. In a flash, it struck her that both she and Diane were women who buried themselves in work, who had found success in business but much less so in relationships. It was her worst fear realized: that she was not so different from her own mom. But the dark diagnosis had a layer of comfort. Diane's relentless pressure for Kelly to get matched up had long been a source of irritation and self-doubt. But to insist, even in the loudest, the most grating, the most repetitive of voices, that her daughter have better than she had—that was a form of love.

"But of course, it's probably just nerves," Diane continued, lassoing Kelly around the hips with the tape. "You always did let your nerves get in the way of your enjoyment. Ooh, I'm getting such good ideas for this dress. I'll have to order more fabric than I had anticipated. I may be overdoing myself. But I can't wait!" She gave an excited squeal.

That brought Kelly right back down. She was going to have to try on something that looked like the shearings of a whole dog show's worth of white poodles. At least that sort of thing always seemed to sell well in her mother's shop. She consoled herself that once she revealed she didn't need it, her mom would find some other female who actually loved it, and the labor wouldn't have been for naught.

After receiving Diane's strict instructions to do something about those dark circles, Kelly drove north on the freeway to home. She had slowed to a crawl, sandwiched between a beat-up purple Volvo with ironic bumper stickers and a Bugatti. Last year she had tried some self-enrichment app that promised to "free the fighter within." The app had included an exercise in which the user attempted to make decisions by scrutinizing his own physical reactions to an idea. She had gotten frustrated with it at the time, branding it as silly and turning it off. But now she tried the technique again on her own. What did she feel when she thought about her mom making her dress? A twisting in her stomach, a twitch at the corners of her mouth that could be excitement or could be frustration. What did she feel when she thought about the wedding? The twist moved up to her heart, sharpening her breath, accelerating her heartbeat toward panic—best not to linger on that one while she was driving.

What did she feel when she thought about Ethan? And there it was—that tingle. She pulled up Waze on her phone to check how many minutes it was until she got home.

Kelly knew that she should spend the rest of that weekend doing something productive, like putting in extra work on Confibot, or finally organizing that pile of old paperwork that had been sitting in the corner of her bedroom for so long its bottom layers were a different color than the top. Or getting rid of Ethan. She should be distancing herself from him, not spending more time with him. But after a week that was basically "brought to you by the creators of your own nightmares," she just wanted to have a nice day. No pressure, no work, no wedding talk. Just the two of them and the world.

Kelly had always heard legends of the natural opportunities afforded to residents of the San Francisco Bay Area where she had been born and bred. She had always been indoorsy herself, but supposedly there was this thing called the beach? Maybe some mountains? Despite having lived there her entire life, Kelly had to make heavy use of TripAdvisor, Lonely Planet, and WebMD to plan a day of outdoor activities in her own hometown. She would be her own judge of this "fresh air" thing.

"I didn't realize you liked the beach," Ethan mused as Kelly finally found parking. "Why haven't we gone more often?"

"You'll see once I bring out the sunscreen," she said.

Ethan spent a good ten minutes coating every inch and crevice Kelly didn't even know she had with an SPF higher than her credit score. Even with a water shirt on to cover his back panel, Ethan attracted some stares from other beachgoers, male and female, as he set up shop, arranging their towels and beach bag, while Kelly rubbed on some high-SPF lip balm, just in case. Then they stared at each other.

"What do we do now?" he asked.

"I think we . . . go in."

Ethan mimicked her cautious pace as he followed her into the water, an inch at a time. Kelly hadn't done this in years. The face-numbing cold instantly reminded her why. But her flesh started to unfreeze as she forced herself to stay under, wading around a little. Actually, it was kind of nice.

"Are you having fun?" Ethan asked.

"Yeah, I am."

"Are you all right? Do you need more sunscreen? I can go back and get it." He made as if to return to shore, but she pulled him back.

"Stop, I'm fine. Just stay out here with me."

Kelly looked out across the stripes of water undulating toward them, one after another, almost musical in their rhythmic succession. But Ethan was looking at her. "You're beautiful," he said. "Your hair—"

"What? Oh." She fingered her hair; she could feel its natural waves returning in the sea spray. "I'll straighten it out again later, it can't be helped right now."

"No." He reached out and stroked it gently. "This is good."

There was something about being surrounded on all sides by ocean water, supported by it, that made everything else feel impossibly far away. San Jose became Atlantis. The fluorescent-lit offices of AHI were a legend unconfirmed. The orange light of happiness melted all the way to Kelly's toes. She flicked the water playfully at Ethan and he laughed, splashing her back.

That afternoon they went hiking, or struggle-walking in Kelly's case, in the rolling foothills near Mount Hamilton. Ethan let her lead the precarious way up a path winding along the side of a steep hill, the air tingling with the smells of clean, fine-grained dirt and silvery desert plants. Kelly was starting to regret this choice—her calves were not used to exercise that didn't involve getting into or out of a chair—but she pushed forward. They emerged onto an overlook.

Seldom was the sound of traffic so far off—it was more of a hum here, a feeling rather than a noise. A panorama of red hills, spotted with tough shrubs and spiky, geometric growths, stretched from horizon to horizon, the peaks dipping toward and away from each other like waves frozen at their crest. It had been a long time since she had seen something so still.

"Isn't it beautiful?"

"It is beautiful," Ethan said. "Thank you for taking me with you here."

"You don't need to thank me." Kelly looked around, letting herself sink into the moment. She looked at Ethan. "Aren't you happy here?"

He smiled at her. "I am if you are."

What would her life be like after Ethan? In her first twenty-nine years, she had never found anything close to the intimacy she had with him. He was literally her perfect match. He picked up on her every desire and molded himself after it. But was making someone who became perfect for her the same as finding her perfect person? She thought back to all her hours of research on the health impacts of loneliness—the shorter life span, the dementia, the depression. She knew that finding love was challenging. She knew that she herself was not an easy person to love. She could imagine a version of herself going between her home and office, day in, day out, for years, until she could no longer go anywhere but home, living out her days on her own. Loneliness was a real and heavy threat. But was it enough to be with someone who molded himself after her desires? How could she know if he had any true desires of his own? Was it enough to be with someone if she wasn't sure if he was . . . someone?

Kelly tried to shake off the thoughts clogging her brain and just enjoy the moment. She turned from the view to search Ethan's face. But it was impossible to tell if the happiness on his face was more than a reflection of her own.

As the next week went on, it was easy enough for Kelly to push her decision about Ethan to the side. There were too many other demands on her attention at work, including those from Robbie. But when the weekend came, what should have been a pleasant, freeing emptiness just meant a lack of excuses. And so, on a sunny April Saturday, while Ethan did laundry in the next room, she slid into the computer chair at her home desk, a mug of coffee in hand, and opened a blank document. She needed to get organized, to make a plan. Writing out what she needed to do in logical, discrete steps might make the daunting process seem possible. "Complete step one" was much friendlier than "Kill your fiancé."

An hour later, she felt much better. She had her plan written out and pinned to the background of her phone. The list was neat, precise, and orderly, and she was right on schedule with Item A: the mother.

She had decided to give the "tell Mom that Ethan is moving away" tactic one more try. She straightened her shoulders within her pressed white button-down and breathed in through her nose before pushing open the boutique's door—an astringent, cleansing breath.

As soon as she entered her mother's shop, she felt out of sorts—the place always had that effect. But Kelly would not let that deter her. She was maintaining a clean mind. She was on a mission. Just like that time she had come here determined to tell her mom that Ethan was history and instead ended up with a fiancé. But she shoved the thought away—this time would be different. This time had to be different.

Her mother wasn't in the front area, but Kelly thought she heard a rustling in the back. She pushed past the pink-flowered curtain and saw Diane, back toward her, in the workshop, a small, square space cluttered with an impossible variety of fabrics, threads, and notions in a veritable rainbow of white.

"Hey, Mom," she said.

Diane turned, surprised. "Kelly! I didn't know you were coming over. What a nice surprise! You never just drop in. Is everything okay? You should have warned me." She edged in front of whatever she had been working on, blocking Kelly's view, fidgeting a bit.

Kelly focused herself with another cleansing breath and got straight to the point, in accordance with her plan. "There's something I need to tell you about Ethan," she began.

But Diane wasn't listening, still moving nervously, swishing some fabric behind her, which she seemed half determined to hide and half eager to show. "I wish I had known you were coming—it's really not ready for you to see yet. A lot of it is still just tacked in."

"What is?"

"Your dress."

"That's okay, I don't need to see it anyway. I need to tell you something." The last thing Kelly wanted right now was to have to find something nice to say about a dress that looked like a Pomeranian with a growth-inducing gland disorder.

But Diane didn't seem able to contain herself any longer. She moved aside. "What do you think?"

At first Kelly wasn't sure what she was looking at. Where was the solid shell of blinding crystals? Where was the giant skirt? Could it not fit in the room? Was this the slip? But the dress she was looking at was actually . . . lovely. It was as if Kelly, who had never in her life pictured what type of wedding dress she might like, was suddenly seeing the exact dress she'd dreamed of all along. Soft, ivory silk flowed from the modest straps into a lightly fitted bodice and then a trailing skirt. The V-neck and dipping back were complemented with delicate pearls. It was a bit flowier, a bit dreamier, than any garment Kelly typically found herself drawn to. Yet somehow, it was just right. When Kelly looked at the dress, she forgot entirely why she had come into the shop that day. All she could imagine was herself, in that dress, walking down the aisle toward Ethan.

"Well?" her mom asked anxiously. "I know it's simpler than what I usually design, but it just seemed like—you." And Kelly was amazed to see that her mother knew exactly who that "you" was.

"It's perfect," Kelly breathed.

Diane must have pumped some sort of brain-addling chemical through the vents of that godforsaken shop to impair all decision making. That was the only explanation for why Kelly had done this yet again. And for how her mom got women to spend fifty dollars on a garter belt. That night, she was back in her room, ostensibly writing the investor dossier for Confibot. But her eyes kept going out of focus as she stared at the screen. All she could think about was how she had landed herself back in the same boat with Ethan yet again—a boat that was unmoored, directionless, and about as seaworthy as a sieve. Her brain knew that she shouldn't keep Ethan; it was why she had gone to see her mother in the first place. But her heart was still refusing to listen.

Ethan knocked lightly on the open door, awakening her from gazing blankly at the computer, which had blinked into sleep mode. "Want me to start dinner?" he asked. "I'm assuming you want to stay in tonight and work."

"Yeah, sure," she said absently.

"Is everything all right?"

She waited a moment before replying, her eyes still raking the screen. "I got into a fight with Priya," she began slowly. She still hadn't told him. Scrunching the whole business back into the corners of her brain made it so much easier to deal with.

"Over what?" He came and sat on the edge of the bed as she rotated her chair to face him.

"Over—" She had been about to say "Over you," but a sense of delicacy held her back. "Just work stuff," she continued. "She was supposed to show up for something for me and didn't. I mean, I guess she's asked me to do stuff too and I haven't. I've been so busy, I've kind of been in my own world."

"You work so hard," Ethan said consolingly. "It's remarkable you can make time for anyone else at all."

"Yeah, but I haven't been making enough time for work, either. I'm falling behind with Confibot."

"I have some great articles on productivity I could read to you.

There's one about structuring your day in triangles to achieve maximum efficiency; it's fascinating—"

Kelly waved him off. "I don't have time to read articles on saving time. What would really gain me some time is if I could get my mom to back off with the wedding planning stuff, but I feel like I've already been kind of rough on her lately, and she is doing a lot. She's only trying to help."

"And you're only trying to take care of the things you need to take care of," Ethan responded sagely.

"But that's not how my mom sees it," Kelly insisted. "Not everyone is as nice and as reasonable as you. Pretty much no one is."

"You are."

"No, I'm not!" Kelly wasn't sure why she felt such a need to make him understand this. His compliments weren't helping. No matter how sincerely he believed them, she knew that they weren't true. She had always felt that Ethan understood her more than anyone, that she could show him sides of herself that she normally hid away. He knew her as well as she knew herself. But maybe that was the problem. His ability to judge her came *from* her. As innately rational as he was, he was still predisposed, more and more as time went on and he was around her, to understand her perspective and support it no matter what. She began to wonder if she would ever be able to grow in a relationship with someone who was so close to her. There was a fine line between closeness and being closed in.

"You're too hard on yourself." He reached out and smoothed her hair; she caught his wrist affectionately as his hand came to rest in the nape of her neck.

"Why don't you get started on dinner? I'll join you in a minute," she said quietly.

When Ethan left for the kitchen, she softly pushed the door until it was almost closed, picked her phone up from the desk, and retreated back to the far side of the room. There was no good reason why Ethan shouldn't hear her conversation. Still, she felt sensitive about it.

"How did the farmer find his sheep in the tall grass?" Gary asked as soon as he picked up the phone. He waited a long beat for Kelly to say something, but she didn't, so he went on, finishing emphatically: "Satisfying." He guffawed, but Kelly didn't laugh. "Kelly? Are you even there?"

"I'm here," she answered.

"No laugh? Tough room."

"I'm just not in a joking mood," she said, plucking at the hem of her shirt.

"What's the matter?"

Now she laughed, a dry, sarcastic laugh. "What isn't?" And she found herself spilling out everything—almost everything. She didn't tell her brother the truth about Ethan, but she detailed her stress over the wedding and her work troubles, all the way back to Dr. Masden's evisceration of her all those months ago. The more she talked about her worries, about how much she had left to do on Confibot, and how stuck she felt with the project, the more overwhelmed she became. By the end, she was nearly breathless. "Anyway, I know you can't do anything about any of this, and you've got enough of your own stuff going on," she hurried on, "but I just kind of wanted to vent. I haven't really had anyone to talk to about all this."

"You haven't talked to Ethan? Or Priya?"

"Priya and I, um, had a fight," she confessed. She carefully avoided addressing Ethan.

"So? I know her well enough to know that she'd still want to help you, even if you had some kind of fight. *I* can't tell you how to make a robot, but she can. Just ask for her opinion."

"I'm telling you, she's not going to want to help me right now."

"Have you tried? Or are you too proud to ask?"

"What are you talking about? I'm not too proud to ask for help."

"You're not even willing to take my help right now." A silence fell after Gary's words. Kelly could hear the bright, metallic tones of a Baby Einstein video in the background before he started speaking again. "I'm just saying, not to minimize your problems, but I think you're making things harder for yourself. You've got a great brain, but you need to get out of it sometimes. Honestly, Kelly, it sounds like the psychologist guy acted like an a-hole, but that he wasn't that wrong—about the robot or about you."

Kelly was fed up with people questioning her choices—Dr. Masden, Priya, Anita, Gary. If one more person questioned her thinking, she would—she would—she might just believe them. She glanced at the cracked bedroom door, Ethan on the other side. The conversation with him had been so much easier than this. But it felt hollow in comparison. Gary's words had weight. They sunk into the skin.

"I do appreciate your help," she said finally. "I'm listening. Thank *you* for listening."

"You know I'm here whenever you need to vent. There is no 'I' in 'brother.'"

"True, yet also completely irrelevant."

"All I'm saying is, you don't have to do this alone. By the way, have you talked to Clara recently?"

"Umm—no, I guess not." Kelly searched her memory. She couldn't remember the last time she and Clara had spoken. Her sister had missed the last family dinner. Kelly had noted the absence as uncharacteristic, but had been so wrapped up in her own worries that she hadn't dwelt on it.

"She just sounded off when we talked last week."

"I'll text her," Kelly promised. When she got off the phone, she shot Clara a text to check in, then chucked the phone down on the bed. But something stopped her. She turned around, picked the phone back up, opened her contacts, then froze. She really didn't know if she could make this call.

She was a grown-ass woman. She could make this call.

"Hi, Dr. Masden," she said when he picked up. "I really need your help."

twenty-four

• • • • •

"What do you think Confibot should be?" Kelly was seated opposite Dr. Masden in the control room, sharing the same set of chairs in which she and Anita had had their come-to-Jesus. She was almost as nervous now. And she wasn't even thinking about the rakish way his hair fell over his forehead, or how close he was sitting to her, or the fact that there was a patch of hair on her knee that she'd missed every time she shaved for the past month. She was nervous because she knew that he could respond in literally any way to her question, and that if he responded in a way she didn't like, she would not be able to simply veto his ideas in the wake of everything that had gone down between them. She couldn't control what he was about to say, but she would be forced to give it a chance.

But he simply raised a skeptical brow. "Are you sure you want to know?"

"I'm asking, aren't I?"

"It's just that we didn't exactly leave on a positive note last time. I got the impression you never wanted to see me again." He ran a hand wearily through his black hair. "I really couldn't blame you. I've regretted what I said to you since then. It was rude, it was unprofessional—"

"Which is exactly what I was," Kelly broke in. "And I am sorry. I called you here to ask for your opinion, right? Isn't that enough to prove that I mean it?"

"My opinion's not scientific," he warned. "It's not in your data set."

"Look." Kelly swiveled to her computer, pulled up the folder with all her months and months of research, and dragged it into the recycle bin. She resisted the urge to clutch her bosom and scream "My baby!" and forced herself instead to look back at the psychologist, who smiled.

"All right, then," he said. "I'm going to do a very psychologist thing and turn the question on you: What do *you* think Confibot should be?"

Kelly resisted the urge to roll her eyes. "I think he should have a face that's the most pleasing to the greatest number of people and—"

"Not other people. You." The doctor looked around and gestured to Dot-10, who waited lifelessly in a corner of the room. "Dot-10's big right now, right? Why do you think that is?"

"I have no idea. Her functions aren't even the most advanced on the market."

"I can guarantee you that it's not about her functions. It's about how she makes people feel. So how would you want Confibot to make you feel?"

Kelly considered carefully. "I would want to feel comforted," she said at last, "like I could trust him to take care of me and live in my home. I mean, I'd be trusting him with my life, really, if he was handling my medical care. And I'd want to feel stimulated, like I could have intelligent conversations with him, but that I also wasn't intimidated by him. And—what are you writing down?" Dr. Masden was scribbling notes as she talked. Kelly worried that he was preparing another gut-wrenching diagnosis for her. But he lifted the notepad with a smile.

"*This* is your data," he said.

Kelly had started the day with a sinking feeling that she could be heading toward another dead end. But as she and Dr. Masden worked together, her skepticism shrank and her optimism grew. The more the doctor elicited her ideas and talked through his own, the more she started to realize, begrudgingly, that he could actually be right. Together they were sketching out a vision of a robot who could be sophisticated and multifaceted, interacting with users on a deeper level than just blasting them with digital trophies like Dot-10 did, yet still fun and broadly likable.

As she threw the data set out the window and just listened to what she, and Dr. Masden, really wanted, she was called back to that manic weekend when she had made Ethan. She saw now, suddenly, how she had been making the process of designing Confibot so much harder than it needed to be. She had been tying herself down, ignoring the value of her own ideas—and as an engineer, a creator, ideas were her currency. This was what she was here for, what she loved about this job: the adrenaline of invention, the ability to open her mind and imagine anything in the world she wanted, then magically make it happen in the flesh (or in the silicone, as it were). Unshackling herself from the data put the art back into her science. It put the humanity back in the process of creating a robot.

But a buzz from her phone pulled her down from her high. Left cheek, Q3 motor. Now. She pursed her lips, imagining Robbie sitting there at his desk, issuing commands like he was Genghis Khan or something. If Genghis Khan ate unflavored oatmeal every morning and drove a Prius. She would never make any real progress if she was constantly being interrupted, and daily now she was having to stop what she was doing to satisfy Robbie's demands. This was his third text in the last half hour, since she hadn't responded right away.

"You're popular," Dr. Masden remarked.

"For someone with antisocial tendencies," she answered, looking up from her phone to smirk at him.

He laughed in response. "Okay, I'll give you a revision: How about 'selectively social'?"

"I'll have it printed on a T-shirt." She grinned in return. "But I do have to get this. I'll be back."

She pocketed her phone as she stood decisively. This was ridiculous. If Robbie was at his desk, he was right down the hall from her. They dated for six months, for Pete's sake. Asking Dr. Masden about his thoughts had helped. She should just ask Robbie too.

"What do you want?" she asked as she marched up to Robbie's cubicle, not bothering to keep her voice down; most of the other engineers were off at lunch.

Robbie startled, spinning in his chair. He recovered himself, assuming his "you may kiss the ring" face. "Was my order not clear enough?"

"I don't mean what part, I mean what do you want from me? What do you want from—all this?" Kelly whipped her hand around, gesticulating.

"I want to be allowed to complete my own work in my own cubicle without being molested."

"I'm not here to molest you, Robbie," she said firmly. "I just want to talk." And now his face took on an infuriating air of judgment, as if he were calculating just how much of his time Kelly had earned. But she stood her ground—though she did throw in a "Please?" He did have the upper hand, after all.

At last, Robbie relented. "I don't have much time," he said in a clipped tone, pushing his chair aside to make room as Kelly dragged her own over to sit next to him. It was a tight squeeze. She wasn't sure how Robbie had managed to secure a different chair for himself than any of the other engineers had: a spare, Scandinavian piece in blond wood. If anything, it looked less comfortable than the squishy black ones the company had probably mass ordered from Office Depot. He had Robbiefied his whole cubicle, filling the shallow shelves with his Fitbit, smart air filter, digital calendar, personal coffee press, all of the silvery gadgets that regulated his days. Kelly had always known that Robbie took a particular interest in transhumanism, forever looking for ways in which humans could transform and better themselves through machines. She had understood his attraction to the field on an intellectual level—she herself found the advances in the area exciting. But now, eyes skimming over the possessions he used to upgrade every facet of his life, she wondered if there was more to it on an emotional level. Maybe Robbie did this work because he thought that humans on their own, himself included, weren't good enough.

She took a deep breath and forced herself to look at him. "Why are you blackmailing me?"

"We're in direct competition. This should be obvious."

"You strike me as someone who would want an honest win."

"You have wrought your own demise. I would say that that's still fair." Robbie's face stayed still and serene, but his right foot jiggled beneath him, his shoe making an infinitesimal squeaking noise, like a baby mouse.

She shook her head insistently. "It still doesn't make sense. You could just tell Anita what you know and get me out. What you're doing isn't really helping you." She pointed at the demo video of Brahma running silently on his desktop in the background. "And you don't even need the help! You're doing well on your own."

"What was it you said about Brahma? That he's what happens when the production line at the robot factory gets stuck?"

Kelly blushed. It was true, Brahma at first glance looked like too many robot parts had ended up on one body. Rows of metal arms bristled from his back, and digital eyes ringed the entire circumference of his head. And sometimes she and Priya did joke about Robbie in the lab. But he was always so utterly placid that she thought he didn't notice, or didn't care . . . Maybe she had mistaken his tendency to not show his feelings for him not having any.

"Maybe I'm not doing so well," Robbie burst out, his foot going overtime. "Anita has scheduled me for a performance review. She said we need to block out an hour for 'a good chat.' How am I supposed to take that?"

"Well, I mean, you could take it as her wanting a good chat. Anita's tough, but she's fair, and she'll give you a second chance even if you've messed up. I would know."

"Oh no, what if I've messed up?" Robbie's thin chest began moving rapidly up and down below his starched shirt.

"Robbie, stop." Kelly leaned forward, clasping her hands. Magically, having to manage his anxiety seemed to dissipate her own. It was kind of nice not to be the one trapped in a vortex of panic for a change. "You've been doing well, you always are. You don't need to freak out. For that matter, you don't need to sabotage me to do well in the competition. You're good at your job, you're good at everything."

"I wasn't good enough for you." The words seemed to burst out before Robbie even knew they were there.

"What do you mean? Like, when we broke up?"

Robbie's own internal struggle played out in the tortured movements of his lips. Finally he spoke. "At least I was real," he exclaimed. "But that didn't stop you from throwing me away to 'focus on your career.' Now here you are, ready to throw out your career for a guy who's not even real! He's—he's a talking hat rack!"

"I never tried to throw you away, Robbie," Kelly protested. "I honestly didn't think you were hurt when we broke up."

"We didn't break up. You dumped me. And yes, when somebody tells you you're not good enough, it hurts."

"You're telling me! You know what I love about Ethan? For him, I *am* good enough!"

Kelly and Robbie stared at each other for a moment, neither sure of what to say. His foot had finally stopped jiggling.

And then the naked emotion on his face locked itself away. "Must be nice," he sneered. "If you're done, I do have work to complete." He turned firmly back toward his computer and began going through the video. Onscreen, Brahma was zooming around a kitchen on his wheels and extending various arms and levers, washing dishes, stirring a pot, observing a visitor at the door via a camera and directing the smart lock to unlock. He was doing many of the sorts of things that Confibot was meant to do, but much faster and more seamlessly. With a new feeling of nervousness, Kelly rose from her chair.

"Yeah . . . so do I." Once she was out of Robbie's line of vision, she nearly ran back to the lab.

The rest of that week, Robbie stopped asking her for parts. In fact, he didn't speak to her at all. And the knowledge of *his* knowledge, the unpredictability of what he might do with it, the silence, was almost worse than his relentless demands. What if he waited until the day of the presentation to do her in? She had an inkling now that his feelings for her ran deeper than she had given him credit for; that his ire at her relationship with Ethan was more than just poor sport. And she understood, finally, why Robbie had blackmailed her, asking for parts from Confibot and Ethan, slowly and steadily impeding her progress rather than just exposing her straightaway to Anita and eliminating her wholesale from the competition. It gave him power. For once in their relationship, a relationship that she saw now was strangled by his inability to love her, or anyone, when he so thoroughly hated himself—for once, he had been the one in control. Those sorts of feelings ran deep. She herself felt some sort of psychic resolution from their conversation, and it was possible that he felt the same. Or it was possible that his feelings would rear again.

But all Kelly could do right now was her job. Over the last few days in the lead-up to the presentation, she put in what felt like a thousand hours on Confibot, rewriting codes, reworking her entire demonstration with Dr. Masden's assistance, and actually giving the poor robot a decent face. It was dizzying, but also exhilarating: finally Kelly was seeing her vision come to life. Confibot was shaping into someone who was professional, polite, and gentle, yet still able to crack a joke or play games; capable and intelligent, yet not intimidating. By nine p.m. on Thursday, Kelly was so sleep-deprived that she thought she saw the Wicked Witch of the West fly past the office window. Some light hallucinating would not have been enough to convince her to pack it in for the night, but some-thing else was nagging at her. Clara gave only a terse response to her text the other day, then hadn't made a peep since. And she could no longer put off her own concern, so she set about quickly sealing Confibot up. Eyes blurring, she reattached the last metal plate and wire she had removed and buttoned his shirt on to cover the whole mess of knobs and filaments. She stumbled out of the lab, convinc-ing herself that some particularly loud NPR would wake her up on the drive out.

The only thing she forgot was the screwdriver she had left lodged by the central command switch, right in Confibot's chest cavity.

Kelly couldn't remember the last time she had been to her sister's apartment. Was it right after she and Jonathan had moved in together? That's right, and Clara had tried to make some elaborate meal for the family but burned it beyond repair, so that she had ended up ordering pizza instead. Somehow she had laughed and smiled through the whole thing. Kelly would have stuck her head in the offending oven.

After she rang the doorbell, she realized that she had no idea what to expect when the door opened. Was Clara sick? Was she even here? Was she avoiding them all for some reason? With a pang, Kelly thought back over all the little jabs or testy moments that might have hurt Clara. She couldn't blame her for pulling away. And, suddenly anxious, she began to pull away herself, bouncing a little on the balls of her feet, edging her weight back from the welcome mat, thinking she could just call tomorrow instead—

"Kelly. Hey." Clara seemed understandably surprised when she opened the door. Her strawberry-blond hair had been hastily pulled back, and her normally sparkling eyes looked flat. "Come in."

"So what's up?" she asked once Kelly was inside. Kelly looked around—it really had been a while since she'd been here. Furniture was shuffled around the living room, new pop art posters colored the walls, a string of unlit white Christmas lights had been strung around the picture-window frame, and a new coffee table composed of painted packing crates, evidently some kind of debatably successful DIY project, sat precariously in the middle of the room. What Clara lacked in funds or decorating skill, she tended to make up for in gumption.

Kelly stammered. "Uh, nothing. What's up with you?"

"But I mean, you're here. Is something wrong?" Clara asked.

"That's actually what I wanted to ask you." Kelly perched on the arm of the white cotton sofa. "Gary and I noticed you had been kind of incommunicado lately."

"Sorry, I've just been busy." Clara had plum-colored grooves under her eyes. She looked tired.

"So, uh, everything's okay?" Kelly asked.

"I've just been working a lot lately," Clara said. "A lot of overtime." Kelly was confused—certain times of the year consistently had Clara working heavy shifts at the vintage boutique, but this wasn't one of them. "And I've actually got an early shift in the morning,"

Clara went on. Her eyes flickered to the door. Kelly jumped up from the couch.

"Oh, sorry, I guess I'll get out of your hair."

Clara looked suddenly guilty. "No, you're fine, it's just I wasn't expecting company."

"I'm not company. I'm Kelly," she said awkwardly. She was used to her sister being loquacious, but Clara just looked at her, twitching the hem of her shirt. Kelly waited before bursting out with "Are you *sure* everything's—"

The opening of the bedroom door interrupted her as Jonathan came out. "Just checked the bank statement—oh, Kelly, hey." The extra day's growth of his stubble and the crease between his eyebrows suggested that he was every bit as worn out as Clara.

Kelly seized her opportunity. "Hey, Jonathan. I was just coming by to check on you guys. Gary and I hadn't heard from Clara in a while and wanted to make sure everything was okay."

Clara gave Jonathan the tiniest shake of the head "no," but he turned to Kelly. "We're fine, we've both just been pulling extra shifts. We need the money." Clara looked ready to protest, but he went on. "It's okay, Clara. I made a bad investment; we lost everything we had. It was with a friend whose judgment I trusted and, well, Clara trusted mine. And with my student loans coming due, we're in a tough spot."

"Oh. *Oh.*" Kelly crossed her arms now, looking at Jonathan. "And now my sister's working herself half dead to make up for your mistake and your debt?"

"Kelly, don't." Clara laid a placating hand on her arm. With her other hand, she squeezed Jonathan's before pulling Kelly aside into the kitchen. "It was a mistake," she told Kelly. "Everyone makes them."

"This sounds like a pretty big mistake."

"Listen, we're broke. It sucks." Clara laughed a what-can-you-do laugh. "But we're here, and we have each other, and that's what matters."

"But it's not your fault. You shouldn't have to pay his way. You didn't know."

Clara looked up, surprised. "Oh, I knew about the debt. And I agreed to the investment too. I had some doubts, but I trusted Jonathan, and I still do."

"Really?"

"Of course. This isn't his problem, it's our problem. Every day, we choose each other," she said simply. Seeing the doubt in Kelly's face, she took her by the hands. "We're fine, Kelly. We're both working hard and we'll get through this together. It's just a bump in the road. You and Ethan would do the same, wouldn't you?"

"Sure . . ." Kelly said. In truth, she didn't know how she would react if Ethan ever hurt her. She had no data from which to judge.

Clara's face relaxed a little and she started busying herself in the kitchen, putting dishes away from the drying rack. "I'm kind of glad you know, at least. It's less stressful now that it's not a secret. And I do want to be involved in your wedding, you know." She looked back at Kelly. "It's just there's not much I can do right now."

"No, of course."

"Just think, a few years from now, we'll both be happily married. Maybe our kids will be playing together. Yours can tutor mine in school." She laughed. "You and Ethan want kids together, right?"

"Yes," Kelly blurted before she knew what she was saying.

"Oh my gosh, can you imagine how Mom's going to be with three sets of grandkids? She'll be in heaven."

"She'll be reserving their wedding venues the day they're born." Kelly laughed too. She located the silverware drawer, grabbed a handful of cutlery and started sorting it in. As she and Clara talked, she marveled at how easy it was—so often they talked as shared offspring of the same parents, not as sisters. Maybe they were finally at an age where the "wolf cubs competing for the same scrap of meat" instinct could be put aside for friendship.

But something held Kelly back from truly enjoying the moment. The golden future Clara was outlining with her words was a fantasy. Kelly could never have children with Ethan. More and more, she was wondering what she could truly have with Ethan. Logically, she had known all along that she couldn't stay with him forever, though she may have entertained some hypotheses to the contrary out of wishful thinking. Now, finally, her emotions were beginning to accept the same truth.

On her drive home, she pieced her thoughts together in the silence of the dark car, the streetlights fanning over the dashboard in waves. Clara and Jonathan chose each other every day. And every day, by refusing to destroy him, in spite of the risks, Kelly was choosing Ethan. But he could never choose her. It was true, she reasoned, that at any given moment, he empowered his own words and actions. But every action is guided by a want, and she could distinctly remember programming in his every want with her own hands. And she knew, in the pit of her stomach, that love couldn't be love without free will. His love toward her was so unfaltering. Maybe that was because it could never be love at all. Someday, some robot might have that ability. But not Ethan.

Suddenly, Kelly felt sick. She pulled over and rolled the window down so she could take deep, heaving breaths of the night air. A sob lurched north in her throat. She knew that real love, the kind that Clara and Jonathan had, was out there, and as much as she had always thought it wasn't for her, she wanted it. She had put up walls against it, she had run from it, and finally she had tried to build it with her own two hands. But if engineering was a human discipline . . . then love sure as hell was too.

A sports car zipped by Kelly, nearly sideswiping her. She wiped her eyes, checked her mirrors, and pulled back onto the road.

When she walked in that night, she expected to see a dark apartment. It was nearly midnight. But the lights were on and Ethan was wide awake in the living room, a notepad and several torn-off pages full of notes on the coffee table, a blouse and skirt laid out carefully on the arm of the couch beside him. He popped up when she entered.

"Kelly! I was wondering where you were. Not really, you're always at work. Hopefully after tomorrow you can take a break, right? Of course you'll be busy when you win and get to make Confibot into a global phenomenon. But you'll at least get a weekend, right?"

"What's all this?" she asked tiredly, strolling to the couch.

Ethan's face took on an excited grin. "I wanted to get everything ready for your big day tomorrow. I thought this would look great on you." He gestured to the outfit. "Professional, but still sexy. Just like my lady. Then I did some research on the investors who are going to be there and put together some talking points in case you have to chat them up or something. I know you hate that schmoozing stuff, so I thought this would make it easier. Like, hmm, let's see"—he picked up the notepad and riffled through the pages of his perfect penmanship—"Alfred Cochran from Pine Capital is also on the board of the National Beet Growers Association. So you could talk about that beet salad you had last week at Karma Café, only leave out the part where you hated it. Oh, and I want you to have a good start in the morning so, madam"—he located a fresh page on the notepad, pen in hand—"may I take your breakfast order?"

Kelly's heart squeezed as she took in all his work. She took the pen and paper from his hands and laid them on the table. "We'll worry about the morning in the morning." Then she kissed him. "To-night I just want to be with you."

twenty-five

. . . . . .

Kelly was so consumed with anxiety on the day of the presentation that she briefly entertained the idea of retreating to the hills, never to be seen again except by hikers who would forever after boast of having glimpsed the Hill Crone. The plus side of this was that she didn't have any room for her feelings about Ethan. The investor reception prior to the main event passed in a blur of alpha-firm handshakes, understated but overpriced power suits, and anxious titters of laughter from the engineers. These people held Kelly's future in their expensively smooth hands. They were so uniformly polished, eternally smiling-yet-not-smiling, that it was impossible to tell what they thought of Ethan's schmooze lines as she spouted them. If nothing else, at least she remembered not to mention her distaste for the beet salad.

The reception ended and the engineers moved backstage, clustered in the awkward funk of being forced to share a small area while not wanting to interact. Today, the competition that had over-hung their usual camaraderie for months could no longer be ig-nored. They skated by on thin surface statements and avoided eye contact like it was catching. But Kelly escaped even the obligatory "good luck"s, being in the fortunate position of having scouted a crack in the curtain through which to peer out at the intimidating audience. She could be using this time to take deep breaths and visualize success. Or she could do what she was doing: staring relentlessly out at the descending horde.

This auditorium, with its broad, curved stage and state-of-the-art lighting, was considerably more slick than the site of her third-grade play, yet flashbacks of that day haunted her. If she couldn't even play a convincing tree, how was she going to convince these international, billionaire investors that they should pay attention to her, let alone give her their precious money? But Confibot did look great, propped and waiting in a chair backstage, his hair immacu-lately groomed.

She felt her phone vibrate and pulled it out to see a video call from Diane. "Mom, I can't talk right now," she said as soon as she pressed the green icon. "My presentation's about to start."

"I know!" Kelly squinted at the image pixelating into focus on her screen and realized it was her entire family—Diane, Carl, Clara and Jonathan holding hands, Gary and his girls—all gathered in the Suttles' living room. They waved at her, the image jostling violently as Diane waved with her non-phone-holding hand. "We're all here watching the livestream," Diane went on excitedly. "The kids got a day off and I made chickpea chili. It's just like the Super Bowl! But without the little tight pants or the halftime show. Is there a halftime show?"

"Just us nerds," Kelly replied. "I didn't think you guys were going to watch."

"We wanted to surprise you!" Part of Kelly was piqued to see her family assembled: if she flamed out spectacularly, in true third-grade-stage-fright fashion, knowing that they were watching would only make her demise that much worse. But she couldn't help but be touched at their interest. She wondered in particular how her dad might respond to her work, if he would be impressed.

"Well, you did." She laughed. "Thanks for watching. I'll try not to bore you." They waved good-bye.

Robbie was up before her, which was at least a distraction, though he displayed a level of self-importance heretofore un-achieved even by Robbie. He began with the stage washed in dark-ness, the spare notes of a sitar playing in what was presumably a reference to his project's name. "Brahmaaaa." A recorded voice echoed over the audience as a single spotlight appeared, aiming down at the contraption itself, positioned center stage on a pedes-tal. The curves of the machine's arms glinted, half lit, half shadowed, making the robot look hulking and spidery. As the rest of the stage lights faded up, revealing Robbie, Kelly almost laughed at the con-trast between him, with his neat shirt and pleated pants, and the Batmanesque machine beside him. He appeared to have scrubbed his face so hard that morning that he had revealed a fresh, naked layer of skin.

"Welcome," he began, spreading his arms, as if today's whole event were his. "I thank you for joining me here today for a very spe-cial birthday. The birth not just of Brahma—but of a whole new era of robotic technology." He began putting the robot through his paces on a mock kitchen set, demonstrating that his glinting carbon-fiber arms could lift a whole refrigerator, yet also had the fine motor control to separate an egg. The crowd murmured appreciatively—the display was impressive. Kelly practiced her calming breaths.

"As if Brahma weren't special enough, I have another special guest for you today. Please welcome Melvin to the stage." Robbie gestured to stage left, and Kelly waited. And waited. Finally, Melvin made his way to the center of the stage with the help of his walker. He had the pace of a tortoise, as well as the shriveled, benevolent face of one. "To truly appreciate Brahma in action, you need to see how he interfaces with a user. So our guest, Melvin, is going to demonstrate how much simpler his life will become with Brahma in his home. Melvin has never seen Brahma before, correct?"

"That's right," Melvin replied, looking warily at the robot.

"So you can all see just how easy and intuitive it is for even an elderly person to use Brahma. All you have to do is talk to him. He's just like a person—only far better."

"Brahma, will you make me an omelette?" Melvin asked the robot. He practically yelled it, enunciating each word loudly and slowly.

"Of course," Brahma replied. He began making preparations, switching the stove on and whipping eggs, smoothly and rapidly.

"That's pretty neat!" Melvin said. Robbie beamed. "Can you make it with cheddar cheese?"

"Cheddar cheese has six grams of saturated fat per ounce," Brahma replied. "I will prepare it with spinach." Melvin's face fell slightly.

"Brahma is designed to not only help you live your life, but to live your best life," Robbie explained to the audience.

Brahma thrust a plate with an omelette and fork on it at Melvin, who reached out slowly to take it, his old elbows creaking. Almost before he had it in his grasp, Brahma pulled away and shot over to the cabinets. Melvin was just managing to grab the plate when Brahma was back, shaking pills into his hand. "Your medication must be taken with food," he instructed rapidly.

"Thank you," Melvin said, struggling now to juggle the plate and the pills, but Brahma was already across the kitchen again, filling a glass with water, then wheeling back to hand it to Melvin.

"Ten ounces of water should be consumed at every meal," the robot said.

"See?" Robbie enthused. "Under Brahma's meticulous care, users will reach optimal health."

Melvin dropped a pill to the floor with his shaking hand as he tried to grasp the cup. "Could you—" he began, but he started when the screen on Brahma's torso lit up with a flash.

"Notification: your daughter is calling," Brahma intoned.

"Ooh, I'd like to talk to her," Melvin said.

Instead, a lightning icon blazed onto Brahma's screen with a sound like a thunderclap. Melvin jumped and spilled his water. "Alert: thunderstorm watch in the area," Brahma said.

"But where's Jennifer?" Melvin asked.

"GPS request. Would you like me to locate Jennifer?" Brahma said rapidly while zooming around the kitchen, cleaning up after cooking.

"Yes—no—I'm not sure." Melvin was clearly getting overwhelmed. It was too much, too fast. "I—I don't think I want to live my best life anymore."

A few bursts of laughter ascended from the audience. Panic

washed over Robbie's face. "Don't be absurd, everyone wants to live best life."

Melvin shook his head, setting his plate and cup down on the counter and gripping his walker to make his way offstage. "Slow down! Read a book!"

Now the audience erupted in laughter. All color had drained from Robbie's face, leaving him as white as his shirt. Part of Kelly knew that Robbie had brought this on himself in his hubris. Part of her knew that his failure here meant a surer chance of her own success. But mostly she felt sorry for him: he had gotten the technical part of his project down perfectly, but had missed the mark on the human element. She could relate.

The tap on her shoulder from behind scared her so much that she jumped.

"Ethan!" There he was when she whirled around. His hands were held behind his back. "What are you doing here?"

"Sorry, I didn't mean to scare you," he said, his voice low. "I snuck in. The guy at the door thinks I'm Alfred Cochran from Pine Capital. All that research paid off. I just had to wish you luck and give you something before you go on. I know you like all those bouquets I make for you on the computer, but I realized that I've never brought you actual flowers before and, well, digital is not the same as the real thing, right?" From behind his back he pulled out a bouquet of poppies, all velvety reds and pinks.

Kelly took the flowers, looking down at them. "Ethan, they're—they're—I love you." She looked up. It wasn't until the words had spilled from her lips that she realized she had never said them before, not to Ethan or any other man. She wondered how long she had been feeling them.

"I love you." He smiled at her. She searched his face: the trusting eyes, the lips so ready to smile her way. His words were an exact reflection of her own.

"Kelly Suttle!" Anita's voice drummed her out of her reverie, pulling her up as if from underwater. She hastily set the flowers down.

She reached the center of the stage laboriously. In the lowered lighting of the auditorium, the faces of the investors stared back at her, all watching eyes, like creatures lurking at the edge of a forest. Kelly caught herself, trying not to think about forests, anything but that stupid third-grade play. She paused under the spotlights, forcing herself to inhale and exhale. The audience could wait for her for one second. Everything was going to be all right.

And then somehow, amazingly, it kind of was. She turned to the watching crowd. "Thanks for joining us today," she said. "I want to show you something I've developed—actually, more like *someone*. There are other caregiver robots on the market, but there's nobody quite like Confibot. I think you're going to like him. I sure do. Of course, I'm kind of biased." The investors laughed.

"Confibot started as a machine, but he's developed into so much more. He truly has the potential to develop substantive relationships with human users. Trust me when I tell you that I know how meaningful that can be." Kelly couldn't resist glancing back, stage right. There was Ethan, expression alight just in watching her.

"So—let's meet him," she said. A light came up on stage left, carving Confibot out from the sheath of darkness. He was seated facing her, hands resting on his thighs, face molded to a pleasant, neutral smile. And he looked good. Kelly heard the audience murmur and stir—after all the functional wizardry they had witnessed today, there was still something viscerally impressive about the level of human realism she had achieved. She felt a little warmth—this reaction was good, this was what she had counted on all along. Fleetingly, she hoped that Confibot's appearance translated through the video feed so her dad could see. She suddenly imagined Priya watching, too, probably crunched into a conference room at AHI with the other engineers from her division, all cheering and jeering in turn.

She had his routine all cued up—all she had to do was start the conversation. "Hi, Confibot, how are you today?" she asked.

Like a flower sprouting in a time-lapse video, the robot stirred to life. "I'm great, Kelly, how are you?" This time the audience's reaction was louder. It was one thing to make an android who looked good from onstage, but the subtle fluidity of Confibot's movements, the ease of his intonations—this was not the Hall of Presidents. In the wings, Anita glowed. She looked positively hungry.

"I wanted to ask you a few questions," Kelly continued.

"I'm great, Kelly, how are you?"

The script was so entrenched in Kelly's head that it took her a second to realize he had gone off it. There he was, still smiling blithely at her. "Sorry, you must not have heard me," she said, more to the audience than to Confibot. "I said, I'd like to ask you a few questions."

"I'm great, Kelly, how are you?"

The audience was talking, all right, but their tone had changed. They maintained a polite hush when they were making positive remarks, but apparently forgot to bother when things turned negative. Kelly couldn't help herself; she glanced at Anita, who had descended with frightening speed into full-on "off with her head" mode. Kelly's gaze went irresistibly back to Ethan, who was knitting his forehead. His whole being was focused on her success.

"Confibot, I wanted to ask you a few questions," Kelly repeated more slowly, as if that would help. The adrenaline surging through her body made every muscle feel weak and loose. She had no other moves. She had no clue what was going wrong. After all the preparation she had done, all the thousands of simulations she had run, he chose this time to develop this problem . . .

"I'm great, Kel—" Kelly took her phone from her pocket and used it to switch him off before he could finish the sentence. Now she wasn't just confused, she was lost. And scared of the look on Anita's face. But just as Anita swooped forward to come out from behind the curtain and call the disaster off, Kelly looked at Ethan again. She had built him just to service her as a wedding date, and at every turn, he had done so much more for her than she had asked or anticipated. But it was time that she started doing the right things for herself. She had to ask him to do one final thing.

"It looks like we're going to need the help of one more person to pull this off," she said. Anita hesitated. Kelly faced Ethan squarely. "I'd like you all to meet my fiancé. Ethan, can you come out here?"

Ethan shrank back as if unsure she meant what she said. She nodded at him encouragingly, trying to show more confidence than she felt, then took his hand as he approached, leading him toward the center spotlight. "Ethan, how about you and I chat for a bit instead?"

"Of course, Kelly. What did you want to talk about?" Ethan lowered his voice, though it was still audible to the crowd through her microphone. "Is this part of the plan? I thought you hated audience participation." The audience laughed. In the wings, Anita was so tense, so ready to jump in and pull the plug, she was practically levitating.

"No, no, let's just—talk. How are you?"

"At the moment, I'm confused." The audience laughed again.

"Um—" Kelly looked around wildly for inspiration. "Come on, let's dance!" She wrapped her arms around a completely befuddled Ethan and swung him around the stage.

"Are you all right? I thought you hated dancing too."

Kelly ignored him. "He's an excellent dancer!" she called loudly to the audience. Then she abruptly stopped dancing. "What's 5,789 times 4,362?"

"25,251,618," Ethan replied immediately. "But why—"

"When did Andrew Jackson die?"

"June eighth, 1845."

"What's my favorite time of year?"

Ethan slowed, looking at her. "November," he said. "You love cloudy days."

The audience was stirring, confused. "We get it, your boyfriend's a catch!" one of them called out, to uneasy laughs. Anita stepped swiftly forward, but Kelly gestured firmly for her to stop, surprising herself with her boldness even more than Anita. She felt sick at what she was about to do, but she was sure. She took a breath and faced the crowd.

"He's not a catch. Oh, he's great—intelligent, good-looking, easy-going, funny. He's the best-read person you'll ever meet, but he's not above doing laundry. Everyone who meets him loves him. I love him." Kelly forced herself to meet Ethan's eyes. "But a catch would imply he's someone I found. And that's not quite true."

She looked out at the faces of the crowd, glowing palely in the dark auditorium. "Confibot appears to be having a glitch today," she said. "I made a mistake. But it's okay; I know that I can still make him everything I'm promising that he is, because I've done it before. I have another model here to show you."

She lifted her hands to Ethan, but froze, unable to do what she needed to. But he caught her eye and gave her the faintest nod, the faintest smile, as if he knew, as if he was giving her permission. Obediently, he turned his back to her. Kelly took a breath and lifted the back of his shirt, the starched cotton faintly warm from his skin. She located his control panel, and before she could stop herself, she flipped the switch. Immediately Ethan powered down—lifeless, still, head bowed stiffly atop his neck like the top arm of a crane, dormant on a work site at night.

The audience gasped. Kelly swiveled Ethan's back to them, lifting his shirt so they could see the control panel.

An image flashed into Kelly's mind of her family watching at home, their shocked faces all in a row. Anita shot onstage with the closest thing to gracelessness Kelly had ever seen her display. "I'm sure you can all appreciate my engineer's eccentric sense of humor," she assured the investors. "She maintains the purity of her genius by isolating herself from all human society. I promise you, this is not her real pitch."

But the same investor who had heckled Kelly earlier burst to his feet. "I've got to see this!" He pushed his way down the aisle and bounded onstage, examining Ethan closely. Kelly flinched as the man jammed his sausage fingers all over Ethan's face. "Absolutely unbelievable!" he cried. He strode to Anita, hand out like a blade. "Let's talk."

As Anita watched the rest of the crowd trickle from their seats, rushing the stage, she transitioned seamlessly to a silken smile. She had planned this all along. This was all the carefully architected outcome of her calculations, not a coup by some engineer, some cubicle citizen. She grasped the man's hand. "My pleasure." In the midst of the turmoil, Kelly noticed Robbie gawping like a gutted fish. She knew that if anyone's heart was thumping harder than hers in this moment, it might be his.

Kelly's gaze found Confibot in his chair. In a way, despite being neglected for Ethan, he was the center of all of this. Through her daze, she realized that her project was real now. Confibot was happening. The bold investor fought his way toward her. "Incredible work," he half shouted over the din. "You have an office model yet?" he joked. "I could use someone who actually spends more time filing than on Snapchat."

"Yeah, I'll bet. Excuse me—" Kelly turned back toward the center of the stage, distracted. In the madness of the throng, she couldn't see Ethan at all.

twenty-six

· · · · · ·

Kelly wasn't sure if she would ever see Ethan again. But she didn't dare ask Anita what she had done with him, and barely had the luxury of thinking of him at all during the daytime. Time passed in a vortex of investor meetings, team hirings, budgetary allocations, marketing plans. At first, watching so many other heads come together to get hands-on with her project, her baby, was almost physically wrenching. Nobody else could understand Confibot like she did. What if they screwed it up? They were obviously going to screw it up. But the more Kelly worked with the various experts joining her team, the more she realized that they knew what they were doing. Confibot was growing and changing, becoming something different from what she had expected—different, but bigger and better. Kelly was learning how to cede control. She was pleased with the newfound respect with which Anita, in her own, tempered way, began treating her; thrilled to finally have her own office, aka closed door behind which to eat Cheez-Its; and ecstatic at the early glimpses of the ways in which her technology, with the ample funding now coming to it, could change people's lives. Watching what had started as an ephemeral idea in her own head become a reality, something that would be in people's homes, improving their quality of life, that would employ countless others in manufacturing and shipping and marketing—the whole thing was magical. She even got a write-up in *Wired* magazine—not bad, she considered, for someone who was only thirty.

As exhilarating as all the work on Confibot was, it was also exhausting. Every night, when Kelly dropped into bed, the thoughts that she could push to the side during the day came rolling forward: the light in Ethan's eyes when he had said "I love you," the trusting way he had turned his back to her right before she had shut him off for good. She knew that she had done the right thing, but she couldn't shake the sadness that overwhelmed her when she thought of him. She missed him. All she could do was push ahead.

D r. Masden stayed on as a consultant, and Kelly not only got used to working with him, but began to enjoy it. One day when they were preparing for a meeting, shortly after the presentation, Kelly could tell he was holding something back. "What is it?" she asked.

"I just can't believe that you built a robotic boyfriend," he burst out. "There's so much to unpack there." He put his hands up. "But don't worry, don't worry. I won't analyze you again."

"It's okay." Kelly laughed. "I know it's a crazy story. Believe it or not, it all started with—"

"Your mother."

Kelly stared at him. "How did you know?"

He leaned forward. "Kelly, I'm a psychologist. It's always the mother."

One hour and six Freudian slips later, Kelly was laughing as he told her a funny story about his own mom.

"So you've got family . . . psychoses—or whatever the clinical term is—too." She shook her head.

"I think the word is 'issues.' And I think everyone has them."

"So if I'm essentially Confibot's mom, does that mean he'll have issues with me?"

"Don't worry," he assured her with a smile. "I'll still be around to help when he's a teenager."

Kelly rolled her eyes. But having someone around to help—it was kind of nice.

Another day at lunch, Kelly sneaked into the lab to get some work done. With all the extra meetings in her days now, she appreciated these pockets of quiet. But just as she rolled a chair up to a computer workstation, Robbie appeared suddenly from behind a rolling rack, brandishing a screwdriver.

"I'm in here," he announced quite loudly.

Kelly gasped, hand at her chest. "Robbie!"

"I wanted to alert you to my presence to avoid startling you."

"That ship has sailed," she muttered.

"And how is Confibot progressing?" he asked, sitting beside her at the counter, his back ramrod straight.

"Pretty well, actually," she answered. "How's Brahma?" In spite of Robbie's own efforts to the contrary, three separate investors had liked Brahma enough to throw some dough his way as well, and the project was on its feet.

"Extraordinary. I can't tell you what it's like to be building such world-changing technology."

"Wow, yeah, I'd love to hear what that's like sometime," Kelly replied, trying to keep the sarcasm in her voice at a low volume. Robbie, whether he meant to or not, could push her buttons, jam them and pummel them and wriggle them, more than just about anybody else.

She didn't say anything more, worried that she wouldn't have anything nice to say, but Robbie suddenly spoke from the silence. "You did the right thing," he said. Kelly set down her pliers, looking at him in surprise. "Even though I know you only got rid of Ethan because of me, I believe you'll be better for it in the long term." He kept his eyes trained down on his work as he spoke.

Kelly hadn't been thinking of Robbie when she'd powered Ethan down—honestly, his blackmail had been the furthest thing from her mind when she made her choice. But what would she gain by setting him straight? Why not let him have this? "Well, I'm doing all right," she replied.

"I do wish you happiness," he said carefully.

Kelly picked up her tool again with a small smile. "Thanks, Robbie."

Moving on was a bigger problem with Priya than it had been with Robbie. Kelly had tried assiduously to avoid her since their fight, treating her like just another coworker in their sparse interactions. They traded a clipped "Hi" when they passed in the hallways. On occasions when they were forced to share lab time, they passed each other tools without eye contact. And this was a million, bajillion times worse than fighting.

After the bridesmaid dress debacle, Kelly had half expected Priya to shower her with apologies. When no apology came, she took this as proof positive that her conjectures had been correct all along: if Priya didn't apologize, that meant that she didn't realize she had been wrong, which meant that she was oblivious of Kelly's feelings, which meant that their entire friendship had been a ruse. Thinking about it, Kelly smoothed her blouse and refocused on her computer.

Kelly's ability to distract herself from her own feelings had always been something of a point of pride. And she made a gorgeous, gung-ho effort that Saturday: she put in a full day's work at home, catching up on TechCrunch, digesting journal articles, and doing a Skype interview for a German news company interested in profiling Confibot. She tried out a new hairstyle that allowed more of her natural wave through. She even pulled out her ultimate distraction weapon, a marathon of old-school Olsen twin movies. But no matter how hard she tried to convince herself that she was totally good without her best friend, a thought kept surfacing, like a body discarded in a river. Maybe the presupposition to her entire argument, that Priya was wrong to jilt her at the fitting in the first place, had been false. Maybe Priya hadn't apologized because she'd had nothing to apologize for. Yes, she had let Kelly down and, yes, she had said some harsh things, but hadn't Kelly done the same? Hadn't Kelly been neglectful of the relationship for a while at that point? It was logical to look at the evidence of all her friendships and to conclude that this friendship would likely fail. But such a conclusion was based on the pattern of Kelly's own behavior. And if she could change that variable, she could change the equation.

A rencontre at work was clearly not an option, given the avoidance games they were playing. Her texts and calls went unanswered, Priya was mysteriously missing at their usual shared lab times, and she must have been spending an arm and a leg eating lunch out because when Kelly picked up her salad du jour in the cafeteria line, she was never anywhere to be seen. And so Kelly tugged on her big-girl panties and decided that the only way to get her friend's attention was to do what Priya had been begging for all along: hang out outside of the office. A quick perusal of Priya's Instagram revealed two things: that she was back with Andre, and that she would be at an open mic night with him that night.

It's totally fine, Kelly thought as she stood in line backstage at the cigarette-scented club, waiting with the other comics for her turn to go up. Yes, that's right, Kelly Suttle was doing an open mic night. Most of the other participants were reviewing their notes on their phones or on little scraps of paper, noiselessly rehearsing their routines, but Kelly had something better. She had a straightforward plan. She had already seen Priya and Andre settle at a table, Andre bumping fists with friends in the crowd. All she had to do was get onstage, a platform from which Priya could not avoid or ignore her, spout her apology, and get off. She wouldn't even have to tell a joke, she consoled herself. She inhaled deeply as she advanced to the front of the line. Time to get this over with.

And then she saw Priya's long hair flip behind her as she disappeared into the restroom—right before the emcee called out, "Kelly!"

Kelly froze. She couldn't go up until Priya was back in the

audience. She tried to stall, shaking her head furiously at the emcee, but he just laughed and ushered her into the glare of the spotlight, forcing her out. She stared wildly into the packed house. She wasn't supposed to have to tell any jokes. A joke? What was a joke? Who are words?

"What—what's black, white, and red all over?" she asked quietly.

"We can't hear you!" yelled a guy in the audience.

"A newspaper!" she shouted. She tried to bring it back down a notch. "Newspapers, right? Who remembers those?" She stared into the audience for a long minute, hoping that someone would say something helpful, such as "I do!" They did not.

"All right, give it up for Kel—" But Kelly had to stop the emcee. She had to stay up here until Priya was out of the restroom. She thought desperately back to what had made Ethan laugh.

"My sister fell out a window! I mean—no, wait, it's a joke—" Just in time to hear this, Priya emerged and saw Kelly onstage. She halted, looking as shocked as if she had walked out the door into Oz.

"Priya!" Kelly exclaimed. "I'm sorry! You were right about Ethan, and I should have listened earlier but I freaked out when things didn't go my way. I'm trying not to do that anymore. It's been hell not having you around. I want to talk to you. I want to meet Andre. Hi, Andre." She waved at him. He waved back numbly, very, very confused. "Will you give me a chance? I promise I'll make more time to hang out together. I'm here, right?"

Priya crossed her arms. "Tell me a joke," she called out.

Kelly searched. Suddenly she thought back to the model number of a certain vibrating motor she had once witnessed Priya, in one of her self-titled moments of genius, construct in the lab: 3X2D5L. "What are the ingredients of a perfect date night?" she asked. "Three

Xs, two Ds, and five Ls." Priya stood there for a moment. And then she got it. She roared with laughter, bending at the knees. The rest of the audience was starting to boo, restless, but Kelly didn't care. She laughed, too, even while the emcee physically guided her from the stage.

"Come here, come here," Priya gasped weakly, gesturing her forward while grasping her own side. "I've missed you, you moron." And Kelly didn't even notice the stares of the audience as she made her way toward the waiting arms of her friend.

As difficult as it had been to avoid Priya, ignoring Kelly's entire family was even harder. As the next family dinner loomed on the horizon, her mother's voicemails and e-mails multiplied, backing up Kelly's phone like a rest station toilet. The phone had buzzed as she sat in her office, designing facial prototypes for a female Confibot. She had silenced it, irritated at the visions that floated unbidden into her mind of the family ringed around the dinner table, all staring at her. Her amazing, perfect fiancé was a hoax. Her dad sighing and turning his attention to dinner, dryly unsurprised; Gary explaining to her nieces where Ethan went, the girls laughing at their batty aunt; Clara smiling with sweet sympathy, holding Jonathan's hand; her mom clucking with disappointment, making plans to sell the wedding dress to some other girl at the shop—that dress her mom had worked so hard on . . .

Now Kelly imagined her mom alone in the shop, running a duster over the shelves, straightening bolts of silk, the dress staring at her the whole time, fluttery as a ghost. No matter how much her family had pressured Kelly, even belittled her unintentionally, it hadn't been fair to lie to them about Ethan, and it wasn't fair to ignore them now. Kelly knew that her mother did love her. Even if she sometimes showed it the way a two-year-old shows her love for her favorite doll, rendering it bedraggled, crayon-faced, one-armed, and bereft of all will to live. And Kelly did love her family—even if, she mused, she was programmed to, in her own biological way. She knew down inside that they would keep coming back to her no matter what, just like Ethan had done, and that she would do the same.

But that didn't make her feel any less apprehensive as she picked up her phone.

Kelly wondered how exactly she was supposed to start this conversation as the family sat around the table in thick silence that night, cautiously testing their mackerel surprise. Hey, remember that time my fiancé turned out to be a robot? Kelly noticed Clara lean in toward Jonathan, nudge him, and point to her plate—some inside joke. They smiled at each other. Both looked considerably fresher-eyed than they had a couple weeks ago.

"Your boyfriend died," Bertie declared suddenly into the silence. She stared unblinkingly at Kelly as she spooned applesauce into her mouth with a slurp.

"Bertie—" Gary began reprovingly, but Kelly stopped him. She had no idea what the consequences would be, but she knew that she needed to own this. She was taking a risk—but this time, it was a smart one.

"Listen, I understand that what happened at the presentation was probably a nasty shock for all of you, and I—I'm sorry. I didn't do any of this because I wanted to lie, or trick you. I was trying to make things easier by having a date to the wedding and, I don't know—I just didn't want to disappoint everyone anymore. Guess I

301

blew that." She looked down at her plate, running her fork through the sauce and letting it drip slowly off, like molasses. Time dripped just as slowly in the silence.

Carl wiped his mouth with his napkin and put down his fork. "Well, I for one was pretty damn impressed," he declared.

Kelly looked up at him. She couldn't have been more surprised if he had opened his mouth and belted out a Verdi aria. "You were?"

"Of course," Diane agreed. "You *made* Ethan. How could that disappoint us? I mean, how on earth did you do it? He was a masterpiece."

"I've never seen such technology in my life," Carl affirmed.

"Yeah, but . . . he wasn't real. I was never actually engaged," Kelly said blankly.

Diane sighed. "I know, that's the sad part. I went ahead and packed up your wedding dress already to make sure it doesn't get damaged—acid-free paper and everything. That way it'll be in perfect shape when you do find a man. Or make one!" She patted Kelly's hand across the table. "Whoever he is, he's out there," she said gently before returning to her food. Kelly felt embarrassed, seeing in a flash that this whole debacle must have exposed the true loneliness she had felt, the frustrations with her own inability to find a partner, to her family. But maybe letting her family understand her vulnerabilities was not such a bad thing.

"So how did you do it?" Clara asked eagerly.

"Yeah, can I have one?" Gary asked. "I could use some male company around the house. The other day, I shaved one of my legs without thinking about it. Then I had to shave the other one, or I wouldn't have looked right."

The whole family was looking at Kelly with full attention. Tentatively, she began to open up.

"Well, believe it or not, I put the whole thing together in one weekend."

"No way," Carl said. Kelly put her own fork down, beginning to smile.

"Yeah. Though I had to make some modifications later. He did some pretty odd stuff in the beginning . . ."

That night was possibly the most pleasant, certainly the most animated conversation they'd had at family dinner for as long as Kelly could remember. It was a delightful surprise, seeing how well her family took the whole thing, how impressed they were with her work. But Kelly knew better than to sink herself too wholly into the high of this approval. There had been plenty of times before at this table when she had felt low about herself, and there would almost certainly be such times again. Even if the whole family had been angry with her for this transgression, or further entrenched in their view of her as the hopeless, forever single one, she would have been okay, she reflected—at this point, she'd certainly been through worse and come out the other side. Her family's opinion mattered to her. But it was beyond her control, outside of her. It wasn't who she was.

Kelly went to the trouble of fixing herself a special dinner one night after work, making a lasagna from scratch. She enjoyed cooking when time allowed these days, even without Ethan around to pitch in, or to playfully shoot a cherry tomato into her mouth from across the kitchen when they mixed the salad. But nothing would ever make her tastes normal. When the lasagna was almost finished, she melted a few slices of cheddar cheese on top.

Maybe it was because she hadn't gone out and done anything special in a while, with no one to do anything special with, but she felt like doing something different that night. She stayed in her pencil skirt and blouse from work rather than changing immediately into something wonderfully comfortable and frightfully unsightly. She ate at the table rather than in front of the television, or at her desk. She even lit a candle, but after a few minutes, she blew it out. Even for her, pumpkin spice didn't sit well with lasagna.

She still thought about Ethan every day, though not as much. As the light that streamed through the windows redressed her apartment in the golden hue of May, the memories that every room held changed, too, melting into a hazy distance. But try as she might, she couldn't go back to being happy with spending her nights alone.

The free trial she'd accepted on that dating site, which seemed like a lifetime ago, had of course expired. The credit card form stared at her expectantly from the screen. It was asking for $19.95 for a month of use. One month, in the course of what she could reasonably anticipate to be a long lifetime, was statistically quite small. And $19.95, in the sum of a lifetime of earnings, was really not significant. And some risks, demonstrably, were worth the taking.

Kelly almost laughed when she saw the profile she'd set up before. It was like reading the biography of a stranger. The picture she'd used was small and blurry, barely showing her. She uploaded a new one, the picture she'd submitted to be used with the press release about Confibot. It captured her in a fleeting moment of hair glory.

She remembered filling out the section about herself with

basically whatever she thought would sound normal and nonthreatening. It read stiffly, like something cooked up by an alien trying to convince everyone that, really, he promised, he was not an alien. It was true, she did now occasionally indulge in a walk through the mountains, but this biking business she had written about—she doubted her foot would ever touch a bike pedal unless at gunpoint. She supposed her mountain walks could count as hiking—she put down hiking. What did she do for work? Well, that had a long answer and a short answer. She went with the short answer.

I'm a robotics engineer, kind of like the people who created the Hall of Presidents. If you're interested, I'd love to tell you more.

Then came the part where she described him—what was she looking for in a guy? She skimmed down the long list of requirements she'd made. Love of Twinkies? Wears V-necks? Her eyes blurred looking at the list. Even Ethan hadn't had half of these. And, sadly, Robbie had several. All those rules didn't mean much of anything, really. She frowned and considered. I'm just looking for someone who will like me for me. Maybe it was cheesy, but she pressed Submit before she could change her mind.

While the wheel turned and turned, Kelly's stomach felt like it was doing something similar. She almost impulsively reached out and clicked the red X at the top of the page, but just before she could, her results came up. Results, plural. Amazingly, this time, she had matches. She wondered skeptically if these were actual, real men or just some sort of bot. Then she realized that if they were bots, she really had no room to judge.

Some were clear nos—the guy wearing a ninja mask in every picture, the man whose bio was simply "Girthy," the one who looked eerily like her own father. But one picture caught her eye. Michael was washing a sheepdog, laughing and ducking as the dog shook and sprayed him with foam, what looked like his family in the background. His profile indicated that he was looking for:

Someone who's smart enough to know when my jokes are dumb, but who laughs at them anyway.

Kelly took a breath and clicked the Like button.

It only took a minute of her scrolling through other options for Michael to message her.

Hey, Kelly! Okay, your description of your work has me intrigued. I'd love to take you out sometime and hear about it.

Kelly blushed instinctively, smiling to herself. She typed a reply.

Sure.

Too simple, this was her first impression and it had to be strong.

Let's do it!!

Too strong. She sounded like she was already hurtling through the streets of San Jose to arrive at their date, panting and desperate.

That sounds fun. I'd love to hear about what you do too.

That could work. What was wrong with that? Nothing was wrong with that. Okay, let's go, let's push that Enter button like the goddess of love that you are—

But Kelly's finger froze over the key. She couldn't do it, and it wasn't because she was waffling over the wording of her message. Something else was holding her back.

Kelly was not prepared for this. All she had been looking for was a tiny gear. She had a hunch that this instrument would allow her to give Confibot the newest advance she was working on—the ability to ever so slightly raise his ears. A small thing, literally and figuratively, but humans could do it, and so should he. But if her hunch was right that this particular gear was the missing ingredient, it would require some digging, as this particular gear was so specialized that it was rarely used.

And so Kelly found herself down a deserted, vaguely creepy hall, looking for the fabled second storage closet. She had never actually used this closet before; the closest room that got any real traffic was the small bathroom that, by virtue of its out-of-the-way locale and by unspoken agreement of the whole office, was reserved strictly for laborious poos. Her journey took her past the bathroom and down the following hall to the end. When she unlocked the door to the closet, she shrieked.

There was Ethan. Turned off, he was stuck between a plastic shelving unit full of overordered screws and a stack of cardboard boxes so old the cardboard had started going soft and pulpy. He was exactly the same as when she'd last seen him on the day of the presentation, a good month ago—hair neatly combed, even wearing the same clothes. But somehow, he was changed. To Kelly, his skin looked oddly dull under the closet's single bare bulb, like a plant that had gone a few days without water. The gloss of his hair was doll-like.

Foolishly, her first thought was that she wished she were wearing a cuter shirt, and that she'd shaved her legs that morning. She shook herself out of it. After glancing quickly behind her to make sure no one was coming down the silent hall, she stepped a little closer to Ethan. "Hi," she whispered, as if whispering made it less weird. She ran the tip of a single finger down his cheek—it was soft, with the give of collagen, but cool. When she brought her finger back, it wore a thin scrim of dust.

Hands at her sides, she leaned in on tiptoes, shut her eyes, and kissed him. She almost missed, catching just his bottom lip. Without him participating, it was hard to handle all the navigation herself with her eyes closed. For a moment, she paused. She realized she was waiting for something, but she didn't know what. His eyes—those eyes that she had selected herself, months ago—only met hers if she situated herself just right within his gaze. Whatever it was she was waiting for, it wasn't going to happen.

Oddly, she felt almost as if she were seeing him for the first time, not as a person or as her personal opus, but as an object—a work of art, really. He was beautiful, and exquisitely human in every detail: the plushness of his skin around the perimeter of his fingernails, the fine hairs that feathered down to the nape of his neck. She felt a surge of pride in knowing that this was her creation. But that was all she felt. That was all he was: a creation, and he could never again be anything more to her. Perhaps he had been a projection all along—someone to love being in love with. Finally, Kelly felt the full force of the loss she had suffered, with all its permanence and weight. Ethan had died, she realized—the part of him that could die, which was the part that had been alive to her. Something had been torn away from her, but something had also been lifted. She felt equal parts sadness and relief. There was a hope, fragile but lively, like a newborn bird, in knowing that the space he left behind in her heart was open now for new things.

With a hand, Kelly gently closed his lids.

That night, Kelly did what she had done every night for the past week: she opened the dating app and stared at Michael's message. There it was. No, it had not changed. No, it had not become any less intimidating.

At this point in the routine, Kelly typically exited the app and found a sensible distraction for the rest of the night, like drinking too much wine and going on an internet deep dive that ended in her donating sixty dollars to a Flat Earther society. But tonight, something was different. The message was still intimidating, but not un-approachable. She sensed that a door had been opened, and she was ready to walk through.

Hey, Michael, sorry for not replying earlier, I'm just seeing this.

Kelly wondered if it was wise to start a relationship with a lie. Then she wondered if this was a relationship. Then she told herself to stop wondering and start writing.

I'd love to go out sometime.

Fifteen minutes later, while she was nervously dipping a Cheez-It in Nutella, she got a notification that Michael had written back.

Awesome! I'm free this Friday if you are. Is there anywhere you'd like to go?

This was Kelly's opportunity to micromanage the moment. By mandating the date's location, she could mitigate the risk of over-priced restaurants, thumping club atmospheres, or—the horror—bowling. She could eliminate any unforeseen eventualities and allow herself to predict the entire night's course of events and pre-pare for any pitfalls that might arise.

Instead, she searched her mind, smiled, and typed.

Surprise me.

acknowledgments

I set out to write an offbeat love story and along the way, I received a fascinating education in robotics, product design, and AI. Thank you to Professor David Heaton of the University of Chichester, Dr. Luis Ponce Cuspinera of the University of Sussex, and Dr. Suzanne Gildert of Sanctuary AI for so generously sharing their time and insights with me.

The whole publication process started when Abbie Greaves of Curtis Brown plucked my manuscript from the slush pile. Then Sheila Crowley jumped in with all her warmth and wisdom, and together the two have been the best agents a writer could ask for. Their brilliant reshaping of Kelly's story continued in the hands of Tara Singh Carlson of Putnam, whose precision, thoughtfulness, and dedication beautifully transformed the book and gave me a new love for my own characters. A big thanks also to Helen Richard of Putnam for all her work to help make this book a reality.

Along the way, several others have contributed their time and expertise to help me improve the book, most notably Zac Allard, Kelsey Lahr, Jules Hucke, and Chelsea Hawk. Thank you for the notes and the writerly commiseration.

Last but not least, thank you to my family: to Gunnar, for being my champion through the high points and the low; to Lewis, whose presence on my lap while I work is always the greatest part of my job; and to Mom, Tom, Dad, Lana, Elyse, Jason, Sheyenne, and Zivon, for your support and never questioning my (probably questionable) decision to be a writer.

How to
Build a Boyfriend
from Scratch

SARAH ARCHER

A Conversation with Sarah Archer

Discussion Guide

BOOK
ENDS

PUTNAM

A Conversation with Sarah Archer

1. This novel is so fun! How did you come up with the idea?

I was living in Los Angeles at the time, so the idea came to me when most ideas did: while I was sitting in traffic. It was an inspiration that immediately grabbed me, so that I thanked the red lights for giving me snatches of time to scribble down notes. At first I thought of it as a reversal of the John Hughes movie *Weird Science*. But I knew right away that I wanted this story to be more relationship-driven, less of an out-and-out comedy. So as I started to think about what kind of character might gain something meaningful from a relationship with a robot, Kelly came to the surface.

2. Kelly's voice is very relatable. Do you identify with her character? Is she based on anyone you know?

Kelly isn't based on anyone real, but I can relate to her introversion and passion for her work—though I don't think I would ever cut it as a robotics engineer! Personally, I've always been inclined to the humanities and gray-area, artistic thinking, so one of the fun challenges of writing this book was getting inside the head of someone who approaches life and relationships in a concrete, logical way. Thinking in terms of things like the scientific method or the order of operations as applied to solving equations helped me develop her voice.

Some facets of Kelly's voice and humor do overlap with my own, but really, I think she's an amalgam of so many people of her generation. Something about living in the internet age has pushed many of us to be equal shades of neurotic, overly analytical, and sarcastic, but ultimately durable.

3. As a robotics engineer, Kelly is a successful woman working in the sciences. Why did you decide to set the story within this world?

Artificial intelligence is a topic that fascinates me, so while I wasn't actively looking for an idea set in the world of the sciences, when one came to me, I jumped on it. I loved exploring what a robotics company in Silicon Valley might look like and what sorts of projects the people there might be working on.

I'm a firm believer in giving characters as much conflict as possible, so by creating a female protagonist working in a competitive, male-dominated industry, I could believe that Kelly's career would be that much more hard-won and she would be even more afraid of doing something to jeopardize it. Anita, Kelly's boss, is slightly older than she is, so her trajectory would probably have been even harder. I like to think that the difference of even a decade or so allows Kelly and Priya to feel more at home in the tech industry than Anita might have felt when she started.

4. What kind of research did you do for the novel?

I was fortunate to speak to several experts in the robotics and product design fields about their education, the work they do, the challenges they face, and how they think about their contributions to the world. These conversations were so illuminating. I'm an English major to my core, so I'm still a long way from truly understanding Kelly's work, but these interviews gave me a window into her world. Then, as with everything in my life, I turned to Google to fill in the gaps, consulting journal articles, interviews, and blogs to answer questions that arose along the way, including those about life in Silicon Valley. The latest developments in AI and robotics are intriguing, intimidating, and exciting—it was tough to avoid getting lost in research rabbit holes on the internet.

5 Before writing the novel, your background was in comedy. Why did you decide to write a novel? Did anything surprise you about writing fiction?

I began writing this book at a transition period in my life. I had just relocated from Los Angeles, where I was working crazy hours in the entertainment industry, to St. Maarten. Even after moving to a Caribbean paradise, I managed to overcommit myself with work immediately, but I still had more time in my day for writing. So I finally decided to attempt a novel, something I had always wanted to pursue. On a creative level, I wanted to try this idea in novel form because I sensed that Kelly's voice could be a major part of the story and I was eager to play with that on the page.

Having focused on screenwriting for years, I found writing fiction delightfully freeing. I still sometimes feel guilty when I just come out and *say* what a character is thinking. Poetry is another passion of mine, and I relish the chance to really climb down into the language and walk around among the words, something that's harder to do in screenwriting. But writing humor definitely requires an adjustment for the page versus the screen: you can't rely as much on the visual and on the manipulation of timing.

6. As you portray it, the modern dating scene—particularly in Silicon Valley—is a bit grim. Have you lived in Silicon Valley? Why is it so hard for Kelly to meet relatable men?

Here's my confession: I've never actually been to Silicon Valley. San Francisco is as close as I've gotten, but I did live in Los Angeles for years, and I think LA and Silicon Valley are similar in that both are industry towns. In terms of the social and dating scene, that can be a negative: many people care only about what they can get out of you professionally—they care more about knowing you for the sake of knowing you than about really *knowing* you. There's a tendency to flex and talk oneself up, and there's an atmosphere of artificiality, where image rules. But on the plus side, when you live in that kind of area it's easy to meet like-minded people, people who are so passionate about the things you're passionate about that they were willing to uproot their lives and move there to pursue their dreams. I met my husband at a networking event for writers in LA—it's not all bad!

7. Without giving anything away, did you always know how Kelly and Ethan's story would end? How did their relationship evolve as you wrote their characters?

The central arc of the story line came to me pretty much fully formed and never altered, even while so much around it did through various drafts. The place where Kelly and Ethan end up felt right to me from the beginning, but how they got there evolved. I think their relationship became deeper, more passionate, and more human, ultimately challenging Kelly at a more elemental level. My focus was always on her character arc, so it helped to play with Ethan's arc as well, and with how he might force changes in the relationship through his own evolution.

8. *How to Build a Boyfriend from Scratch* **is terrifically funny, but it also**

tackles serious questions about love, loneliness, work/life balance, honesty, and the power of expectations— both our own and those of our fami-lies. What was it like to keep up this balance while writing?

I like to include both drama and comedy in almost anything I write, because life has such a mixture of both. It just feels natural. But balancing the two and maintaining a consistent tone is always difficult. It helped me to use Kelly's voice as a sort of filter—thinking about how she would view a situation, what she would find funny and in what ways, or where she would be emotionally in different moments. Thinking about your audience is another useful filter. I wrote the first several drafts of this book just for me, with no audience or commercial concerns like genre categorization in mind. As I advanced in the process and fixed on a more refined sense of who might actually read the book, I was able to make some appropriate adjustments.

9. What do you hope readers will take away from Kelly's story?

First, I hope they have a good time with it! But on a deeper level, for me, the heart of the book is the idea that love is a choice. I believe that one of our greatest gifts as humans is our inalienable ability to love, and our greatest responsibility is to decide how we exert that power. When Kelly comes to make different choices about how she loves, her relationships are transformed, not just with Ethan but with family and friends too. As artificial intelligence evolves into the future, I think we'll face many questions about AI beings' ability to "feel" emotions (and about what that even means) and to make choices. I'm so curious to see how we as a society will approach these issues.

10. What's next for you?

I have some screenwriting projects on the back burner, but my focus is on diving into my second novel. I can't wait for it to come into the world!

Discussion Guide

1. When we meet Kelly, she's struggling to make her voice heard, both at work and at her family dinner. Why do you think this is? Do you relate to Kelly? Why or why not?

2. Why do you think Kelly hasn't found love before? What changes as she gets to know Ethan?

3. Kelly's mom is certain she just wants what's best for Kelly (p. 11). Do you agree? Why do you think Kelly feels she has to lie to Diane to make her happy? Is their relationship different at the end of the novel?

4. When Kelly tries online dating, she finds herself limited by the qualifications she thinks she's looking for in a man (p. 56). Is this kind of profiling helpful? Does Kelly come to understand differently

what she's looking for? What qualifications in a partner would be on your list?

5. Why does Kelly struggle to finish Confibot? How does Ethan help her think differently about her career?

6. Kelly teaches Ethan to eat Nutella and Cheez-Its, her favorite snack. Do you have a surprising favorite treat? Is there a particularly memorable time you shared it with someone?

7. Priya is Kelly's best friend, but things become complicated after Kelly creates Ethan. Why does Kelly feel she has to lie to Priya? How does their relationship change? Have you ever felt that you had to lie to a friend? What happened?

8. Were you surprised by how Kelly and Ethan's relationship evolved? How did you think their love story would end?

9. If you were in Kelly's shoes, what would you do with Ethan? Do you think you would make the same choices she did?

10. What do you think the future holds for Kelly?